Clara O'Connor grew up i
inspiration was on her doc
legend, a place of druids ai
crossroads. Clara worked in publishing for many y
before her travels set her in the footsteps of Arthurian myth.
The world she never expected to explore was the one found
in the pages of her debut novel, *Secrets of the Starcrossed*, the
first book in the *The Once and Future Queen* trilogy.

Once Upon an Algorithm is her first spicy romcom.

instagram.com/clara_author
x.com/clauraauthor

ONCE UPON AN ALGORITHM

CLARA O'CONNOR

One More Chapter
a division of HarperCollins*Publishers*
1 London Bridge Street
London SE1 9GF
www.harpercollins.co.uk
HarperCollins*Publishers*
Macken House, 39/40 Mayor Street Upper,
Dublin 1, D01 C9W8, Ireland

This paperback edition 2024
First published in Great Britain in ebook format
by HarperCollins*Publishers* 2024

1

A catalogue record of this book is available from the British Library

ISBN: 978-0-00-865367-5

Printed and bound in the UK using 100% Renewable Electricity
by CPI Group (UK) Ltd

For the Greek chorus in all our lives, who cheer us on, support us,
tell it like it is and know when to bring the really good cheese!

Chapter One

'Hot date?' asks 1B as she gives me a blatant up and down on her way in the front door, taking in my mascara and heels … after six p.m.

'Yeah,' I say blithely, as if we have similar exchanges all the time.

We don't. But in that moment, I can't possibly admit to my newish neighbour that she is the only woman under this roof having regular sex.

Actually, scratch that, I am probably doing Mrs Morely upstairs a major disservice. She's eighty-four, and Mr Morely must be pushing ten years older, but they're the most blatant flirts I've ever met in my life. I told them so once when dropping in groceries. Mrs Morely informed me with a solemn twinkle that meeting in uncertain times tends to create a unique pattern in a relationship; expecting a bomb to drop out of the sky while your new husband is fighting a war set the tone of their relationship. Every moment is cherished in a life that happily turned out to be long-lived.

The closest I ever get to any action is suffering through the noises leaking through from my new upstairs neighbour.

Curse you, Victorian floorboards.

Some people find love in times of crisis; I couldn't catch a cold in a pandemic, much less a relationship.

Pulling my collar up against the wind blowing up the street, I exit Richmond station, pausing outside the real estate agent's window to look for a house I'm not quite ready to buy.

We are meeting a mere twenty minute walk from her house, yet Alicia can still be counted on to be the last to arrive. Before children, Alicia believed she could bend time. After children, we started to tell her we were meeting half an hour before any of us planned to get there. And she is still late.

I'm early because the subterfuge leaves me feeling anxious that she will arrive to an empty table so I am inevitably the first to arrive. The pub is one of Richmond's most iconic – a Georgian two-storey with big windows and a beer garden that floods at high tide. I bag a window table and throw a jacket across a couple of the seats opposite.

There are only a few occupied tables, but the office crowd will be tumbling in soon for a warming Thursday evening drink, an early start to the weekend. Tomorrow evening it will be the younger office crowd and locals as everyone else retreats to their own corner of London.

I order a bottle of red and five glasses for the table, while outside the last amber rays of evening glimmer across the water as the lights on the bridge glow into life.

'Leonie!' Nessa flaps down in a whirl of bags, coats and scarves, and a quick air peck by the cheek. Somehow she always gives the appearance of someone running late while multitasking a million things: scattered bag lady on the outside, high-flying City lawyer on the inside. She's explained her job to us a gazillion times, but all I really understand is that she works in the City and takes no shit from anyone.

A dark-haired, slim woman hovers behind her for a moment before taking a seat with a crooked smile towards me.

'I'm Isabelle.' Her tones are as warm as Nessa's. As she stretches a hand across the table, I hesitate a moment too long before she gives a small shake of her head and withdraws her hand, giving a small wave instead. 'Sorry, I was living in a remote area for the last couple of years and so never quite had to deal with...' She waves her hand to indicate the greater number of people in the city around us.

'You're visiting from Australia?' I guess, as Nessa busies herself with more immediate matters than introductions by pouring two glasses of purple-toned ruby liquid into the waiting glasses.

'Just moved here.'

'Dumped the ass she married out of high school and is finally getting around to the great Australian tradition of a year in London,' Nessa explains succinctly after her first restorative sip.

'Wow.' She was at least a decade later than most of her

peers. It would have taken some nerve to walk away from the life she had lived for most of her twenties. 'Welcome to London. How are you finding it so far?'

Isabelle's expression lights up in the same way Alicia's did when she had her first child, or Kristen's when she came out of lockdown. Lovestruck.

'It's everything,' she pronounces. I remember first coming here myself. Londoners never understand what those from sunshine-bathed locations see in their sprawling grey city, but there is something about the teeming metropolis, pulsing with history and culture. Here you can walk in the footsteps of Henry VIII and attend theatres still faintly echoing with the applause of the audiences of Shakespeare and Wilde who stand listening in the wings. Music, words and world events flutter in front of those newly arrived from distant quieter shores and they act like a drug, both revelatory and addictive. There is always a new corner to explore, a previously unknown fact to overturn, in a city where nobody watches or comments on what you do or whom you do it with.

I smile back. 'I get it.'

'You're the American.'

'Yeah, I've been here about ten years but I'm originally from Los Angeles, California.' She does that twinge of the brows everyone does when I add Cali on to the address. It's been a decade and I still haven't broken myself of the habit. It drives people this side of the Atlantic nuts. They know where LA is. But there's plenty of call for it back home. The pioneers and frontiersmen did not think things through when they honoured the old world by naming new towns

Paris, Dublin, and Athens. No European ever expects the Paris you're referring to to be in Texas.

'What have you been up to?'

'Exploring mostly.' She shrugs. 'Looking for work, meeting people. Nessa let me tag along to her book club last night. Those girls are hilarious. I'm terrified of them, but they say I can come back next time.'

I laugh. 'I hear they're big drinkers.'

'You haven't been?' she asks, glancing at Nessa who is pounding something into her phone. I'd hate to be on the receiving end of whatever that message is.

'No, it's too far north for me. Finchley is practically in Scotland to me.' I quickly allay her fear that she's somehow misstepped by revealing an invitation that has never been extended my way. 'I live near here in Barnes, just up the river. I keep meaning to look into something like that locally. It seems like a good way to meet people and read more.'

'You gonna get a cat too?' the newly arrived tall redhead asks acerbically as she removes her coat before taking the remaining free seat. 'Hi, I'm Stella.'

I refuse to take the bait as Isabelle introduces herself.

'You don't need to read more books, Leonie,' Stella continues with a quick smile to Isabelle and Nessa. She gives one of the uniformed girls weaving through the now-bustling bar a quick signal that another bottle would be appreciated when she has a moment.

'Everyone could do with reading more, and I promised myself I would read more than just Product and Design books this year.' My to-be-read pile has diversified since

January, but I'm not progressing through it as quickly as planned.

'You promised yourself a lot more than that,' Stella pronounces before looking directly at me. 'Well? You get any dick yet?'

I wince inwardly, squashing down my reflex annoyance. This again. It may be for my own good but arghhhhh, I'm so sick of fending off my friends' persistent intentions. No, that's not fair. I'm the one who informed them of my resolve to shake off my chronic state of singleness; they're just holding me to account. It's their job.

'I've been busy,' I throw out my first line of defence as Kristen arrives, standing at the end of the table with a pronounced look-at-me air, which is not like her at all. She extends her hand across the table, which is odd because, of all of us, Kristen is the most religious about what she touches. Isabelle's eyes flick to me for guidance, wanting to avoid repeating the faux pas she made on arrival. My brows draw together in a frown to show that whatever it is, it is most definitely not an invitation to shake hands. I look back at Kristen, so busy trying to decipher her expression that I miss what Isabelle does not.

'Great ring.'

She is right. There is a gorgeous smoky stone set in gold on the hand held out to us, the stone an almost perfect match to Kristen's own gleaming eyes. Tears spring into mine as I bring a hand to my mouth.

'Oh!' Stella jumps up, her long red hair swinging as she embraces the slightly stiff Kristen with a squeal as Nessa and I also jump to our feet and wrap our arms around her in shared joy. Protocols are one thing, but our girl just got engaged.

Nessa unwraps quickly and runs to the bar to get in the bubbles.

We retake our seats, beaming. 'What? When?'

'Wait, wait for Nessa,' I hush Kirsten's attempt to answer. The smile on my face wins the fight for supremacy over the lump in my throat.

'Congrats,' Isabelle offers, filling the waiting silence with a self-introduction. 'I'm Nessa's cousin. I just moved here.'

Kristen nods at her, taking a moment herself, her eyes bright with unshed tears, her nose scrunching as she says hi.

Nessa plonks an ice bucket with two bottles of champagne in onto the wooden table.

'It's a school night, Nessa.'

She dismisses me with a wave of her hand.

'It's a landmark occasion. Hush.'

I have at least two client calls to make in the morning, but Nessa is right. It's a big night and deserves to be marked accordingly.

'Tell us everything. When did this happen?' Stella asks, pulling Kristen's hand towards her to examine the ring more closely.

'Valentine's Day.'

The table groans. 'Really?'

Kristen's elegant shoulder shrugs as her pale skin pinks. 'Really. We went to this cottage on the coast last week and Camille made this amazing stew and we curled up in front of this blazing fire and she asked. And I said yes.'

She said yes. Our normally reserved friend fairly glows with happiness.

'How did you meet?' Isabelle asks. Despite her own recent breakup she seems to be one of those naturally warm people who is always more interested in learning other people's stories than telling her own.

Kristen glances shyly around the table. We all knew the story, had lived through it in real-time. But that doesn't mean we aren't happy to hear it again.

'They were flatmates,' Nessa begins.

'I didn't really know her,' Kristen picks up. 'She moved in shortly before the LD.'

'The LD?' Isabelle questions, before throwing her head back in recognition. 'Oh, you mean the lock—'

'Ah,' I stop her, 'we don't say those words lest we call the next one down.'

'Like Voldemort?'

The table gasps in unison.

'Did she just?'

Isabelle guffaws before silencing her laugh and raising her hands. 'I'm just going to sit here and say nothing.'

'Where were we?' Stella asks. 'Ah yes, the dickless flatmate.'

Kristen throws our overly blunt friend an exasperated glance. 'Yes, my female flatmate. Camille rented a room in my flat. She'd been there two months, and we occasionally had a glass of wine and watched a movie together but between work and my boyfriend—'

'The last dick ever,' Stella interjects in dramatic tones.

'Stella!' all three of us admonish in unison. She throws

us an unrepentant grin. She has made her views known repeatedly that she doesn't entirely understand Kristen's ability to move forwards in life without pecs and a penis. Stella is married to the sweetest, mildest man I have ever met, but he keeps his outspoken wife happy in the sack, and if you believe Stella, that's all she needs in her world.

'Anyway,' Kristen continues, taking a sip of the golden bubbles as if to fortify herself. 'Then the LD came, and I was working all the time. Camille was working from home and when I got home from work, there was always a meal waiting for me, or a note that made me feel better when it felt like the weight of it all would crush me.'

'Did you get sick?' Isabelle asks, her voice cracking. Her eyes, like all of us, are shadowed with the lingering trauma of that time. Maybe not the confinement and germ awareness of a big city for her, but instead the intense isolation of a rural bubble in company you no longer enjoyed.

Kristen shakes her head. 'I... No, but, as others did, I was working longer and longer hours. I wouldn't get home for days. You know how bad it got. And Camille would make these boxes of clean scrubs and meals and bring them as far as security would let her. I lived for those packages.'

'Then when did you...'

The hum and buzz of the busy pub recedes as Kristen leans forward and her sharp features soften in remembrance. 'One night I crawled home, showered and made it to my bed. I left a note to say hi and that I was only there for a few hours' sleep and would have to go back in the afternoon. When there was no sign of me by afternoon, she knocked on my door to rouse me. I could barely wake up and when I saw her face I burst into tears. I have never been more glad to see anyone in my life. She was beautiful and alive and … well, I couldn't stop crying or let go of her. So she crawled into bed with me. And after a while I was ready to get up and go again.'

Isabelle clasps a hand to her chest as she listens, as if her heart needs the support. 'So when…?'

'Did she cross the border to the new country of Lesdom?' Stella offers.

'Shut up, Stella.' Nessa and I groan at her. She's ruining the story but Stella is full of crap; she's as caught up as any of us.

'Well, when I made it home, I needed… She was the only person I could touch and somehow she let me sleep with her and never made a move. Then, one night, I had this patient who recovered and I couldn't wait to get home to tell her and when I finally did, I wasn't telling her the story, I was kissing her.'

Kristen lifts her glass none too steadily to her lips, smiling into the flute. 'It went on for a while … that night, and nights after.'

'You weren't…?' Isabelle pauses delicately.

Kristen's cheeks flush violently as her smile widens. 'Oh no, we totally were. But it was … we didn't talk about it. Then things started to calm down at work, I came home one night and Camille was waiting. She told me she was in love with me, and she understood that maybe for me it wasn't like that, but if it wasn't then she needed to know. It terrified me that she might leave, but I never really had time to process it. She was my liferaft in a storm. With the storm gone, it hadn't occurred to me I no longer needed the liferaft. Or rather, what I realised was that she wasn't a liferaft; she was my solid ground.' Kristen shrugs, blowing her cheeks out as she finishes her story.

There is silence as we all wipe away the tears on our faces.

'To Kristen and Camille,' I say, raising the delicate glass of golden bubbles in my hand. Their story makes my heart burst. And selfishly reminds me momentarily of my situation, making me feel like a terrible friend. Kristen, in the worst time of her life, made a leap into the unknown for love. I've sworn to do the same. 'We should do something special to celebrate.'

'Celebrate what?' Alicia asks. She is, as predicted, atrociously late, and scanning the table she stills in the middle of decloaking. 'Oh no, what have I missed?'

'Guess who got engaged?' Nessa hands her a glass to join our toast.

Alicia whips around to Kristen. 'You did?'

After hugs and ring admiration, she finds a free seat and drags it across. 'How about a weekend in Paris? We haven't been away together since *before*. Camille can show us around, we can get to know her better and I can escape the monsters.'

'How about weekend after next?' Nessa is already checking her phone, peeking from under her lashes directly up at me. 'The Six Nations will be on in Paris, and the city will be overflowing with men. Well, not overflowing, but there's bound to be some extra men in town for the game.'

Inward sigh. I love my friends dearly but lately it feels like they never miss an opportunity.

'I don't know. My stepbrother is coming to town and he's asked me to consult on some work,' I demur. I don't have the closest family and my stepbrother has never asked me for anything before so I don't like to refuse.

'Priorities.'

'C'mon, you have to come.'

'How come you have to work on the weekend?'

I exhale. 'You're right, you're right. I'm in.'

'Speaking of being right,' Stella opens. Here we go. 'How goes the plan to find a guy before the next apocalypse?'

'I've decided on a cat.'

'C'mon, Leonie.' Nessa laughs. 'You said it yourself. A girl can't survive on memes and chat groups alone.'

My own words are thrown back at me. I am planning to do something, I really am. But ... life.

Stella turns and runs her immaculately made-up eyes up and down me. 'I'd do you. You are one bangin' chick.'

I cringe at her use of heavily dated American slang.

'You just have to sell yourself.'

'I can't, okay?' If I was able to do that, wouldn't I be in a relationship already? I am confident at work, have great female friends, but somehow I hit my late thirties manless. Oh, I date, but it never goes anywhere. I never meet anyone who seems like the one I want to spend the rest of my life with. Barely even one for the rest of the evening.

Nessa looks at me assessingly, shushing Stella. 'Let's do your world.'

'What?' I have no idea what that's supposed to mean.

'What's the product? You're a product manager, so what's the result you're looking for?'

Alicia nods, as a marketing manager in a digital company she often works closely with a product. 'What is it you want to build?'

I laugh. This is easier, abstracting me from the chronic state of my singleness. 'A relationship for the next apocalypse.'

Kristen smiles in encouragement. 'What would you do first if this was a job?'

'Well, after I'd decided on the problem to be solved, I suppose I would evaluate the needs and requirements and then do some market research.'

'Boom.' Stella bangs on the table and we all make a grab for our tall swaying glasses. The wooden table is sturdy, but the uneven floorboards make it less than stable.

Alicia pulls a pen out of her Mary Poppins handbag. 'What are the needs and requirements?'

'You should do a top ten,' Isabelle chimes in. 'I did one recently. We all have things we want. It's interesting to write them down, to see what's really important.'

No time like the present, it seems. How have we moved on from the celebratory talk already?

'A good screw.' Stella directs Alicia to start writing. 'Good in bed.'

'That's not the first thing on the list,' I object. If they're going to do this my way then the list needs to be in priority order.

'Then what is?'

I know exactly what I want. I pull the paper towards me. It will be easier to write my criteria for the perfect man than to have to list each aspect out loud, here in the crowded pub, even if my audience consists of my closest friends.

<u>The List</u>
1. At my stage in life – i.e. interested in long term.
2. Educated.
3. Tall.
4. English, maybe American.
5. Good communicator.
6. Well-travelled.
7. Open to children. Maybe.
8. Good-looking.
9. Good sense of humour.
10. Fine. Good in bed.

I hand it over for their perusal. It's not exciting, granted, but I don't need a unicorn, just a regular guy who is decent enough. A minimum viable product.

'This seems doable,' Alicia announces before Stella plucks it out of her hands and pshaws loudly before handing it to Nessa and Isabelle, who look up at me speculatively.

'Are you kidding?' Stella explodes while Kristen takes her turn. 'You put sex last. What is wrong with you?'

'I'm more interested in having company I enjoy than sex.'

'You can't have one without the other,' Nessa advises sagely.

'Leave her alone. We can do something with this,' Alicia intercedes on my behalf, scanning the list. 'It's a start.'

I squirm as they continue to debate the merits of my list until talk turns to the logistics of our Paris trip once again.

Finally, two bottles of France's finest consumed, we don coats and scarves to brave the outside.

'You need to join at least two dating apps by the time we go,' Stella insists as she gives me a hug. 'This is on. You will have a date by the wedding.'

A deadline. Great. 'Tell me you haven't set a date yet.'

'Camille likes June.'

Right. Four months. That's doable.

Isn't it?

TWO

———

We are barely settled into our seats on the Eurostar before the grilling begins.

I hold up my phone to prove the apps are loaded as agreed. Not the most difficult assignment to begin my first step into 'Operation Do Something'. Nessa immediately snatches it out of my hand.

She opens one of the many dating apps that litter dusty corners of my phone. Profiles created in moments of positivity, which then malinger for eons before I get around to deleting them. Okay, I never quite delete them; that would be admitting defeat and it's not that I believe I'll never meet anyone. It's that I just don't believe I'll ever meet anyone.

'What about this one?'

I scan the profile; he looks nice enough. 'He's short.'

A few moments later and Nessa has found another prospect. I glance at it. 'Too tall.'

I'm not saying it to be funny. I dated a guy that tall once. No heel in the world could save me from the neck crick.

Another. 'He doesn't look very interesting. What would we talk about?'

Glasses guy. 'Too hipster.'

Broken-nose guy. 'Too sporty.'

Muscley guy. 'Too gym buff.'

Bearded-black-T-shirt guy. 'Too heavy metal. No way.'

Studious guy. 'Yikes, too straight-laced.'

Car-selfie-from-bad-angle guy. 'Too lazy.'

Alicia puts up a hand to pause proceedings. 'Harsh. How do you make that out?'

'So he wants to find a date, potentially a life partner, but can't even take the time to find a decent photo? Pass.'

Nessa flashes up another candidate. Pretty guy. 'Not straight enough. No offence, ladies,' I throw to our guests of honour.

Naked-torso guy. 'Only in it for one thing.'

'You are too fussy.' Camille raises a brow. 'You don't know until you try.'

'I'm not new to this. I've tried plenty of frogs. I think I can at least spot Prince Charming potential. And I don't see the point in wasting time on someone I know won't work out.'

Kristin links Camille's hand, and they exchange looks. 'Or Princess Charming potential. You never know.'

'Don't you dare swap sides as well.' Stella levels me a glare. 'I can't be the only one complaining about men.'

'You never complain about Derek,' Alicia says. 'I, on the

other hand, left the house today and turned my phone off so no emergency calls could lure me back.'

'You've left Tom without backup?' I can't believe it. To hear Alicia tell it, Tom does nothing with their two children.

'His mother is twenty minutes away, though he swears he doesn't need her. Anybody game for a little sweepstake on how long he lasts?' Alicia turns her phone over on the table to allow her to see any incoming messages now that we have pulled out of King's Cross and she can't be called back.

'Focus, people.' Stella brings everyone's attention back to the conversation around my love life, or lack thereof. 'So, to sum up, Leonie, on top of the list you already gave us he must also be: not too trendy, engaging, into similar musical and other entertainment tastes, work out but not too much, and not on dating apps for just a good time. Have I left anything out?'

'You are way too picky,' Nessa agrees with Camille's assessment.

'It's not that I'm picky but I would like to meet someone who I can see myself spending the next forty years with. As it stands, I never need to compromise: I get to choose who I see and what I do. Would life be better with gym guy? Yes, he might have an amazing body but would he want to go to the theatre, or share a cheese plate with me over a glass of red wine?' I lean back, satisfied that I've made my case.

'I don't like the theatre,' Stella announces, 'and you still hang out with me.'

I eye her critically. 'You're right, I can't recall why we're friends.'

She pulls a face and then reaches into her bag. 'Cos I bring the stinky cheese.'

Out of her bag and onto the small train table between our seats she deposits several chunks of cheese. I spy a veiny blue Roquefort and… I turn over a round one with an orange rind.

'Epoisses,' I say. 'You are the queen of all my friends.'

Camille looks at the table and then up at Stella, her face screwing up in an exquisitely French expression of horror. The one they pull out when you admit to liking cheese singles or spreadable butter. 'You are bringing French cheese on the train to France?'

'There's an English cheddar in there,' Stella defends her choices stoutly, which only earns her a very gallic *pfffttt*.

'You can't eat those on the train,' Alicia protests looking around to see potentially offendable travellers. Our nearest neighbours comprise two businessmen on calls and a family deeply involved in a board game.

'Not without something to wash it down.' Nessa pulls out a bottle of red and some cups, while Stella dives into her bag a second time to produce a baguette, two knives and some napkins.

The cheese is exceptionally stinky and after a few smears of pungent goodness we re-wrap the Epoisses and the blue, sending the businessmen some apologetic glances.

'It's so good, for something that smells so very, very bad,' Stella says, tucking it back into her bag.

'It's true.' Camille throws a shoulder. 'All the best things are.'

Nessa casts me a speculative glance.

'How's Isabelle settling in?' I enquire, heading her off at the pass. Isabelle, it turns out, is doing very well. She's secured a job in a marketing agency and is looking for a flat.

———

Conversation stays with less difficult topics as we emerge from the tunnel and settle back to watch the French countryside roll by – immense fields and the occasional row of tall, thin cypress trees, so much a signature of France and Italy. As soon as they come into view I relax, as if it would be an affront to them for the mind not to ease of all its stresses and turn to thoughts of beautiful foods and wines.

We pull into Gare du Nord, the last of the cheese and empty wine bottle gathered and disposed of as we tumble out into the light of the great station with its vaulted ceiling and follow Camille out where she wrangles us a car big enough to take us all together to our hotel in the Marais.

Even in the cold – and it is colder than London – there's something about Paris. What little girl doesn't dream of someday living there? After my first weekend trip to Paris from London I signed up for a language class. This was before language apps and those audio programmes that promise to have you speaking like a native if you just do their online course while going about your day; back in the day of evening classes and mass repeating of lines back to a teacher. I thought it would be like Colin Firth in *Love Actually* jumping from a scene of him in the Tube speaking aloud to himself to assembling sentences that the whole restaurant laughs at even as he still makes himself understood well enough to propose. Well, it wasn't like that. It was a cold hall in Putney for an hour one evening a week with three other people and an English spinster type who winced every time I spoke in my American accent. I did not get much further than *Je m'apelle Leonie. Je suis Americaine*.

But you don't need French to stroll around the Marais to kill a couple of hours before we meet up again for dinner. It might not be the most sociable thing to do but I pull on my sneakers and head out on my own. I know they mean well, but I need an hour off from the dating advice.

Walking out of the hotel I turn right. The joy of the Marais is wandering about until you lose yourself in the tangle of streets, but with my phone in my pocket I will still be able to make my way back in plenty of time to get ready for dinner.

I meander through the streets with windows displaying out-there jewellery and mannequins draped in bright clothes that beg for attention, along streets where the tables of the cafes overflow into the streets, eventually popping out along the grey-green of the Seine.

Down on the stone banks are the usual couples walking along and groups of students lolling about. I visited Paris on a school tour for our big Senior European Trip and swore that when I came again, I would be one of those people, walking arm in arm, laughing together, looking impossibly romantic. I have been here many times since, on weekends with friends like this one, occasionally for work. Never in the company of the love of my life.

I let myself wander across the beautiful bridges to the

Isle de la Cité and past the scaffolding around Notre Dame. The memorial to those stolen from Paris during the Holocaust sits behind the cathedral. It is a strange subterranean monument, a hidden place in one of Paris' storied sites. There is something about the thousands of lights in the darkness... I don't know what the artist intended or how it is received by others but I've always found it strangely poignant. A reminder of those lives stolen, but still hopeful. I drag myself onward enjoying the effect of the lowering sun turning the sky dramatic streaks of red reflected in the darkening grey of the river.

Unable to resist, I hop over to the Left Bank to hit up Shakespeare & Co. I just about have time to find one – not work-related – book and then, if I hustle, I'll be back in plenty of time to get ready for dinner.

Floor-to-ceiling books, crumbling walls, old chandeliers... I could happily spend the rest of the evening just wandering around the shelves. Under pressure, I struggle to choose the perfect tome but I always like to pick up something to support the old bookstore when in town so pluck out a lucky dip book from the basket. S & Co. was founded by an American expat so I've always felt something of a connection. Sylvia Beach, the owner of the original S & Co. is best known for publishing *Ulysses*, she also fell in love and spent much of her life in a discreet relationship with a Frenchwoman, and I hope she is looking down and can see the occasion that brings us to town.

Not so long ago Kristen was meandering through life, successful in her career, occasionally so in her relationship status, and now she is getting married. Because she was brave enough to see love where she never expected to find it.

As I wait at the kerb for the light to change, I unwrap the mystery book. Kerouac's *Big Sur*. A laugh huffs out of me. Only I could come all the way to Paris and get whacked across the head with a reminder of home.

I should ring my mother.

Later, for now I need to hustle, as my blue dot is far too many blocks away from our hotel and our dinner reservation is in forty minutes.

'What sort of research approaches would you take at work?' Nessa circles back to the topic that seems to spring out at me every time we sit down. The waiter makes that slight bon-appetite bow as he backs away from the table with our order.

The candle flickers as even more wax glides down the side of the old wine bottle. The interior is cavern-like and the music is low. It is the perfect spot for Kristen and Camille's celebratory meal, and we are back on this. Again.

I pick at the bread while I think.

'There are different ways to research potential products. You can look at the market and see what's already out there.'

'You've already done that.' Nessa acknowledges my spotty dating history – apps, set-ups, random encounters, I have tried them all.

'Or you can see how people engage with products to see

how successfully they interact with them. Light users and heavy users, for example, may have entirely different ways of engaging. Often it's about looking past what people say they want; you have to watch them interact with products that are familiar or less familiar to them. You can use the results to validate ideas or disprove them so you can prioritise what features are most important.' I can see Camille and Kristen glazing over. 'Take remote controls. There used to be a hundred buttons, because, when asked, people said they needed all those things. But look at remotes now; they have like four or five buttons on them because actually that's all you really need for most tasks. Everything else is now is hidden in the settings section.'

Even as I say the words, I am drawing parallels in my mind. What are the features I think I want and what do I really need?

'It's about being open-minded rather than seeking to validate your hypothesis. Everyone brings bias and it's about trying to see past that.' I sum up the best approach for early research.

'How do you do that?' Camille, an accountant, is interested in a world so different from her own.

'A/B testing has been very popular for the last few years. You try two different versions, maybe one that does things close to your hypothesis and one that changes things up. Lots of the big websites use this, so you might see a page that looks one way and Stella might see it laid out a different way, and then over time a pattern emerges, data proving which is the most successful. Sometimes your assumptions about people's preferences can be overthrown.

What people say they do and what they actually do when unobserved can be miles apart.'

'Huh, so what you say you want and what you actually need may be two different things?' Stella's tone has a good deal of the ah-ha about it. 'I propose a little on-the-ground market research.'

Stella and Nessa exchange a glance, smiling at each other in perfect accordance, and my stomach dips.

'What?' My eyes flick from one to the other without moving another muscle in my face, not wanting to turn my back on either of them.

'How about a guy who's wrong in every way?' Nessa proposes, holding up her hand before I can speak, change the subject, or shut her up. Anything to put brakes on the direction this conversation has taken. The atmosphere suggests resistance is futile.

'What?' I lift my wine glass and take a fortifying mouthful.

'Isabelle is hitting London like a tidal wave. She's on three or four apps, including the ones you showed us earlier.' Nessa leans into the table. 'She told me about a new one called Opp/Att. It's going for the opposites attract angle. Instead of giving you the guy you think you're looking for, it gives you the opposite. You just need to enter your criteria and handily enough we already have your top ten.'

'I like it,' Alicia concurs, snatching up my phone before offering it back to me. 'Open.'

'No.'

She pulls it back to herself across the table, punching in

some numbers. Red. She tries again. Red. Her eyes narrow contemplatively before she makes her third attempt.

'What's the wrong guy?' Camille asks, her accent giving verve to words that shouldn't sound nearly so interesting.

My screen traitorously reveals itself.

'A guy who will throw you up against the wall,' Stella throws out quickly. 'And leave you unable to walk the next day.'

'A man who can show you a good time. No talking about existential bullshit all night. He's got to make you laugh,' Alicia adds, despite being all too busy on my phone and occasionally consulting her own phone.

'Someone unexpected,' Kristen adds. 'With beautiful eyes.'

Camille bats her lashes and pecks her on the lips. '*Merci, Kristen amour.*'

'Anything else?' I ask dryly. This list is considerably shorter on criteria than my own.

'Good-looking. He must be able to tempt Leonie to be naughty; she likes pretty things.' Camille's eyes crease at the corners as she gives a little moue.

'Ha. No one knows you like we do, baby,' Alicia crows. 'This is the wrong guy.'

She holds my phone up to the other two.

A dark-haired, blue-eyed, blunt cheek-boned, very good-looking face flashes before me.

'Put it down.' I speak like I'm admonishing a naughty child.

'But he's perfect – sexy, young.' Alicia looks correspondingly crestfallen.

'What did you put in to get *him*?'

'Exactly what you asked for.' She holds up a photo of the ten-point list I did in London.

He's the opposite of what I asked for? I knew what I wanted long term, but short term? I'm tempted. Would it hurt to step outside the safe zone, add a little zing…? It's only for one night. No, there's no point. I'm here with my friends, not to spend an evening with some stranger.

'That's the wrong guy?' Maybe if I go along with her, she'll leave me alone. Act like I'm game until they get bored and we move on to the next subject. 'Sexy, young, what's not to like?'

'Right?' She puts the phone down in front of me. A message flashes up to notify me of the match.

'What is the point of going out with someone I would never approach in real life?'

Kristen reaches across the table and puts a hand on mine, her eyes compassionate.

'Darling, when have you ever approached someone in real life?'

I flick her hand away.

'I would.'

'Then why not this one?'

'Are you kidding? Too young, too hot,' I splutter, aware that this is not a winning argument. 'What would we talk about? Why would he even agree to meet me?'

In true movie-style timing, an incoming notification pings. I'm beginning to believe that somehow my phone is in on this.

I pick it up and watch with horror as a message rolls in.

MeetMeInParis: *Hi!*

'He exclamation marked "hi",' I say dismissively.

Alicia snatches my phone up. 'So have you.'

My phone tings again. '*You in Paris for long*?' Alicia reads aloud before tapping in a response. '*One night only.*'

The other two nod, happy with the tone she's setting.

'We'll need her back tomorrow for the marché,' Camille reminds Alicia.

'*Me too. You nearby?*' Alicia reads as she continues to torture me with my phone's help.

'Ah, he is. In the fourth.'

'Oh, my god. Please stop.' I reach for the phone, which Alicia laughingly holds away from me, and Stella picks up the baton to ensure it is firmly out of my reach.

'*Le Noir Maison in an hour,*' Stella reads before putting my phone down on the table. '*Fait accompli.* Job done.'

Picking the phone up, I subject her to a withering look. 'I don't think so.'

I flick through the phone, looking for the green logo'd app they'd been using. It is but a matter of moments to apologise and set this guy straight.

'You deleted the app,' I realise, stunned disbelief locking my body. 'I have no way of contacting him.'

'I know.' Stella smiles knowingly. 'And you would never leave anybody sitting on their lonesome in a bar in a strange city. You'd never stand him up. Think what it would do to your karma.'

'I'm not meeting him,' I say resolutely. 'I can't believe you just did that.'

'Why not? Drastic action is called for.'

'Don't make us tell you how long it's been.'

'C'mon, it's not a commitment for life. It's one night.'

'I won't even have finished dinner,' I protested.

'Oh yes you will.' Nessa beams as the uncharacteristically efficient Parisian waiter arrives with our first course.

'You may have to look elsewhere for dessert though.' Stella winks.

Chapter Three

At the bar sit three potential candidates, but the one at the end of the bar watching the door is definitely my guy. Unlike in the photo I oh so briefly glimpsed, his dark hair is practically a buzz cut, but no one would mistake this guy for someone who's served. He leans on the bar as if it was built for the sole purpose of bearing his weight. The bluntness of his hair is a plain frame for the well-cut angles of his face and his lip curls upward in a greeting that creases his cadet-blue eyes.

'Hi, I'm Jack.' He leans forward to kiss me on the cheek, catching me by surprise. The slight stubble rubs against my cheek. His voice is a slow, dark river that you want to run your fingers through to break its caramel perfection.

'Jack,' I echo. 'Not really?'

I can't help myself. He is the epitome of Jack-the-Lad, and he has that Robert Downey Jr, Guy Ritchie vibe to him. An odd combination of fresh-faced and hard angles, a smile accompanied with a glint in his eye that says he knows how to be bad, and how to be very, very good at it. My stomach twists. I exhale. Loudly.

'How old are you?' There's that glint. His lips hook upward as his eyes light with a darkly mischievous gleam.

'Old enough.' He steps into me. Despite any gap in our ages, I have no doubt he has more than made up for it in experience.

I bite my lip nervously and step back to get a moment to think. This is not what I was expecting. I didn't take a close enough look at the picture. Hadn't been able to. But the glimpse Alicia flashed before me had been of his face. I'm going to kill Alicia; I'll put good money that they weren't the only photos on this man's profile.

I have a feeling there is at least one other on there with hard abs and bared tattoos.

I did not sign up for this.

Before I can take another step back, he takes my hand in his and rubs a calloused thumb down the inside of my palm. The touch skitters through me.

'One drink,' he says, pre-empting my imminent retreat. 'You're here now.'

Right.

He raises an eyebrow at the bartender, who immediately looks expectantly at me.

'Ah, a red wine, *s'il vous plait*.' Hold on, no. Black teeth alert. I'd only just remedied this with some magic handbag wipe Alicia donated to the cause. '*Pardon*, no, ah, I'll have a cocktail, please.'

My mind races to come up with a cocktail. I rarely have them – normally black teeth is a price I am happy to pay for a luscious full-bodied Bordeaux. And while in France it's practically a sin to drink hard liquor. Focus. Occasionally, I have a Cosmo, but I have an inkling it is deeply old school, not to mention that tricky table-to-lip coordination required. Has anyone even ordered them since *Sex & the City*? Stella's go-to cocktail is a gin cocktail, which has a better glass shape, sophisticated ruby colour, and cheeky curl of orange.

'A Negroni, please.'

Jack orders a beer.

I casually look over at Jack to find myself being surveyed by a heavy-lidded gaze.

'Hi.'

'Hi, yourself,' he responds as I take the bar stool beside his.

So far, so good. My eyes flick up and down his face: thickly lashed eyes, mobile mouth, eyes lightly crinkled at the corners, forehead barely lined and I can already tell he raises his eyebrows when he speaks. I should warn him that that will cause premature lines when he's older. Cos, he's not. Older, that is. I swallow a mouthful of the drink discreetly placed in front of me. It's sour and I cough as it hits me with force in the back of the throat, and the heat wallops my stomach.

'You okay?'

I raise my hand to wave dismissively as I cough repeatedly into my elbow. I take the drink of water he hands me and smile weakly as I sip gingerly to soothe my affronted throat.

'You didn't use an old picture,' I say accusingly.

His mouth tilts at the corner. 'No.'

'Why not? Everyone uses an old picture.' I glare at him. I'd seen he was younger but half assumed he'd fudged like so many app daters do. 'How old *are* you?'

'Does it matter?'

I assess him. He's right; this is a one-night thing. I'm not looking for forever from him. I'm not even looking for all night! An hour here should placate the girls sufficiently. Hell, I'm lucky if I make it through an hour. He's, what, maybe six years younger than my impending forty. Okay, maybe more like seven or eight.

He leans forward and his lips touch mine, a light brush before he eases back, meeting my eyes before leaning in again. He puts a hand at the spot where my jaw meets my neck, not holding, barely cradling, a feather of a touch as he deepens the kiss. His lips are malt and there is the tinkle of glasses behind me.

He pulls back, his eyes darker than they were moments before.

'Doesn't seem to matter.'

'What?' I feel mesmerised by the liquid eyes gazing back at mine. I'd forgotten how good that is. That meeting of lips in a kiss.

His smile widens.

My thoughts are utterly scrambled by that one touch. I swallow and try to focus. 'Are you in town for the rugby?'

His eyes crease at the corners. He looks amused and possibly a bit offended at the same time.

'I'm not English,' he says in a definite manner. The city is full of white and red-clad men for the Six Nations rugby. He tacks on as an afterthought, 'Or French.'

'I didn't think you were French.' Not for a second. He's not smooth enough, far too earthy.

'So you thought I was English?'

Of course he isn't; that would have met one of the requirements on my list and the point of tonight is for me to go off piste, to try a flavour I don't normally go for. He speaks English natively though, so there are only so many countries he can be from – most of which I avoid dating because the accents, while charming, usually take me too long to decipher.

'Scottish?' Am I finally going to have my Jamie Fraser moment? Please be from the Highlands, I could extend my English criteria to British for a tartan clad man. My college self is already clasping her hands together in joy.

He shakes his head ruefully. 'No, but you're getting closer, and also further away.'

Okay, so he's definitely from one of the other two Celtic countries. Welsh, maybe. I don't know too many Welsh people. Possibly Irish. There is something of the Colin Farrell about him. Dark-haired, olive-skinned, but for a Celt he's pretty tanned. Dark-blue eyes watch as I work to make my next guess my last.

'Irish?'

'There you go. You have it.' That slightly lyrical inflection is unmistakable this time, his tones rich, like chocolate swirled in more chocolate.

'Your accent isn't very strong,' I comment. It isn't; it's there, but nothing like the rapid rhythm of my friend Niall who hails from somewhere on the southern coast and whose speech is more akin to some kind of performance art than regular communication – an up and down lilt, hands moving expressively as if to conjure the words I cannot catch.

'I don't live there, and I got tired of repeating myself.'

I wince. I regularly have to ask Niall to repeat himself. Well, sometimes I guess at what he's saying and it mostly seems to work out. In my defence, I can nearly always tell what he's saying now, but sometimes I get distracted by the rhythm of his speech and just lose myself in the cadence.

'I'm American.'

'Yes.' His eyes gleam at me, as if that is all too apparent. Humph. I've lived in the UK long enough now that when I go back to the States, I am sometimes mistaken for English. This rarely to never happens on this side of the Atlantic though.

He leans forward a little to hear what I'm saying over the background noise of the increasingly busy bar, and his denim-clad knee brushes against my own. A flare of awareness shoots through me, and it takes me a minute to pull another question together from the few facts I have gleaned.

'You don't live in Ireland now? Where do you live?' Please don't say London, please don't say London. I absolutely cannot do this if there is even the slightest chance I will meet him again. Which is madness. I've lived in London for eleven years and have only bumped into someone I know once, at Portobello market.

'America,' he says deadpan. Touché.

'Big place,' I note dryly. If he isn't going to offer

information, I refuse to sit here like the Gestapo pulling answers out of him.

'Northern California.' He narrows it down. His T-shirt flexes across his chest as he turns to the bar to lift and take a sip of his drink, the strong column of his throat on display as he tilts back a stubbled but clean-lined jaw. What is wrong with me? I never do this, never objectify men, but all I can think about is what he looks like when that shirt comes off. Tattoos? He has that vibe to him, and I will bet any money that what is under that shirt is worth adorning.

He replaces the dark bottle of beer on the bar and is waiting for me when I meet his eyes again. Totally caught.

What did he say? Oh yeah.

'I went to school in Northern California, to Sta—' He slightly hunches and his lips tighten as if he knows what I will say. And doesn't like it. 'Okay, no schools.'

He slants me a twisted smile in acknowledgement that I read him correctly. I get it. I went to school on my stepfather's dime, always felt a little like I didn't deserve the education I received and am all too aware what a privilege it is. Once I throw out Stanford, we're on the road to establishing who we are in terms of social and economic status. I'm happy to take a night off from that.

'What brings you to Paris?'

If the school question made him defensive, then this one totally pisses him off. He picks his drink up and finishes it before answering, mouth turned down like the happiness has emptied out of him.

'Nothing, as it turns out.'

I don't know where to go from here. I've touched a

nerve with what I thought was a fairly innocuous question. I glance casually around the bar. Why is there never a clock on the wall? I've nearly finished my drink. Is it too soon to make some sort of exit?

He closes his eyes briefly. 'Sorry, I've just had a bad day, and I thought maybe meeting someone for a drink would make it better. But all I'm doing is wrecking your night as well.'

This is it. This is my out. My friends are a ten-minute walk away, having fun, and this is hard work. But I also don't want to leave him like this. I've had bad days. Being alone never makes them better.

'It's just drinks.' I shrug, still not sure of my intention, but setting the boundary for the night nonetheless.

He catches the eye of the barman.

'A whiskey, *s'il vous plait*. You have Jameson?' The barman nods. He arches a brow at me and I nod. Okay, I'm staying for another. 'And an Aperol spritz.'

I raise both my eyebrows. 'Ah, did you just go all Humphrey Bogart on me?'

'Bogart?' His lip twitches. 'I don't plan to drink it for you.'

I frown. Oh, he thinks I'm referring to the stoners' term for when one person is hogging the joint. Do people still use the term that way?

'I meant, you know, all'—I do a swaggering accent—'Here, little lady, let me order your drink at this here bar. I know exactly what you need.'

His lip twitches again, eyes gleaming as the barman drops the two drinks on the bar. 'I think you'll find that's

John Wayne.' He laughs before leaning one shoulder more heavily on the bar, eyes drooping as his voice husks. 'Between us, we both know you weren't enjoying that drink. Go on, do it, damn it. Take a sip.'

On the 's' his lip curls and he lisps it a little. He's right; that is a far better Bogie.

Despite myself, I laugh and lift the bright-orange drink to my lips. Dear citrusy goodness. I practically sigh in the enjoyment of the sparkly, tangy drink, sweeter than the Negroni and substantially less alcoholic. Too many more of those and the night wouldn't be long coming to an early and embarrassing end.

A scene springs into my head and I lean forward and impulsively press my lips to his.

His brows draw together. 'Whatcha do that for?'

I laugh aloud as on cue he gives me the line from *To Have and Have Not*. Even though we've already kissed, I give him the line back. 'Been wondering whether I'd like it.'

He laughs in response to my much better Bacall impression and his head goes back, the strong column of his throat exposed, a sight which I enjoy almost as much as the kiss.

'I get the feeling the drink isn't the only thing that isn't your usual tipple.'

I bite my lip. He's right. I need to stop. I'm here to step out of my usual lane. I need to stop reacting every time he surprises me.

'You do this often?' he asks, somehow indicating the impulse hook-up with a swirl of his finger.

'No, just wanted to try something new.'

His eyes meet mine, amused before something pinches it from his face and he's looking at me seriously.

'What?' I ask.

'I wish I was new.'

I don't follow and tilt my head for him to explain.

'I wish I could be new again.'

New. Like we're just two blank slates here in this moment, a moment where I'm not weighing up whether this date is someone I will see again, because we've already established we won't. He lives on the other side of the world. I don't need to judge whether he could be The One, because he can't be. Besides the fact that he is the opposite of everything I'm looking for in a potential partner, this evening is already marked out as a one-night thing. It was before I ever stepped into this bar.

'You mean, like we just appeared fully grown in this bar and don't have the history of our lives to pull up and lay out in front of each other?'

'Yeah, no history, no baggage, no trying to figure out what is or is not being shared,' he concurs.

'Like we're eighteen?' Shiny and new, unburdened by what we do and where we live. Except most of my scars came from before I was eighteen. The last two decades have been pretty wound free. Work comes first, but I don't want to talk about work and I sure as hell don't want to talk about my lack of relationships. So I'm in.

'Sure. Like we're eighteen.' His eyes are more sombre than his tone, which is upbeat and flirtatious. His eyes say eighteen probably wasn't the time of his life either.

'I was awkward at eighteen.'

'You? But you're a goddess!' His smile is broad and cheeky.

'I am not.' I groan. 'You were one of those guys?'

'Who were *those guys*?'

'The ones who had it all figured out, all *look at me, I'm hot and you know you want me*.' The guys who went to my school, all loose-limbed, athletic, confident gods who strode about the school like they had everything going for them. Which they did.

His smile widens, 'Like a jock? Nah, I was more of a lad about town.'

'Same thing, no? Cocky, got all the girls, good at sports, king of the school.' He chuckles hard and dark at my assessment as if I couldn't be more off base if I tried.

'Nah, not me. Well, some of that.'

'The girls?' I guess. His smirk tells me I'm not wrong. I was out of my depth with guys like this at eighteen. Has anything really changed?

'Mmm, the girls were around all right. But not too much of the sports for me.' His eyelids hide whatever other truths existed for him at that age.

'No fair. You can't pick the age and then refuse to tell me anything about yourself from then either.'

'I didn't pick the age, darlin'. You did.' He swirls his whiskey round in his glass, watching the golden liquid catch the light from the candles on the bar. 'You're right though. It's not fair. Can we just say I wasn't up to much good at that point in my life and leave it at that? It's not particularly a time I look back on fondly.'

'Me neither,' I admit. 'I … never felt like I fit in. I went to an LA high school where nearly everyone was wealthy and golden and I was this other being, a gangly beanpole trying to merge into the walls to avoid drawing attention to myself.'

He blinks before twisting our hands together, pulling me up from the bar stool, as he stands eye to eye with me.

'Seems like it worked out in the end. Elegance from top to toe'. As if to seal his assessment he lifts my hand to his lips where they move over my knuckles before he takes a bite of the skin on the back of my hand, which travels like a hit of fiery whiskey all the way through me.

'I didn't go to a posh school in Dublin. But I know what it is to feel you're not the same, not enough,' he eases back onto his stool casually as if paying homage to women in this way was an everyday event. I blink. At him, perhaps at myself, I don't know why I told him that, it's such an adolescent wound and I can tell he isn't sure why he is reciprocating either. Normally I would be evaluating what that revelation says about him, about out potential future. But I'm not. I want to know more, explain more, learn more. Just because.

Dragging in a deep shuddering breath, I pull my hand back in an apparent need to use it to lift my drink. Obviously, I could use the other one, but I think I need it back to regain my balance, to firmly push the lid down on the strange impulse.

I take another sip of my drink to wet my far-too-dry mouth.

The music in the background has gotten louder since our first drink.

His head tilts to one side and his lip pulls up.

'Do you dance?'

My eyelids flick heavily at him. I love to dance, but it's late. This has been fun, or something, but I should go.

'Let's go dancing.' His tone is half-suggestion, half-order.

I'm not sure. However, if there's one thing I miss about my twenties and early thirties it's dancing, dancing off the alcohol, moving to the music.

Live a little, an insistent voice inside my head urges me. I watch him watching me, waiting for my answer, willing me to say yes.

'Okay. I'm in.'

'All right, give me a minute.' He nods toward the toilets in the corner behind me, easing past, inside my space, his hand almost touching my leg as he goes by as if physically reluctant to move away from me. His near touch leaves tingles in its wake.

He really wears those jeans.

I pull my phone out of my handbag. I cannot believe I'm doing this. I came to be with the girls. I'll be exhausted tomorrow.

My screen is awash with messages. I scan down them, a dozen or so requests for updates.

Me: *All good. He's*

I pause.

Nice isn't right. He's not nice; there's an edge to him. He has been considerate and easy to talk to but if we were to walk down the wrong alley, I have a feeling he can handle himself; that it won't be the first wrong alley he's ever been down.

My fingers trace out some more letters.

Me: *He's fun. Cute.*

I hit send.

Cute. He isn't cute. He is terrifyingly attractive. He makes my toes curl and my stomach flip and if I'd walked into a bar where he was sitting on his own on any other night, I wouldn't have looked at him twice. Once for sure, but as someone whose life would not be touching mine in the real world. If he was on a TV screen, I would binge that bad boy on repeat. Oh wow, I am so far out of my comfort zone I don't even know the name of the zone I am in right now. Danger, danger.

I breathe out a calming exhale. At least, it's meant to be calming, but it stirs up the flock of butterflies inside me and sends them up and out in a swirling cloud.

Stella: *Typing…*

I can still leave, be gone before those blue eyes and well-shaped jeans return.

Me: *We're going dancing. I'll be late. Don't wait up.*

That last one will send Stella wild.

He still hasn't come back though. Has he left while I sit here daring myself to stay?

We're staying in a hotel so the girls will have no idea what time I get back, whether I bail in ten minutes.

Alicia: *dancing girl emoji*

Or later.

Stella: *egg plant emoji x3*

'Aubergines. Just drinks, huh?' a voice whispers in my ear. Heat rises through me.

'Shouldn't you be calling them eggplants by now?' I toss back, he's lived in the States long enough, though to be fair, I still can't bring myself to call them aubergines in England.

'You say tomato…' He chuckles and an arm wraps around me and scoops me off the chair, which is no mean feat as I'm no pixie girl, and as he sets me down a barely there kiss flutters against my bare neck. I always thought going weak at the knees was a cliché in supermarket romances, but in this moment, I swear if he didn't have his arms around me I could swoon to the floor.

Get a grip, Leonie.

I lift a brow in what I hope is a dead cert for Lauren Bacall and finish my drink before stepping out of his arms to put my coat on.

He leans across the bar to talk to the barman, presumably getting directions for somewhere to go dancing on a Saturday night in a city neither of us are familiar with. His jeans stretch with him as he leans across his seat to where his jacket has fallen. I let out a laugh at my perving and just to prove to myself I'm not some crazy ass ogling hussy, I wander outside to wait for him.

My stomach fizzes as I step out onto the cobbles and lift my head up, taking in the shuttered windows of the Parisian buildings above the slightly misty evening. Some men stumble by clad in blue rugby jerseys.

A blond, broad-shouldered man breaks from the group and comes toward me, a smile on his lips, which fades a little in wry acceptance as an arm snakes about my waist from behind. I know I shouldn't enjoy this minor exchange, but I can't help myself; I give my blue-clad almost suitor a rueful smile. *What? I never get to have this moment.*

A possessive kiss lands on my cheek. 'Ready?'

I'm not sure I am, but let him take my hand anyway.

The club is dark and as we step down the stairs, my willingness to prolong the evening is starting to cool. But then the music catches me.

In most other parts of my life I'm self-conscious or constantly aware of the impression I'm making on people around me; in a room full of developers I strive to appear the right level of confident and authoritative. With my friends, my mom, my stepdad, I worry whether I am being the person I want to be or that they want me to be to the right degree in any given situation.

Not on the dancefloor. On the dancefloor, I don't care. I

will shake a leg to Elvis, step to the side with Beyonce or get down on it with Kool & the Gang and I don't care who's watching. I let the music fill me up and just dance.

Jack, it turns out, is a good dancer, and not in that white guy jogging up and down way; he can really move. Patrick Swayze he ain't, but as he wraps himself around me and pulls me in, he has my rhythm. Happiness fizzes up through me as the intro beat of 'Footloose' comes on, my dance partner hooks his shoulder Kevin Bacon style, kicks out a leg, and then he is full-on cutting loose. I burst out laughing and join him doing, de doing de doing doing, throwing my shoulders and hips back and forward in the trademark moves until the big finish and he grabs my hand and swings me in and kisses me.

Not a sexy hey-there kiss. But a sweaty, hot, open-mouthed plastered together breathless kiss that melts my insides. There in the middle of the dancefloor, with its cheesy multi-coloured flashing squares lighting up under our feet as we full on pash on the dancefloor. Hands grabbing at hair and butts and under shirts.

We pull back and stare at each other, breathless.

Someone jostles against me and I fall slightly forward into him. He puts an arm protectively around me and we make our way off the floor to some couches along the mirrored wall. What decade have we fallen into?

'Water?' he mouths at me, lifting his hand in the universal drinking sign that says bottle of water rather than a glass of something stronger. I nod. Good idea.

It's hot in the club and smells of late nights and alcohol, which explains the sticky crunch I can feel under my feet.

What am I doing here with this guy? He's nearly ten years younger than me, and way too ... everything.

He returns and hands me a sealed bottle of water. It's clean and refreshing, water has never tasted so good. I look up to find those electric eyes on me and smile as I retrieve a drop of water from my lower lip with my tongue, a delicious power surging through me as I catch him watching the movement.

His eyes flick back up to mine.

He steps into me and this time his hand comes up slowly to frame my cheek as he pulls me slowly in for a kiss. He doesn't kiss me straight away but seems to breathe me in before coming in for the slowest, deepest kiss I've had in years. He savours it, making it last, like this is the only chance he will have to do this, and he wants to make it count.

'We should go,' he says and I realise he has our jackets. He must have retrieved them from the coat check when he ordered the water.

He's ready to move onto the next portion of our evening. Am I?

Chapter Four

By the time my coat is back on and the cold air has hit my face, I realise I'm not. I can't do this. The occasional accidental night after seeing someone a few times, or at a wedding, is one thing but to calculatedly meet someone for casual sex who you never plan to see again? To deal with the whole awkward morning departure? I can't do it. My head is already shaking as I turn around. His lips tug down as he takes in my expression.

'I don't think we should have sex,' he says, pulling my hips into his.

'What?' Have I misread the signals? I swallow, totally caught out. I find I'm somewhat annoyed. Am I offended?

'Stay with me.'

'You just said you didn't want to...'

His brows slant down and inward, his chin down as he catches my hand, his thumb playing on the inside of my palm. 'I know. But I don't want to say goodbye either.'

I'm not sure what he's suggesting.

'Stay with me,' he repeats.

I look around the almost deserted street. It's late. Do I really want to walk home alone? Get a taxi back to my safe but cold hotel bed?

'No sex?' I ask. Is he asking me to snuggle? That's not the impression he gives out to the world.

His shoulder lifts in a shrug. 'I won't tell if you won't.'

'Is this some ruse to lure me back to your room?' I ask. 'It would seem to me that given we met up for a drink after one brief exchange in a strange city you weren't looking for cuddles. Or...'

Maybe he has some strange fetish and has to work up to it. What am I suspecting him of, being some serial non-sex dater? How twisted has the world become?

Or how twisted have I become that I...? I don't know him. Sure, there is something about the way he meets my eyes, the way he speaks to people, that assures me of his integrity. Or at least a basic humanity that leads me to believe I won't be floating in the Seine in the morning if I indulge this one basic need. He holds a hand out to me. Human contact. A night wrapped in arms I have admired all evening. What's the worst that can happen?

If nothing else the walk to his hotel fulfils my fantasy of strolling hand in hand with a man through the dimly lit back streets and empty boulevards of Paris.

'Tell me about your first time,' he says into the hush of the room. His arm is around my T-shirted waist, and he smells

good. Salty. Woodsy. His length is curled about me and …
who am I kidding? The pressure of his touch is making me
crazy. All I want to do is turn around and inhale his bare
flesh. Is it bare? The light was off when he came in and I'm
in a T-shirt. His legs are definitely bare, the rough hair of
those muscular legs looping over mine. It appears no
touching isn't part of the night's guidelines.

'What? Why are we talking about this?' Even after all
these years my entire body cringes at the awkward
memories.

'Eighteen-year-olds talk about this,' he reminds me of
our earlier agreement. 'Embrace the game, no complicated
histories, none of the mistakes or misdeeds of the last
decade, or *two*.'

I elbow him in the ribs for that last.

'C'mon, tell me.'

I feel like my stomach has turned into a tumbling mess
and I open my mouth to answer but can't push the words
past my mouth. I can't believe I'm having this conversation.
I can't believe I'm still embarrassed about something that
happened so many years ago.

I huff out a breath. 'I'm not playing.'

'Because you don't want to or you can't?' His voice is
warm with laughter, then his body stills as I fail to answer,
or something about the feel of my body betrays me. This is
why I prefer to keep my clothes on in the presence of others.
Darkness, nakedness, leads to intimacy, leads to
uncomfortable truths.

'You aren't?' he breathes.

Aren't what? What does he mean? I turn swiftly about in

the dark, banging his chin in my haste. I put my fingers up to catch his face.

'Oh no, I'm so sorry. Are you okay?'

One of his hands comes up to cover mine, holding it there for a moment.

'I'll survive,' he says. 'Now answer the question.'

The only light is the faint orange of the streetlights through the open window at my back. At least I don't have to endure his seeing the heat blazing from my face.

'Are you asking if I'm a virgin?' I ask drily. 'That's cute.'

'Are you?'

'Not unless it grows back,' I admit. 'It's been a while.'

I don't want to fool him into raised expectations that I'm all amazing moves and porn star actions when it's more likely I've forgotten what goes where. Well okay, I can still remember the basic mechanics of it all but still, it's been a while, that's all I'm saying.

'How long?'

'No, no, no, my friend. That's not the deal, no pasts, only the eighteen-year-old present.' I groan as I realise what my evasion has led me to. 'So yes, I'm a virgin.'

'At eighteen?' he breathes, his tone utter disbelief.

'High school... I was half a foot taller than most of the guys my age, with wild hair and … a whole pile of chip on one shoulder, awkward on the other.' Am I really defending this two decades on? 'Thankfully, college happened.'

'And?'

'Guys got taller and I discovered hair products.'

'The question is about your first time.'

'I hooked up with some guy at a party and it was a

quick trip to his bedroom and an even quicker trip to the other side of womanhood,' I say, my tone going from offhand to high documentary narrator delivery.

'That sounds like it was an experience to remember.'

'Not particularly,' I wince, 'more a fumble across the line than a score. What about you? Not still a virgin?'

'Sixteen.'

'Ugh, even a decade on you sound pleased with yourself.'

'Oh yeah, I showed her a real good time. In the men's loos at an away game.'

'Did you win?'

'Nah, two–one.'

Silence, as I wait in amusement.

'You meant the sex.' And there it is.

'Obviously yours was one of the great romances of the age.'

He huffs a laugh. 'Sharon, I think her name was. Great big knockers she had.' His accent gets considerably broader as he boasts of his sixteen-year-old self's conquest.

'Classy,' I observe.

'But at least I was still young.' I can hear the smirk in his voice.

'Mine was a classic college rite of passage. Crossing into womanhood.'

'While I was thrusting my way into manhood from a much earlier age.' Pun clearly intended.

'You must have been quite the experienced old hand by the time you got to eighteen,' I flash back.

'I managed to pick up a thing or two, all right.' His

accent again broadens as he leans into me in the dark. His lips are hovering above mine, close enough that I can sense him there, mere millimetres away but not touching. The banter of moments ago fades into the night. There's nothing but our breaths in the crisp night air and the closeness of our lips.

'I thought you said no sex.'

'Kissing isn't sex.'

His lips glance off mine.

A touch runs up the outside of my leg. A single fingertip, a line of touch under the sheet on my hyper alert skin.

'Your legs.'

I smile against his lips.

'Yes?'

He breathes deeply, his chest barrelling out in the dark, the sheet lifting and slowly dropping as he exhales into me. Everything is soft.

'I like them.'

I want to lift my hand and touch him but he was so adamant earlier that nothing would happen and I don't want to ruin the moment. I want to live on this cliff edge of rising deliciousness forever.

'Leonie.'

'Mmhhhm.'

His lips press into mine and his palm goes to the flat of my back and pulls me in. His kiss deepens as heat licks up through me. My hand is caught, splayed across his chest as he plunders deeper into my mouth and my free hand comes around to hold his head to me. I never want this moment to end. This reaching, hungry finding, exploring. A kiss so natural, so fierce in its first moments that I wonder how we can go higher if this is the starting point.

There's a growl as he pulls back and sets a trail down my throat, my chest, as my T-shirt is discarded.

'I want,' he groans.

We've turned slightly, and he is now across me as his weight goes dead and his body stills. The blaze takes a minute to cool in my veins as I attempt to adjust to the change from sensory overload to nothing.

He turns onto his back and is gone.

'I can't,' he groans.

'Can't?' I echo.

What's going on here? Dread replaces the heat in my veins.

'You're not...' My stomach sinks. 'Are you cheating on someone?'

'I ... no, but ... I shouldn't.'

'You're married?'

His hands come up to cover his face. 'It's not... If you're asking if anyone would be hurt by us being in bed together then no. But I can't. I shouldn't be here. I meant it when I said I just planned to have a couple of drinks. That I just wanted you to come up.'

He turns to me and pulls me in against the length of him. I can feel his hardness against my stomach.

'Do I want more right now? Yes. But ... I'm sorry.'

He hasn't answered my question, but there's something about him that's honest and I want so badly to trust him. Which is odd, because with all the much closer to perfect guys I've dated, I've never felt this visceral desire to trust them. Maybe that's it. Maybe it's that this is just tonight. He lives far away. Is so far from my type it doesn't matter. So I can't have sex with him, but I don't want to go. If we have only this one night, just being here in this bubble has its own charms.

'Okay.'

'Yeah? You'll stay.'

'I'll stay, but that's it.'

'I feel like I'm letting you down. I want to touch you,' he whispers, the rich timbre of his voice vibrating through me. 'I want to run my hands up and down you, over and over. Learn the feel of you, the shape of you.'

'What are you doing?' For a man who moments ago shifted down the gears, the warmth from his tone is gearing things up again. His hands aren't on me but I can remember the feel of them, the hard, calloused touch running up and down my body.

'I can't do anything. That doesn't mean you can't.' His breath is a whisper of heat on my skin. 'That you shouldn't get the release you deserve.'

'What do you mean?'

He pulls the sheet down and my body is revealed, lit by the glow of the streetlight through the window. He sets his teeth in my shoulder and I feel it all the way through my body; the flame igniting once more, the rasp of his stubble on my shoulder. The cold air from the open window shivers across my heated skin.

He takes my hand and places it on my breast. He can't possibly mean that I should … here in front of him.

'No.' I pull my hand away.

'You want to try new things, right? Do it.'

I pull in a shuddery breath and lift my hand back to where he placed it.

'Trace your fingers across your breast. That's it. Now take the nipple in your fingers. Roll it. Tweak it, mmmm hmmm. Now your other hand, move it downwards.

'Are you wet?' His breath is warm, close. 'Tell me.'

'Yes.'

'Say it.'

'I can't.'

'You are though?' I'm mortified, but also really, really turned on as his voice in the darkness directs me, his heat beside me in the bed.

'Press your fingers together.' My pants slide off and he guides my hand between my legs. 'Inside, out, now in. Touch, press. Ah, do that again, again.'

I'm winding tighter and tighter, the sound of his voice rippling through me.

'Now, come for me.'

And I'm gasping for air, arching high as the electric shocks catch me and pull me in before shattering outwards and I lie in his arms shuddering.

I feel giddy and safe and enervated as his muscular arms remain folded around me. I can't believe I just did that. But I did.

I turn and breathe him in.

Chapter Five

The white voile curtain wafts in the room by the open window. I see the dark shadow of the balcony on the other side and beyond that … Paris. Shit.

The weight of a male arm curls around me. Breathe. My lips feel swollen in a good way and my fingertips trace the slight prickle of delicate skin irritated by unfamiliar stubble burn. A smile lingers on my lips. I'm not sure why. Last night went nothing like I expected and normally I would be in the horrors.

Shallow breaths. Don't disturb him.

I lift the arm from around my waist and slowly edge my way out of the bed. I can't believe I did that with him last night. I wish I was one of those women who can take their pleasure where they find it, modern, strong, but no. My one-night stand comes with a solid side of *what did I do with this stranger*. And last night's escapade is a doozey. Straight-up sex would have felt less intimate. I lower myself out of the bed and turn to see if he's still asleep.

He is. The dark outline of his lashes lies on his unguarded face, the stubble from last night is darker, and his chest is rising and falling steadily.

I scrabble around on the floor and can see his discarded clothes, but not my own. I grab his shirt and pull it on; it smells amazing. Of a light cologne and that unique masculine aroma of his skin.

I have a mental image like I'm Catherine Deneuve or Cara Delavigne, some chic woman, hair thrown up carelessly, wearing their lover's shirt. I dread to think what I really look like crawling about on his hotel floor. Hair at full frizz, panda eyes and creased face, no doubt. This room is tiny. Where the hell are my clothes?

My handbag is lying on the floor over by the door where I carelessly dropped it last night when we came home. Arrived. *Arrived* home. I mean, *arrived in the hotel.*

I pull my phone out of my retrieved bag; the girls will be wondering where I am.

A scroll of messages cascades down the screen, and I unlock the phone, opening the app to read the list of questions that might have started off direct at me but at some point became more *about* me as they amused each other regarding my evening's activities.

Alicia: *You alive?*

Stella: *She never came back to the hotel. Go, girl!*

Alicia: *Let us know how it's going??*

Camille: *Leave her alone. She's busy.*

Alicia: *Or dead in a ditch.*

Stella: *Or thrown up against a wall…*

'Morning.' The rusty voice comes above me from the bed. He levers himself up into a tousled seated position against the pillows to see me crouched in my inelegant position on the floor.

'Hi.' Smooth, be smooth. I look down at the white-collared shirt that smells deliciously of him. Whatever he wore is amazing, all sea winds and cedarwood smoke. 'Ah, is this okay?'

'Looks good on you.'

'I'm sure.' What woman isn't at her best after dancing the night away before settling in on a hotel room floor? 'Ah, you haven't seen my clothes, have you?'

He tilts his head in contemplation of my question, as I continue to scan the room. Seriously, how could I have lost an entire outfit in this matchbox?

'I might have,' he admits as he leans back on the pillows.

I narrow my eyes at him as I make my way back to the bed and loom over him threateningly, while in, you know, nothing other than his white shirt.

'Did you do something with them?' Did he hide my clothes?

An amused look creeps over his face as he grabs a wrist and pulls me down on top of him until I'm straddling him on the other side of the sheet. I can feel his morning greeting against my centre and I feel a little breathless. He grimaces and adjusts me slightly into what for him might be a more comfortable position but for me, despite my release the night before, feels like torture.

'They're hanging in the closet.'

'What?' I ask suspiciously. 'You're the type of guy to go in for a little middle-of-the-night tidying? I don't know if you noticed, but you seem to have missed some.'

He glances over the side of the bed to where his jeans and shoes lie abandoned on the floor.

'So I have.'

'Just my clothes then.' Either he is the most considerate man I have ever met or he was guaranteeing I wouldn't be able to sneak out on this weird no-sex one-night stand. 'You holding them hostage?'

He pushes up and rolls me over until I'm lying underneath him, his hands catching mine and spreading them above our heads.

'You seem like the type to make a run for it, unless I trapped you here in my bed.' He gives me a leer and waggles his brows in comic villain style.

I swallow nervously. His eyes have dilated and grown heavy-lidded, and even though I know he doesn't plan to have his way with me, whatever held him back the night before seems not to be at the forefront of his thoughts right now. Why didn't I brush my teeth while I had the chance, or go to the bathroom? I berate myself as his weight presses down on me.

My flight instincts are fully triggered now. This is a crazy idea. The light coming through the window must be showing every crease on my face, every flabby muscle on my body.

'Where have you gone?' His eyes are watching the flickers of expression cross my face.

'I should go,' I say, pushing up, attempting to pull my hands free.

'Damn,' he groans, reacting to the movement against his lower body. 'I wish...'

I can only imagine what he wishes – that he hasn't woken up with some stranger in his bed. Some *older* stranger who he didn't want to have sex with that he now has to get rid of.

'Woah, what is that?' He stills, his eyes watching me intently.

'What?'

'You look like...' He pulls a face. 'Are you sorry you came back with me?'

It's difficult to act casual and nonchalant with six feet of male pressed against me, watching every facial tic and muscle from about two inches away.

'No, I mean, I guess, I'm not sure.' In a moment of madness I speak the truth. 'You, why didn't ... you didn't want me.'

'Fuck.' His eyes look vaguely anguished as he squeezes them tightly shut, and I can't read him at all. 'That's not it.'

'What is it then?'

He releases me and turns over, his hand smoothing back his seal-dark scalp.

'I felt... You ever feel like your life is this single track that loops, and there's a scratch on the record, and it warps

63

that bit of the song every time. Well, last night I just needed not to hear that scratch. And while you were there that song felt new and I didn't want it to end.' He blinks, casting the moment away. 'I'm not making any sense.'

He turns a roguish smile my way.

I'm not sure what to say to this. But the anger and creeping feeling of mortification seep away, and I reach a hand across and lay it flat on his chest.

'Okay.'

He puts his hand over mine and closes his eyes for a moment before opening them and turning his head to smile gleamingly.

'I'll release your clothes if you have breakfast with me.'

'You're resorting to blackmail?' I stretch luxuriously in his shirt, held together by only two buttons. 'Or we could stay here.'

He bursts out in a deep throaty laugh.

'Humph. Tease.'

We exit his hotel and walk down the street to a small café and take a table for two on the street and order two *petite dejeuners*. The waiter swiftly places café au lait, juice and a bucket of bread and jam on the table.

I look at him over my coffee. 'Why are you on a dating app?'

He can't struggle to meet women. We've been here less than five minutes and already two women and one man passing by have allowed their gazes to linger on him. He's not eye-catchingly good-looking, but there's something indefinably magnetic about him.

His mouth pouts as he lets his head drop to the side. He meets my gaze contemplatively before answering. 'Same reason as you, I suppose.'

'I doubt it.' My stomach clenches at even the idea of telling this never-to-be-seen-again stranger the truth of my draught. Especially as nothing really happened. Only I could get naked with a stranger in the world's most romantic city and still come up dusty.

'There are only two reasons to be on an app like that.' I identify two use cases, neither of which I feel apply to him. I'm intrigued. Fine, I'm being nosey, but it's also informative. It's always interesting to understand the outlying use cases for any consumer-facing product.

'Which are?' he prompts.

I narrow my eyes at him in the filthiest look I can muster. I walked straight into that one. Whatever I answer will tell him what my true motivation is.

'Well, I suppose the demographic falls into two categories: those looking for a relationship and those not looking for a relationship.' I smirk back at him for having neatly dodged a personal answer in favour of a more professional observational remark.

Observation 1: Avoids flirting with possible sexual partner. Subject distances with use of professional deflecting manner.

'Which are you?' he asks, sitting lazily back in his chair.

His eye snags on my lips before meeting mine in a challenge. Daring me to admit what I set out to do last night.

'Fine,' I say primly. 'The latter.'

A broad smile stretches across his face. His teeth are very good. Hollywood good, I notice absently.

'You can't say any different. I very much doubt you were looking for a relationship with an older' – please let me look as nonchalant as I sound; I can't believe the girls put me in this situation. He has to be barely… I flinch. I can't even think about it – 'woman in a city you don't live in.'

'No,' he says. 'I was examining the features.'

'What?'

His eyebrows rise as he confesses, amused, 'My UX designer wanted me to check out a chat feature she likes and you have to be on the app to experience it, so she threw up a profile so I could play with it.'

'Right. Likely story.'

'It's true.' He spreads his hands, those calloused, skilful… He doesn't work with his hands.

'You're building a dating app?' Cringe, so I am desperate and needy and he's just doing research.

Observation 2: Subject way too exposed.

Result of Trial 1: Retreat!

'No, a social media app. I think people are tired of the social goldfish bowl. Of other people's best lives being paraded in front of them like a dog show. We're building a social media app that enables smaller, more private social circles, but also provides the openness of an interest group app. Something in between WhatsApp groups and Instagram.'

'That's a great idea.' Focus on what he's saying. It's digital development; you know this stuff. 'So friends and family can still share openly without the fear of being stalked by your weird ex, but you can still meet new people.'

'That's the idea.'

'How far along are you?' There's a long way between talking about an idea and having an app in the app store.

'Pretty far.'

'Oh, yeah?' He didn't miss my 'sure you are' vibe.

'I'm here to meet potential investors,' he says tightly, the wicker protesting as he straightens in his seat.

'You're meeting VCs?' He must be quite far along. Venture capitalists don't throw money at just anyone with a good idea these days. Good ideas come and go; execution is key.

'Met,' he corrects, his face turning to observe the people passing in the street. 'Yesterday.'

'How did it go?'

'Well, yesterday was a bust until about ten p.m.'

His face hardens, the youth seeping away.

'They didn't go for it?'

'Oh, they liked the idea well enough, and what we've done so far. But I don't think they were too interested in me.'

I can see the boy he hinted at last night. His chin is up, his face dark, his lips thin. He looks like he could take a swing at someone or something and keep on swinging.

'What's wrong with you?'

'Not educated enough, not slick enough.'

'I'm sure that's not true.' It isn't about who you are in technology, or whom you know. Technology is a meritocracy; if your product is good it's good. Plenty of the world's most famous companies started in garages.

'Isn't it?' He looks at me, his eyes hooded. 'What about you, Stanford? Do you consider me a genuine prospect? Or am I just a bit of rough for the night?'

My stomach dips. I stare at him, appalled. He's right. He is the anti-Mr Right. That was the whole point. To spend time with a guy who is the opposite of everything I'm looking for. And I let him in and he turned me down. Was it to get even with the world? To make himself feel better?

'Well, if you were, I was short-changed.' As soon as the words are out of my mouth, I want to call them back. Did I open up to him because he's right? Because he's not someone I see a future with? So I went for the jugular because despite our connection of the night before, I felt rejected and I lashed out? Ugly. Ugly.

'Sorry, darlin'. You'll just have to pick up some other boytoy to tumble ya, I guess.' His accent is thick and his face suffuses with blood from the rage that burns through him. My breath is stolen by the gut punch as he accuses me of being some kind of rich cougar… Ugh.

I stand and fumble in my purse, pulling out the first note that comes into my hand, and flinging down the unfamiliar currency on the table.

He looks at it and his face drops.

'Fuck you.' He stands up and his chair clatters to the ground as he swings away wildly

He is gone up the street and around the corner by the time I figure out what made him so angry. It isn't a pinkish ten euro note that would have covered my breakfast, it is a purplish colour. 500 euros.

Every atom of my body contracts in wild embarrassment. He thought... Oh, my god. Did he think I was trying to pay him for a good night out? Is that possible? Did women my age pick up younger men in foreign cities and pay them for sex? Of course they did. I pick up the note stiffly and replace it with a smaller note to cover both breakfasts.

I start to follow him down the street to explain. Explain what? That I hadn't intended to pay him for sex. I pause, my feet sticking to the pavement. How dare he? How dare he think that!

The cobbled streets, which had so entranced me last night, are now a labyrinth of unfamiliar corners and doors. I have no idea of the name of the hotel he is staying in. I feel the burn of tears in my throat.

Research phase complete, it seems.

Chapter Six

'How was it?' Stella is the first to spot me walking into our hotel. She probably had spotters in key positions around the Marais reporting back to her.

'I can't talk about it.'

My feelings and assessment about last night are still all over the place. The endorphins still fizzing confusedly viciously squashed at the memory of Jack's face when he thought I—

I could feel my face heating again.

I lift my eyelids to discover this is not going unnoticed as my friends scour my face for any information they can glean.

'Oh, come on, give us something,' Alicia pleads. 'This is the most exciting thing I've been a part of since the day all the socks matched out of the washing machine.'

'I still can't believe that happened,' Kirsten wonders in an aside. It is pretty miraculous; Alicia's house is utter chaos most of the time.

'You tell me about your evening first,' I barter for time.

'After the restaurant we went for a drink at a little wine bar around the corner. The end.' Nessa gives me the barest of top lines.

'Aww, come on.'

'We were robbed,' Kristen adds.

'What?' The rest nod in sad agreement.

'My mom and dad gave us cash to buy an engagement present while we were here this weekend, something French and expensive. It terrifies them that my taste has become utterly foreign to them. So they threw cash at the problem, but I lost it.'

'I don't suppose this is what you lost?' I ask, pulling the offending article from my purse.

Kristen's face lights up in relief. 'Yes! How on earth did you end up with it?'

'I'm not sure, but I've applied plenty of brain power to the problem. Maybe when we were paying for the taxi from the station?'

It is possible. There was a late dive into purses on arrival at the hotel to come up with the right amount of euros, several notes had ended up in my hand, and I must have used the ones I am more familiar with and tucked the ridiculously big note in my purse without realising.

'So, c'mon, dish,' Stella orders.

I've got to give them something or they will never leave me alone.

'He was nice.' I shrug.

'He didn't look *nice*.' Alicia frowns. 'I must be losing my touch.'

'Did he throw you up against the wall? Did he do bad things to you?' Stella leans forward.

I exhale noisily. 'No.'

But they were right; there is merit to be found in going off-piste.

'He was gorgeous and charming. And ten years too young.' I glare at Alicia at the less enjoyable deviation from clearly marked slopes. I know, I know it's ridiculous to be hung up about it. But it was unexpected.

'And just after one thing?' Stella persists.

'I think he had a bad day and just wanted some company.' I pause as I recognise the truth of this. Last night I was so caught up in my own reactions and how hot he was, but besides avoiding talking about himself, he had almost seemed as if he wanted to put his regular life in a box for one night and lock the door.

Stella waves a hand dismissively. 'You did not stay out all night to give some stranger a pep talk.'

'It wasn't like that. In fact, we didn't really talk about our lives at all – at least not in the normal "what do you do for a living" way.'

'What did you talk about?'

'Never mind the talking, what did you *do*?'

'Who would play him in a movie?'

The onslaught of questions gives me an excuse to shut it down. 'Last answer and then we're getting back to the primary reason we're here and heading out to find the perfect gift for Kristen and Camille.'

I consider the questions thrown at me, and what it would take to get them off my back.

'The test case was a success *and* a failure. Last night I thought the difference in our backgrounds didn't matter; this morning we had a misunderstanding that would never have occurred if he met the criteria on my list.' But I had also dropped my guard more with him than I had with any guy I had met in years. Maybe because he wasn't a real prospect I hadn't put pressure on myself. Or because I couldn't shut down something that was never going anywhere anyway.

No, it was a fail. It had made me feel like shit. In future I would stay en-piste. So what if it was beige? Beige is fine; beige doesn't stalk off the next day.

Nessa opens her mouth to cross-examine me to find out what happened – that titbit was way too juicy – so I rush to distract them. 'I stayed at his last night, and he could be Colin Farrell's younger brother.'

'Colin Farrell? So you did do the dirty.'

'What was the fight about?'

'Does that mean he's Irish?'

I hold up my hand. 'No, that's it. Now, where are we going in search of the perfect way to spend five hundred euros?' I wave the disastrous purple note in the air.

'How about hitting the markets?'

'We should go to the big one in Saint-Ouen,' Nessa suggests, she who never arrives anywhere without thoroughly researched options.

'Non, the one in Montreuil is smaller but better.' Camille shakes her head, her braids swinging. 'Less *touristique*.'

After a short debate, we decide on the larger and more

famous Saint-Ouen as we're spending the entire day there before catching a late train back to London.

On the train, I put my own haul away and pull out my phone to check my email. Having turned off notifications for the weekend, I need to check where I need to be in the morning. I agreed to meet my stepbrother while he's in town; he wants a favour and as I'm between gigs, I can't reasonably refuse him.

'What?' I can't help but mutter aloud, my annoyance needing an audible outlet. There's a reason I never really got on with my stepbrother. Handsome and popular in school despite being thirteen to my sixteen when our parents married, my mother had quickly developed the habit of holding him up as an example of how I should be. The term *golden boy* was made for Eric. Blonde, tanned, and athletic, he was the perfect example of a Cali surfer jock. For the two years we overlapped at high school I had to suffer through people's shock when they learned we came from the same household, despite the obvious difference in appearance that screamed our lack of a blood tie. Though I always felt it was how comfortable we seemed in our skin that appeared to be the biggest challenge for people to get their heads around. Eric was charming and confident and, well, the centre of every party, while I was the awkward, defensive, doesn't-fit-in-anywhere girl. Everyone loved him, and he had grown up into a somewhat entitled smug asshole as a result. In my opinion.

Case in point: having asked me for a favour, which he knew I couldn't turn down in front of our parents on our Christmas video call, he now isn't even going to turn up.

'What's wrong?' Nessa, beside me, glances up from her pre-Monday emails.

'My stepbrother isn't coming.'

'Isn't that a good thing? You're off the hook.'

I've grumbled about this all spring. Instead of going home for Christmas as I would usually have done pre-pandemic, I'd stayed in the UK and gone to the Chilterns for Christmas with Nessa and some other friends, then got guilted into promising to do this nebulous favour for my stepbrother.

'You would think, right? But no, just because he isn't coming doesn't mean I get out of doing him this favour. It just means I have to do it without him.'

'What is it he wants?'

'I'm not sure. He has a company back in the States and they outsource their builds to an agency at the Silicon Roundabout. I figured he was just pulling me in for a couple of days to show off or to make it look to our parents like he's doing me some kind of favour by giving me work.'

Which I don't need, thank you very much. There's plenty of digital consultancy work to go around, and I've built a good enough network that I don't need the distraction of whatever it is Eric is dragging me into. Unlike a proper job, Eric's 'favour' came without a clear time frame, project outline, or ongoing local networking opportunities as the resources here were at the engineering rather than product level.

'Why is the build happening here?'

'Dev resource scarcity,' I explain before continuing when Nessa's look communicated that my words were gibberish to her. 'His company is in Silicon Valley. Developers and engineers there are paid astronomical amounts, partly to cover the ridiculous cost of living in the Bay Area and mostly because they are all gobbled up by the tech giants; most kids have jobs before they've even graduated for money that would make your eyes water. Devs in London make good money, but nowhere near the same level; they're more expensive than the outsourcing options available in Eastern Europe and Asia but they're more self-sufficient here with fewer communication issues.'

'So why does he need you?'

'Damned if I know. He didn't really tell me much about it.' I did ask, but once Eric got my buy-in to help in front of our parents he'd moved on. He's never really been a details guy, more of a wave a hand at a problem and someone will fix it for him kinda guy. 'I guess I'll find out tomorrow.'

'You still have to go?'

'I can't wriggle out of it now. I'll go to the office, show my face. Hopefully they won't need anything and I can get on with my life.' I'd been flat-out since the holidays and had a lead on a project at one of the telecom companies. If I locked that in for a mid-March start, I could take a week off and hunt down some winter sun instead. Pull some books out of my TBR pile, throw some clothes in a bag. If I caught an evening flight out of Heathrow tomorrow night, I could be on a beach by Tuesday.

I've been dying to finish that historical trilogy, and

there's that dense political bio that I'm currently using as a sleeping aid. A week on my own in the sun. I can already feel the warmth on my skin. How far south would I need to go this early in the year? The only downside of an impromptu trip is that it would be solo.

Solo. My TBR pile topples over as a pair of blue eyes flash before me with a devilish glint. I make those books sit up and push back.

It will be nice. Relaxing. Satisfying.

I watch the lights from the occasional house in the French countryside whip by. I take out the vase I bought at the market, unwrapping it carefully. There is a long crack in it. Kirsten persuaded me into buying it, but the crack is worse than I had realised. I trace the line of it through the charming painted scene. I'm not sure I can live with it. I'll drop it in to a charity shop; no point in getting attached.

I never had a big life plan – sure, go to college, live in Europe, but beyond that I never really thought about it. I sort of assumed that life would unfold and I would just be carried along through life's landmarks. *Time and tide wait for no man...* Nessa and I had gone to *Julius Caesar* at The Globe a couple of years ago. The line snagged in my brain. My life ticked away and I seem to have missed the tide that caught others up and allowed them to hit the classic milestones by forty. At least be on divorce number one by now. I hadn't even got around to buying my own place, afraid of committing to somewhere that wasn't quite right. It was the same with work; I flowed from contract to contract, instead of starting my own business.

Maybe the girls are right. Maybe I need to stop waiting for the perfect wave. Catch today's tide.

Not that I will ever admit that.

Chapter Seven

He thought I was paying for sex.

It was my last thought before falling asleep, my first thought this morning. Every atom of my being cringes at the look in his eyes when he looked down at that note. How quickly the mood had gone from flirty to dirty. My stomach folds in on itself. I spent my life feeling like I didn't fit in with the people around me; he was so quick to throw my education at me. How could I have failed to recognise…? Too caught up in wondering why he had stopped short of sex; that's all I had been thinking about. Why he didn't want to sleep with me.

8:10. Argh! I throw myself out of bed and hit the shower. I just have to do this favour for Eric, then I can be on a plane and out of here by nightfall. I've built up a solid clientele so I don't need to worry about where the next job is coming from anymore.

I've got this. My life is fine.

There is a new ad in the real estate agency's window. A two-bed overlooking the river, at the top of the price range I'm allowing myself. The second room is a little small, but it will only ever hold the occasional overnight guest, so that doesn't really matter so much. The main bedroom has a great view; the kitchen is tight, but it's not like I'm going to start cooking family meals anytime soon. My mom will be devastated if I buy a place. Nothing says *I'm not coming home* like buying an apartment on another continent.

She'll be fine though; we aren't that close. She has Mike and their palatial home in Pacific Palisades. She doesn't need me, never needed me. I am the hangover from her misspent youth. The freewheeling seventies that left her far from home in the eighties with a 4-year-old that she hadn't known what to do with. My dad died – I barely remember him – and Mom raised me on her own. We had nothing until she met and married Mike, and he lavished us with all that money could buy.

At Farringdon, I pull up my map and follow the blue dot to the brick Georgian building indicated by the address Eric had sent. The ground floor of the building has a frosted glass front and looks semi-abandoned; the address is 58b, so I check the doorbells to the side of the metal door and see that there's a small one with *Synch* written on it. I vaguely recollect that Eric's latest company is called Synchronicity. This must be it. A disconnected voice answers and when I announce myself, buzzes me in.

'Top of the stairs. Blue door,' a crackly voice directs me.

I make my way up the ageing carpeted stairs to the first landing and the chipped blue door, which is slightly ajar. Inside is an open-plan office where several desks with undisturbed developers sit. Two bikes hang from the ceiling against the back wall. A girl with pink hair and a nose ring approaches me.

'Hi,' she says, sipping from the builders' merchant mug in her hand and waits for me expectantly.

'Hi, I'm Leonie Durant.'

The girl nods and waves me to an empty desk with a monitor on it.

'I didn't realise there were two of you coming, but we can squeeze you in over here. You brought your own laptop, right? You got in last night? You found your way here all right? I suppose this is mad different to California. I've never been there, but I really want to go someday. I hope you brought an umbrella; it's going to chuck it down here this week.' The pink-haired girl finally pauses for breath. 'You want a coffee or anything?'

'A coffee would be great,' I manage weakly. In all that barrage she hasn't offered her name. The seven or eight men sitting at screens with noise-cancelling headsets haven't even looked up. 'I'm sorry, I didn't catch your name?'

'I'm Max. Did you think I was a bloke?' She laughs as she walks away. I frown. Have I missed an intro email from Eric?

I usually work for bigger matrix organisations – telecoms, banks, video-streaming companies – that have enormous buildings and need an assist on a project in their digital department. Start-ups aren't really my thing; I know this is a satellite office, but where's the onboarding? Am I expected to just walk in, take a seat and crack on?

It's the middle of the night in California so a full day will be gone before I can get hold of Eric. I send him a text telling him to call me as soon as he wakes. So much for my Heathrow plan this evening.

Max returns bearing another builder's mug full of pitch-black coffee.

'I don't know how you take it.' She sits down on the edge of my desk. 'You want milk or sugar?'

'It's fine.' It probably isn't fine, but I can pop out for a proper coffee in a bit. This area might look like it hasn't changed in two hundred years, with its tangled streets of brick residential buildings, vaguely boarded-up warehouses and frosted shop fronts, but all the tech worker bees will pour out of these unlikely places at lunchtime. And if there's anything techies agree on, it's the need for good coffee. There will be at least half a dozen good independent cafes within five minutes' walk of here, as well as the usual coffee and sandwich franchises.

'Max, can you help me get set up here?'

She looks at me strangely. 'Just plug in your laptop; you'll be good to go.'

It's my turn to look at her strangely. They're operating on an open network? In the middle of Clerkenwell? Is she being serious? Only one way to find out as she's already halfway back to her own desk, a prime spot beside the window, half-shielded from the rest of the room by some strategically placed potted plants.

I pull my laptop out of the tote bag I carry it in; it's lighter than most laptop bags but also less likely to be snatched. My theory is that while my top-of-the-range MacBook is a prime target, the expectation of paperbacks and random crap that make up the typical contents of a canvas bag makes it less likely to attract thieves.

I connect my laptop to the monitor and turn it on, where, to my relief, I am duly challenged to enter a password to access the Wi-fi. I send my thanks to whoever sat here last for scribbling it on a Post-it stuck to the monitor. I can't access any of the work systems though.

I check my email to see if Eric put an attachment on yesterday's email that I overlooked, with helpful details like what it is he needed or what organisational tools his team use.

No, it's just the note to say he couldn't make it but that he's sending someone else and that the team are great and it's awesome that I'm helping him out.

A notification that my battery is low sends me diving back into my bag for the charger. The desk is out in the middle of the floor but the desk opposite has some cables dropping in between our two workspaces. A quick look under the desk confirms the existence of an extension lead. I plug in the charger and then drop it off the back of the desk so it reaches the plug and then get down on my knees to plug it in. Since it's the first day, I'm in one of my nicer office outfits – a tight-fitting skirt and smart silk blouse. I usually dress up on the first day to get the lay of the land, but it would be easier to scrabble about on the floor in jeans.

Job done, I'm crawling backwards when I hear Max greet a new and more expected arrival.

'Oh, you're here. I thought for a minute you'd gone back and sent her instead,' I can hear Max saying.

'Who?'

The voice is muffled, but something about it makes me reluctant to exit my cave.

I continue to back out from under the desk, aware of the picture I'm presenting in my tight skirt. A pair of scuffed Onitsuka Tiger sneakers stand beside the red Doc Martin boots I recognise as Max's.

'Hey,' I start, as I follow the Tiger sneakers up denim-clad legs and a dark hoodie to still-not-dealt-with dark stubble and a pair of navy-blue eyes.

Why is the floor remaining in place? Oh, for the distinct possibility of the San Andreas of my youth. There's a floor below us; the fall through won't kill me. I can survive with a couple of minor broken bones.

His jaw is locked as narrowed blue eyes survey me. So much for the foolproof plan to meet a guy I would never see again.

'What are you doing here?' His tone is as rough as his stubble.

What am I doing here? What the hell is *he* doing here? 'Eric Simonds asked me to come by and help out.'

Not enjoying my distinct disadvantage kneeling at his feet, I stand up quickly and find myself not entirely better placed as between the chair and the unmoving Irishman I'm practically chest to chest with him.

'Help with what? He never told me.' He is way too

close; I can smell that uniquely Jack smell again, the salty, woodsy smell of him that underlies that tangy cologne he wears. If I take too deep a breath, my breasts will touch his chest, a fact my body doesn't seem to have missed at all as a tingle of awareness crackles along my skin.

'Why would he tell you?' I'm genuinely asking, but from the thinning of his lips I can see that he interprets my question rather differently. As in why would the big boss need to run a new hire by a lowly, uneducated grunt.

'Too true,' he dismisses me, tossing a parting sign off over his shoulder as he walks away. 'You do your thing and I'll do mine.'

What is his thing? He doesn't pause to explain, just pulls up a seat beside one of the devs who looks up long enough to give him a familiar nod as he pulls his laptop out of his case.

Crap.

Crap, Crap. Crap.

I can't believe I'm in the same room as him. My mind is in minor meltdown. He still thinks that I thought... My body breaks out in a sweat. I'm not sure which is more embarrassing: that he thinks I tried to pay him for sex or that we haven't even had sex but what we did do is even... No, what *I* did. He did nothing, I realise. All he did was tell me what to do. I need fresh air.

'Going for coffee,' I murmur to Max on my way out.

At the bottom of the stairs I look wildly about. The chilly wind has picked up and cools my heated face. I turn east and start walking. Coffee. I will get a coffee.

I walk to the end of the street and into a black-awninged

independent with witty quotes on the window. The barista takes my order and hands me my flat white while I stand there blankly.

'I didn't bring any money...' I walked straight out of the office without my wallet.

The fantastically hipster barista nods his man-bunned head toward my phone, which is somehow in my hand. In the event of a zombie apocalypse I'm sure somehow it will still make my emergency grab list, even if ultimately it would only be useful as a missile, like the records in *Shaun of the Dead*.

'Cash is the past. Barter is the future,' he says sardonically, 'but for today there is the mighty phone.'

'Right.' I shake my head, and after several attempts open the wallet app and pay electronically. Picking up the tiny cup filled to the brim with the nectar of the gods, I sit on the bench along the side wall in the tiny café.

Jack is here. In my life. The guy I was never going to see again.

My one-night stand, Mr Couldn't-be-more-wrong, is working for my stepbrother. Maybe I don't have to go back there. It is a loose favour; Eric hasn't even told me what he needs. He probably doesn't even need my help. The whole thing was probably just him showing off on our Christmas video call. Him being the big Silicon Valley hotshot throwing me a bone in front of his dad. That's all. I don't need to be here; I could be on my way to Aruba.

This is crazy. It's no big deal. I can go back there and do whatever it is Eric needs. No big deal.

I can never go back there.

This is what comes of trying to be more adventurous. Of trying new things. New things are a terrible idea.

I pull out my phone and open the group chat with the girls.

Me: *Whose idea was it?*

Alicia: *What?*

Me: *head exploding emoji*

Alicia: *typing...*

Me: *The 'have fun, you'll never see him again' guy in Paris...*

Me: *He works for my brother!!!*

Alicia: *Oh.*

Me: *That's all you got?*

Alicia: *Shrug girl emoji*

Stella: *He is hot, right? Why does this have to be a bad thing?*

Me: *face palm emoji*

I can't tell them what really happened. I wanted more

colour in my life, wanted to lift myself off the safe beige path and make mistakes, add drama to my palette.

Now my life is flashing neon red.

And my coffee cup is empty. *Big girl pants, Leonie.*

I can do this. I have nothing to be embarrassed about. He got the wrong end of the stick. Though who the hell assumes that they're being paid for sex?

That's crazy.

He works for my brother. That is all.

I just need to get through today.

———

Buzzing back into the office, I climb the stairs for the second time and take a seat at my desk. My phone pings in my pocket. Repeatedly.

I can explain. All I have to do is explain it was a mistake. A strange misunderstanding. Multiple chimes emerge from my jacket pocket. I take my phone out to turn off the sound so the entire office doesn't become aware my Greek chorus is in full flow.

'Look, Leonie,' a low, soft chocolatey voice sounds from behind me.

Jack.

I swivel round to face him as my phone pings again.

His eyes flick to the phone beside me on the desk and turn flinty.

He leans in, his hands on each side of my chair, his lips going to my ear.

'Five hundred wouldn't even start to pay for what I'd like to do to you.'

My heart stutters as he pulls away and is gone.

'What the—?' Is he out of his mind? That did not just happen to me. I swirl my seat back to hide my reaction. What the hell? How dare he talk to me like that! Is he for real? My heart is pounding and a slight sheen has broken out on my face. I've never been so mortified, or angry, in my life. Yet part of me is shivering in what feels awfully akin to... *What would he like to do to me?* No, I douse those wayward thoughts with my outrage blanket.

I can't work with this guy.

I can't cede the ground either.

Screw him! Who does he think he's talking to? I may have been late to holding my own in this game but I've spent most of my life in a world where simply being female meant I had to learn how to stand my ground and look good doing it. I didn't crawl away then, and I'll be damned if I do so now.

I stand and walk over to Max. I can feel Jack's eyes lift and watch me across the room. I'm super conscious of the extra sway my heels add to my gait, to the impact the tight skirt makes on the movement of my body. And damn him, I throw an extra wiggle in there, just for kicks.

I even lean into the desk to talk to Max, a little something I'd seen in a Reese Witherspoon movie. I have no idea if men's brains actually work like that but having spent most of my working life playing down my sexuality there's something about the gauntlet that Jack just threw down that has me turning up the dial. How dare he? I don't need to pay for sex; I am attractive and in good shape. I flash a glare in his direction.

Dear god, it works. His gaze is fully locked on my booty. His eyes move and meet mine before snapping away, and his jaw locks a little in reaction at having been so entirely caught.

A small victory smile dances on my face as I turn back to the waiting Max.

'There seems to have been a little confusion,' I begin as evenly as I can manage. 'I'm the consultant Eric Simonds sent. Can you give me access to your systems so I can take a look at everything?'

Max nods. 'I'll put together an email with the various links to the systems we use. Do you want access to the code or just the tickets or what?'

'The tickets, and any documentation you have will be fine for now.'

I give her the email address I use for professional email and walk back to my desk, that slight victory smile still consciously on my lips as I will myself not to look his way.

Sitting back down at my temporary desk, I feel professional and proud that I took the high road. Admittedly, the *Legally Blonde* move may not have been the most mature move but it beat kneeing him in the balls. Waiting for Max to pull together the info I need, I pick up my phone. My earlier alarm call has now elicited a full set of responses – Kristen aside, who may as well be on another planet when she's on a shift at the hospital.

Stella: *eggplant emoji*

Stella: *eggplant emoji*

Stella: *eggplant emoji*

Stella: *eggplant emoji*

Stella: *eggplant emoji*

Stella: *eggplant emoji*

Subtle, Stella. Message received.

Alicia: *side-eye emoji*

Nessa: *He works for Eric? I thought you said he's probably a tradie!*

Nessa: *I'm with Stella. Rock that body.*

I open the app to read the rest of them.

Alicia: *Live a little. What harm can it do?*

I lean back in my chair. What harm could it do? *This* is what happens when you go off-piste. Avalanches. Disaster.

Me: *I have to work with him.*

Stella: *So?*

Me: *Sleeping with a man I work with is not happening.*

Nessa: *That wasn't on the list. Wink emoji.*

Me: *That's implicit in the list.*

Me: *This is the problem with venturing outside the box.*

Alicia: *typing…*

Alicia's typing stops. Then.

Alicia: *You were alone in the box, Leonie.*

My breath catches in my throat. Ouch. I put the phone back on the desk, face down. I do not need any more advice. The chorus got me into this mess to begin with.

Focus on work, make it through the day, recommend someone else to Eric.

Max's email is waiting and I click on the first link. Access granted, I scan the projects presented. It looks like they divide everything up by platform. I open the iOS project to see what iPhone/iPad features look like and sigh.

I can't find an overview of the project, just endless small tickets describing pieces of work to be done. Scanning through them they all seem to be written dev to dev, instructions on how to connect APIs and JSON strings and links to various files and don't really describe the features at all.

Which means that I am no closer to figuring out what they are all so busy building.

I poke around a bit in the other platform folders; the Android and Web projects are laid out similarly. I open various tickets in the diminishing hope that somewhere there are some links to a wiki, a depositary of documentation outlining the project.

Looking up, I find that most of the developers seem to have headed out to take a break from their screens and get some food. Max is also gone from her desk. Jack sits at his, his face intent on what he's doing until he flicks his gaze my way, his eyes locking with mine. I break off first. Damn.

I push back from my desk as if he merely caught me in the middle of getting up from my seat, not just sitting there looking at him.

I pluck my purse from the floor and stride out without looking his way again. I'm halfway across the floor before I realise that if I leave I have no way of getting back in if Max isn't back before me. Without hesitating, I continue down the stairs and back out onto the street. Damned if I'll ask him.

Loitering longer than I usually do over lunch, I search flights. Aruba. Some books. This will all be a funny story I'll be telling in a month or two. Maybe a *year* or two.

I scrunch up the sandwich carton and stand up out of the chair in the brightly lit café. Max must be back by now.

Back at the metal door of number 58, I push the doorbell and sigh as the door buzzes open. I step into the dimly lit stairwell and move back against the wall, out of the way of the guys coming down the stairs. I smile faintly in greeting at the two Indian guys. Were they on the team I'm working with? I haven't really taken in all the faces. The third body stops and my smile fades.

A black hoodie fills my vision from a step above me.

'Lads, go on. I'll meet you there.'

I take another step to pass him, which is a mistake as it only takes me closer as he moves to block me.

'What are you doing here?' His accent is neutral, his voice controlled.

I lock gazes with him again. *Do not look away.*

'I'm doing a favour for Eric Simonds.'

'What kind of favour?'

'That's none of your business.'

His gaze darkens. 'None of my— He an ex?'

'No, he's not an ex.'

'More your type though, right?' He hasn't moved closer, but the stairway seems smaller. 'Rich, fancy college, right background, ambitious, all that stuff?'

All that stuff? My age, my speed. Right. Full of himself, slightly overweight, suited. Is that how he sees me?

Fine.

'That's the kind of guy you usually go for, isn't it, I?' His voice curls into a soft growl.

I raise a hand to his chest and push him back even though as far as I can tell he hasn't got any closer. A wave of heat runs through me.

'That's right, little boy.' I give him a light pat on the

cheek before dropping it to his chest again. So patronising. What the hell am I doing?

He pushes against the hand until it's all that separates us. His heat permeates the length of my body, still cold from outside.

'Not so little.'

'I wouldn't know.' I shove him away and practically run up the stairs to the sound of a dirty chuckle.

'Maybe we should fix that.'

I burst through the blue door, disturbing even those wearing noise-cancelling headsets.

'Sorry.' I give the room an apologetic wave. Professional, work, do work, that's what I'm here to do. Right, some app. Need to assess it. Just get through today.

'Max?' I approach the oasis of green and the pink head pops around the side of her monitor. 'Are there any other designs or documentation I can look at?'

'No, that's it,' she chirps.

'Right. Can I get the contact details for the designer?'

'I'm the designer,' Max says.

'Oh, right.' She's young; I thought maybe she was a college student or something doing a few hours of office management or the like to get something on her resume.

'Can you show me the designs?'

'What, like UX files and stuff?'

'Yeah.'

'Oh, we're not doing that. I'm embedded with the teams and they just ask me and I sit with them and we work together until it looks right.'

Over the years I've trained my face not to react when

clients tell me the crazy trend-of-the-moment approach that they're taking to development. Methodologies come and go, but one of the lessons I learned the hard way was that some documentation was key; amongst other things, it allows people joining the team later to quickly catch up on what you've built, and how you did it. Like me. Now.

'Can I at least get a build?' If they're far enough along, then being able to see what they've done so far will at least allow me to figure out what they're building. The tickets I saw this morning were for an identity system so the product could be anything. 'My test app is against the email address I gave you earlier. If you can send it to me, I can upload it onto my phone myself.'

Max screws her face up. 'We don't let other people have a build on their own phones.'

'Why not?'

'Er, I'm not sure. Confidentiality, I guess.' Max shrugs.

'Can I get a couple of your test devices with the latest build then?'

'Sure. Javid is lead tester; he can help you.' She points to a desk in the corner where yet another guy sits wearing a headset.

Javid provides me with an iPhone and an Android tablet, pointing out the latest version of the RL8 app. The website is being built out of Buenos Aires, so he shrugs when I ask him if I can see it. Not a good sign. If the mobile testing is being done here and the web is being tested by a separate team, the likelihood that the flows are seamless between devices is not good.

Opening the apps, I'm not sure what I'm expecting –

some kind of get-rich-quick mindless time-wasting addictive nonsense. But it isn't; it's good.

The home screen holds bubbles of people's faces joined in greater or smaller bubbles overlapping with others. Even without knowing the people here, it feels like I've walked into a community. RL8 is some kind of social circles app. I explore the available journeys and discover that it feels like wandering into a bar or a social space where I know everyone. Whispers of conversations reach out, some in real time, some archived. It seems to depend on how well I, or in this case 'Jacvtest2' knows the other people. Unless we're connected, I can't see who's there. There are ghost presences in some conversations, friends of friends, I guess. Unlike more traditional social media apps where users throw their own messages on a wall and others respond to them, this feels more organic – conversations rather than profiles of other users acting as the hub or hubs around which RL8 is organised. RL8, *Relate* … cute. It's engaging and charming and… This is Eric's product. How … unexpected.

This was the product Jack was talking to VCs about in Paris. The one he described as living in the space between an interests-oriented app like Instagram and a social groups direct-messaging one. I can already see how it would work in my life, give a combination of private conversations but not so exclusive that some serendipity of interest or new friends are blocked out. He said it was quite far along; it looks like most of the main sections are complete, or nearly so. It's getting late in the day to be looking for new venture capital.

How odd that he took the meeting and not Eric. I would

have thought bringing in investment would be right up Eric's street. Perhaps he hadn't deemed it likely so had sent his engineer instead. Slightly unfair that he set Jack up to fail.

I browse the iPhone and then the Android version of the App, noting where journeys didn't seem quite finished or don't match between the two devices.

By the time I look up, it's dark outside. Picking up my phone I discover buried amongst the ongoing encouragement from my friends to continue my interaction with the Anti-List guy is a missed call from Eric. Damn, I'd put it on silent after lunch. It's gone seven, making it mid-morning on the West Coast.

Pulling on my jacket and winding my scarf around my neck, I shut down and pack away my laptop. Max is already gone for the night, as are most of the devs, apart from Jack, who sits in the green glow of his monitor. The light and shadows make him look like the most deliciously alien dark angel.

Whose attention I do not need to attract.

Am I coming back tomorrow? I can't be sure until I speak to my stepbrother. There is plenty I can help with, but I'm not sure what the goals are. Anyway, without knowing how safe it is to leave my stuff unattended, I can't leave it here. Looking around at the desks I see that most people left them clean; whether they lock kit up here or take it home is unclear.

Better safe than sorry, besides which, maybe tomorrow I'll be in Aruba. I put my laptop in my bag before pulling the tote over my shoulder.

'Bye, princess.' I turn to find Jack giving me a two-finger forelock salute in the manner of a worker to a foreman like he's giving me a final farewell. Grinding my teeth, I continue to the door, a comeback failing to appear just when I most need it.

Stomping down the street for the Tube station, I still haven't come up with a genius response when my phone rings.

'Unless it's a one-finger salute,' I grumble without even looking at the phone. 'Yes, Leonie Durant speaking.'

Still in work mode, I will be embarrassed if this is one of the girls ringing to urge me on.

'Leonie, babe.' The drawled tones annoy me from five thousand miles away. Why did I agree to this?

'Hi, Eric.'

'Just wanted to check in, see how it's going over there.'

Like he's doing *me* a favour. Deep breath. It's just how he talks; he can't help himself.

'Great.'

I roll my eyes at my automatic response. Things are not great and it's all his fault, but old habits die hard.

'Super. I knew you'd like it there. Great bunch of guys – they're looking after you?'

Eric and his ever-present impression of a wall street banker. You know, that oozy combination of everything is always perfect in my sunshiny world, slathered with that complete lack of sincerity of somebody about to sell you something useless.

'Everyone is very helpful,' I trot out tritely. 'I'm just not sure what it is you need from me?'

'Babe, anything you can do to get it all on track. Your mom is always talking about how great you are. Just wave some of that Leonie magic.'

What is he raving about? I have better things to do than lend a magic wand to Eric's latest pet project just because he's bored of it. Every time I speak to my mom, it seems like he has a new thing on the go.

'Eric, it's not clear what it is you're asking of me. The product looks great, I'm sure it will be very successful, but what is it you need me for?'

'Look, Leonie, I'm counting on you here.'

I roll my neck back and look up, screaming soundlessly at the hazy urban night sky.

'Counting on me for what?' I ask in as neutral a tone as I can muster.

'We need to launch in a month.'

'What?' He asked for my help in December but waits until March to tell me he's launching.

'I just found out we have competition and if we don't launch in four weeks we're sunk.'

'Four weeks,' I repeat. That's not possible. The apps I looked at today were pretty far along, but they're still working on major features, like identity. They're nowhere near close to submitting to the app stores, much less launching to the public.

'You're a lifesaver, Sis.' I hate when he calls me that. And I haven't agreed.

'There is no way you're going live in a month,' I caution him.

'What if we get more developers?'

'That won't help, even supposing you could find a load of developers to start in the morning, you don't have enough documentation. It will take weeks to bring them up to speed and in the meantime the devs you do have will lose focus.'

'Can't you do some documentation? We need it anyway – if you could send it over as soon as you've got it that would be super helpful.'

'Do you want documentation or speed of delivery?'

'Both are top priority.'

'Which one is the most important?' Wait for it… It doesn't matter how many times I ask that question, the answer always comes back as…

'They're equally important.' His tone suggests this is blatantly obvious.

'You know how the technology development equation works,' I prompt, trying another tack.

'What? What do you mean?'

'If time and quality can't give, then money is no object?' This is the trifecta on which all tech projects operate. You can go fast, go cheap, or go bug free, but you can't do all three at once. 'I can reach out to some contacts, maybe get you a business analyst and a good UX designer.'

'Ah, that's the thing, Sis…' Why does he keep calling me that? We shared a household for two years before I went to college and during that time, he rarely acknowledged I was alive outside of the house. 'We're all out of capital, but if we launch it before those other guys then I've got a buyer all lined up. They're really interested, but we have to be first.'

'Then why don't you just tell the team? That should

motivate them.' I saw no mention of anything about a potential payday on any of the threads, and if this team is expecting the big sale in just a few weeks, they're unusually casual about the hours they're putting in.

'Well, it isn't like that. We aren't paying them in shares.'

'What?' It's industry standard for start-ups to pay devs partially in shares; you get your team cheap and really motivated that way, and everyone is invested in making it happen, otherwise you have millions to pay for the whole operation out of your own pockets. 'How can you afford that?'

'My partner and I, we're all in, baby,' he says, like he's a high roller in Vegas, giving that down-on-his-luck, betting-big-against-the-house laugh a guy throwing his last roll gives.

'Where did you get that kind of money?' My hand comes up to my forehead as if bracing against the incoming information, dread prickling across the back of my neck.

'Where else, Leonie?'

I close my eyes.

'Bank of Dad.'

'But you must be into this for millions of dollars.' I quickly add up the cost of the three teams in San Jose, London and Buenos Aires, the equipment, the running costs... They'd been working on this for a year, maybe longer.

'Dad will get it all back. RL8 is a solid investment.'

'Yeah, if it pays off.'

'We're so close to the finish line.' Asshole. If they don't get there first, they lose everything. It happens all the time;

movies, apps, books, everyone always thinks they've caught the zeitgeist, that they have a great idea, that they're the only one to do so, and then realise that there will be three Robin Hood movies released in the same summer, or everyone is writing about witches, or the same concept is hitting the market from multiple apps. Movie-goers and readers might be happy to consume more than one version of the same theme, but people tend to only have space for one version of the same type of app and that's the one that makes it; the rest sink without a trace.

'That's why I need you. I need all the wiki stuff and paperwork for the sale. We have to get this done and out in the world, like, stat.'

Stat like he's a goddamn doctor – more like a con artist. I don't know how much money my stepdad has; he paid for my college and that is the last cent I took from him. My mom deserves the pleasant life they have and my stepdad is a good guy; they don't need to face a retirement in which they will have to move away from their friends and start over. The US is no place to find yourself without the safety net you've spent your life building.

'Eric, I thought you were asking me to come in for a couple of days. What you're asking for will take weeks.'

'That's what I figured, but if we need all this stuff, well, I would sure appreciate you stepping up.' He pauses. 'We never ask anything of you.'

We. The family. His dad, my mom.

'You said you were between jobs so I know you have the time, and don't worry, I'll look after you once we sell. Make it worth your time if that's the problem.'

Every bone in my body stiffens at the implication I need to be paid to do anything for our family. At the tone that suggests he is part of the family and I'm only in as long as I get paid. Sixteen-year-old me wants to tell him exactly where to go. But my silence taken for compliance, Eric continues, 'And, Sis, if you could keep the sale on the DL…? Jack is an amazing guy but he can be a bit tightly wound. He already knows about the competitors, and the time crunch; that's why I sent him over. He's great. Real fast. He'll get it done. Don't want to add to the pressure he's under.' He stops then and I can hear someone talking in the background. 'Look, Leo, I gotta go. But you're the best. Knew I could count on you.'

And he hangs up on me. He actually hangs up on me.

Ass. Hole.

I can't believe this. He bet everything on this and now I can't not help.

Oh well, so much for Aruba.

Chapter Eight

Normally I tone it down after the first day. The lay of the land suggests jeans are fine but there's something about the way Jack eyed my outfit yesterday like I'm some slick corporate consultant type that makes me want to live up to his prejudices. He doesn't like suits? Too bad.

My wide-leg pants swish over my slender-heeled court shoes and my tailored blouse fits me snugly about the waist, making the most of my length and curves. I am an Amazon; I have totally got this.

Only Max looks up as I make my way over to the desk I used the day before. Plugging in my computer, I go over to the coffee machine and deposit the freshly ground gourmet coffee I've picked up on my way in. I rinse out the dried-in grounds and set the percolator going. Moments later the smell of rich, dark coffee is wafting into the open-plan room from the little side kitchen.

'This is amazing.' Max perches on my desk, her hands wrapped around a fresh mug of steaming coffee. Putting my pen down on my notebook where I've been jotting down a rough plan of action, I look up at her.

'Glad you like it.'

'You a total coffee addict?'

'Not really. One or two cups a day, but when I do it's got to be done right.'

'Mmm.' Max's eyes gleam appreciatively.

'I was wondering what time you have stand-up?' The fifteen-minute whip around that most teams start the day off with is a good opportunity to introduce myself quickly and try to get a handle on who everyone is.

Max's brow crinkles. 'We don't do a stand-up.'

'How do you coordinate what everyone's doing?'

'Oh, everyone knows what they need to do and gets on with it.'

'Right, and if anyone has a question or needs to co-ordinate with someone else?'

'They do it on Slack.'

I took a quick look at the various conversation threads on the direct messaging app yesterday. They seemed to be organised like the Jira task projects in the platform teams.

'How are cross-team conversations handled?'

'I guess between the devs one to one? I don't really know.' Max takes another sip of her coffee. 'I can intro you round, if you like?'

'That would be great.'

. . .

By the time we've done the round of the room I have a better, if still patchy, understanding of the team. I've also asked enough questions that my suspicions are confirmed.

There is no way this product is launching in a month. If the work is split into traditional two-week sprints, then that means they have two weeks to finish and two to test and debug. Two weeks. My stomach flips at how much would have to be done in that time.

'Who's the project manager?' I ask Max. Maybe I'm wrong. Maybe the team works fast and is totally on track to deliver on time.

'There isn't one; we don't need one.'

Not the first time I've heard that either. Self-organising teams are on trend, as is flat hierarchy, with no one calling the shots ... except someone always calls the shots. There is always a leader; I just need to figure out who it is and not piss off the team before I even get started.

'No worries, I'll figure it out.'

Max's nose twitches, her nose ring glinting in the morning light through the big front window. She wants to know what I'm up to but as I pick up my pen and tap my keyboard to bring my monitor back to life, she mooches off back to her desk.

By the time I head out for lunch, my screen and desk are peppered with coloured Post-it notes as I puzzle my way into the system they've set up.

Mostly it seems good, though the lack of urgency is

making me a little nervous, but the tickets seem to move across the task board at a fairly consistent rate from what I can make out. Vivek and Alan lead the iOS team while Graham and Igor have the most comments across the Android tickets. Looking around the room I can't entirely match the names on all the tickets to those I'd been introduced to earlier.

Most of the directional planning seems to be organised by someone called JEK according to the history of the movement on originating and completed tickets. He seems to be the business analyst or something of the like – at least, he's the one doing the most creation of tickets outlining the tasks the team need to complete in upcoming sprints. The requirements are bare, and largely fleshed out by devs asking questions in the tickets, though even then the features aren't entirely clear so perhaps Max or others are filling in the gaps with face-to-face conversations.

Given how quiet the office is that doesn't seem to be likely though, which sends me back into Slack to see if direct messaging between the names on the tickets is filling in the gaps.

This yields nothing particularly conclusive either. It's like standing on a shore poking sticks into a river to see how deep it is: sometimes I hit the ground but more often I don't, so in some places I get a feel for the river bed and in others my knowledge remains a void. This does nothing to settle the jittery nervousness that seems to have inhabited my bones since Eric's bombshell. My family's fortune is sunk in this project and a day and a half in I'm no closer to assessing how far away the finish line is.

After lunch I take a different approach and go back to

the actual products on the test devices. I quickly list the main feature areas I can see: social, chat, payment, identity, video. Under each of these I capture the key features, so under identity I list the usual suspects: profile, registration, sign in, account management, history. After these have been completed, I put them up on the wall beside the door where an unused whiteboard hangs.

I can feel Jack's eyes on me, but I refuse to look that way. This is a normal day in any office. I never fish in the work pond; muddy waters in my professional life I can do without. Now and always. That doesn't mean I can't sense this particular fish circling me; he's like a shark, casually ignoring me. Meanwhile, I feel very much observed.

I pull my top taut as I take in my work. I flick through the iPhone app and assess how many of the features are already complete before doing the same on the Android phone I have been supplied. Going back to my desk I grab two pads of different colour Post-its and replicate the first set. Shuffling the Post-its on the wall I list them so each feature appears in triplicate under the three device types, iPhone, Android and the website being built.

With a sharpie I then place a tick beside features that appear to be complete and a score out of ten on partially completed features. Some developers nod and smile as they make their way out of the office for the night.

Vivek from the iOS team pauses, jacket on, backpack on both shoulders. He eyes my work.

'You haven't marked the responsive website,' he comments.

'No, I don't have access. Javid just gave me the apps.'

He makes a clicking noise between his teeth, his eye flicking dismissively to the corner where the test team sit. 'Ah, you should have said, I can sort you out. I have to get the train now but I can text you the link. Are you on Slack?'

'Leonie D.'

'No problem,' he repeats, bobbing his head as he heads out the door.

I've been assuming that several settings for the apps are being handled on the web; if they aren't there's no chance we'll launch soon. My eye is caught by the address ticket in the payment section. I flick to the location ticket in profile. Are they duplicating elements of the same service? I sit back at my desk to dig into this while waiting for Vivek to send me the link. He seems like the type to respond pretty quickly to smaller items he can tick off his to-do list.

In fact, I open Slack to check and sure enough I have an unread message already. He must have sent it while walking to the station. I wasted half a day when he could have solved it this easily. A dev team that knows each other can easily identify who can answer a question, but as a newcomer broadcasting to the entire team such a basic question is unlikely to garner me fans. I kick myself. I don't have time to pussyfoot about.

My stepdad is a good guy; he doesn't deserve this.

I click on the link and enter the credentials Vivek supplied with the URL of the unfinished website. My initial impression settles the butterflies in my stomach that go into full chaotic flight every time I think about the impact my failing to get this product across the line will have on my family. My mom struggled after my dad died. She isn't materialistic, being a bit of a hippy, but her 'everything will work out' attitude is challenging when you're nine and starting elementary and the only kid in class without the uniform. She did her best, but life was definitely easier after she met and married Mike. Big, blustery Mike who shuffled into our life and took over, in a good way, for my mom. At sixteen, I doubled down on awkward and felt like everything he gave us was something I needed to keep an account of because someday he might want it back. Nothing is forever.

He tried with me, but he was too loud, tried too hard and I just backed away into my world and ensured I didn't rock the boat. Smooth waters mean no sudden upturns like when my dad died. I was too little to remember but if he hadn't left us things wouldn't have been so hard on my mom. I figured there was no way Mike would leave us, as long as I kept my head down and gave him no reason to. He never did leave and if I could do this for him... I square my shoulders. No way is Jack or anyone else stopping me from helping Eric out of this mess.

I stretch my back. The website, it turns out, is in good shape. I tick off the completed features on the boards and step back.

'What are you doing?' The growl comes from maybe a foot behind me. There are a few people still at their screens on the other side of the room. On this side, it's just him and me.

'I told you, Eric asked me to come in and lend a hand for a few weeks.'

'And this?' I turn slightly to confirm he's indicating the whiteboard and wall now liberally covered in Post-its.

'I'm trying to figure out how close you are to finishing.'

'Close enough.' He scowls.

'Really?' I query as lightly as I can manage. 'Is that close, like a week, or a month, or by summer?'

'We'll be done when we are done.'

I turn to face him. The main lighting is on and the strip lighting seems, unfairly, not to hurt him at all. The scowl darkening his face is at odds with the casual stance he has, one lean hip balanced on a desk, his legs stretched out in front of him. He's wearing that black hoodie again but it has ridden up at the side. My hand itches to reach out and straighten it ... then slip up and around the warmth of the skin it covers. What is wrong with me?

'That's not good enough.' Really not good enough. We're working together, he is way younger than me, not to mention he thinks I'm some predatory, desperate woman. Is that why he didn't sleep with me? Is that what he thought all along? No. That kiss on the dance floor, that scorching moment was real, I'm sure of it.

'What's not good enough?'

I blink and find he's standing in front of me, way too close for my already scattered focus. His voice is husky, lowered, though the chances that the guys working on the other side of the room are listening is non-existent.

'What?'

'Something's not good enough,' he prompts. His lids are low and it feels like he's edged closer.

'The timelines.' Is he talking about me? About him?

114

Focus on why you're here, get a grip, Leonie. 'The timelines ... that is, not having a plan with a clear launch date to work to isn't helpful, especially when it's a race to the finish.'

'Why does it have to be a race?'

'Because you can't be left behind.'

'Finishing isn't always the most important thing.'

'Huh?' I'm not following. Unless I am, a trickle of heat uncurls in my stomach.

'Sometimes you need to step out of the race.'

'What?' Is he talking about the night in Paris? Or the project?

I need to put this back on safer ground.

'If your competitors get their product to market first—'

'Being first isn't everything.' He smiles. 'Being the best is.'

'Best is great but if your competitors launch first, you're screwed.'

His brow furrows. 'What do you mean our competitors?'

Shit. I'm not supposed to mention their competitors. No, that isn't right, it's the sale that Eric is aiming for that I'm not supposed to share with the team.

'Eric said you knew? There's a similar product expected to launch soon.' Isn't the push to beat their competitors to the finish line why he's here in London?

'How does he know?'

I shrug. 'Knowing Eric, he probably heard about it from a buddy. He's worked in Silicon Valley since he graduated; he knows loads of people.'

Jack's jaw clenches. 'Yeah. Course he does.'

Without saying anything further, he marches over to his

desk and grabs his phone. He pulls on his jacket and is out the door before whoever it is has answered.

Good chat. Let's do it again sometime.

Or not, I reflect.

What was all that about? I need to establish some boundaries. We have to work together and confusing exchanges like that one are not helpful. Every time we speak everything seems charged, full of double meaning, and my wayward thoughts are out of control. I'm turning into Stella; all I can think of is pushing him against that desk and straddling him. Oh my god. I exhale roughly. What happened to the girl who put sex at number ten? Fantasising about him is not okay. Lines are blurred because of Paris. I just need to untangle the wires, put everything back in its correct lane. We work together; he's too young; we definitely do not share common interests. What would we even talk about?

Who needs talk?

I close my eyes to block out the images that thought inspires in my mind. I lift my palm to my forehead, practically checking for a fever.

I need to go. It's Tuesday, and if I leave now, I can make my yoga class. I can put today, and everything marked 'Mr Inappropriate' into a box and close the lid.

The Tube is overheated because the weather this week is suddenly mild but the slight drizzle makes everyone damp, giving that vaguely steaming feel to the carriage. A drizzle of condensation makes its way down the curved window opposite and I watch its progress, seeing again the beads of sweat on Jack's temple as we danced together, the beads in the hollow of his throat as he pulled me into him, his hand a solid pressure on the curve of my back.

My phone vibrates in my pocket, the Wi-Fi in the station we have stopped in rescuing me from my wayward thoughts.

Eric: *Leo. I really need you to keep shit together over there.*

What is he talking about? Is that whom Jack called when he left the office?

Me: *I don't know what you mean.*

The Tube pulls away, and my signal is non-existent while we're in the tunnel. At the next station I watch as the Wi-Fi picks up and stare at the face of my phone until the apps connect and messages pop onto the screen.

Eric: *I do not need Jack freaking out.*

Eric: *We need to wrap him in cotton wool. Without him there's no chance. We need to be extra nice to him.*

Eric: *Why did you tell him anything? I told you not to.*

Eric: *Leonie. It's important. I let you into my confidence. It's important you don't let me down. Our family has never asked anything of you. We need you to do this one thing. Please tell me I can count on you.*

I stare in growing outrage at the messages. Wow. Accusation, blame, pressure, guilt trip all thrown at me in so few lines. I literally cannot formulate a response as the rage burns through me.

The train pulls off again, commuters now filling every inch of space in the carriage. The woman standing over me has looped her umbrella around the wrist of the hand that's holding the strap over my head, leaving the umbrella to drip freely onto my lap. I throw her a dirty look, which is really meant for my dumbass stepbrother but frightens the life out of the woman standing over me who apologises profusely and puts the offending umbrella on the ground at her feet, where she will be entirely unable to retrieve it when she reaches her destination.

'It's fine.' I smile vaguely back at her, and I lift the umbrella to rest against my boots where the handle is within reach should she need it. The minor exchange takes the edge off my rage, the overly good manners soothing me. This is London. I live in London. Where people apologise for minor offences and where I am a long, long way away from my ass of a stepbrother.

The train jerks to a stop at the next station.

Missed call from Eric.

Eric: *Leonie. This is a big deal. Can you please respond?*

Jackass.

Me: *On Tube.*

As the train pulls away, I compose a new message to have ready when we hit the Wi-Fi in the next station. The last thing I need right now is to have a conversation with him.

Me: *Eric, the team needs to be aware of the deadline. I have said nothing about the sale. You told me he knew about the competitor. Will smooth things over with Jack tomorrow.*

I put my phone into my bag where I won't be able to feel the vibrations of his response. If he's hiding the sale, it's likely because the team won't keep their jobs afterwards. But if my parents aren't going to be ruined, I need to focus on helping to make the sale happen. The team will be fine; there are always new jobs for good developers and if the app succeeds, it will enhance their CVs and put them in an excellent position to find new work.

At home I throw a ready meal into the microwave – I'll make something fresh tomorrow – and pull on my yoga gear while waiting for it to ping. Unable to resist, I pull my phone out of my bag as I quickly eat before running out the door for my relaxing Yin and meditation class.

Eric: *You are a legend, Sis. Can't do this without you!*

Eric: *If you could be super nice to Jack...? Key to success. Just don't mention the buyers. He thinks of it as his baby.*

Eric: *I'll get him to take you to the pub or whatever you guys do in London.*

Unknown number: *Hey. We need to talk. Eric suggests drinks. I'm game if you are.*

It has to be Jack.
So much for my hope of finding some Zen this evening.

Me: *Love to.*

Chapter Nine

W hile my laptop is booting up, I jot down my loose
plan of attack. If we're going to get RL8 to market
in a month, then we have our work cut out for us. I write
the word *cut* at the top of my to-do list for the day and circle
it. What features can we go to market without? I smell
cedarwood and ocean before I see him as his head leans in
close to mine and he whispers in my ear.

'Still on for drinks later? Eric says we've got to play nice
together.'

I pull away and throw him some major side eye for his
invasion of my space, though this is far from being the
automatic response it should be. I swear, for a moment I
nearly curled into him like a kitten.

'You'll do what I tell you to do?' I ask, my words picked
unwisely, provocatively. I know this will annoy him, but I
do it anyway. It's like a compulsion.

'If that's the way the lady likes it,' he purrs, with a soft
chuckle as I stiffen. If he keeps this up, I'm going to deny

the human race any further propagation of his genes in the most efficient way possible. My wayward thoughts rob me of a suitably cutting comeback.

His lips thin as his glance flicks to my notes.

'And you aren't cutting anything,' he says over his shoulder as he walks away.

Aren't I? This app needs to launch almost immediately, and that's what I will make happen.

Normally, I would go gently now, soothe ruffled feathers, boost egos, do what's needed to bring the team round. But I'm over it. Over him. Who is he anyway? If I hadn't met him before he wouldn't dare speak to me like that. I straighten my back as the spark of his fingers tracing the indent of my spine while I lie on white sheets next to him flashes through me intensely. His fingers were calloused, his skin rough as they trailed lower. I shake it off. I'm better than this.

I set a meeting, subject *Estimation*, and invite the entire office.

As the room gathers around the wall where I stand waiting, I can sense that my brutal approach has not gone down well with everyone. A one-word subject line may not seem brutal to most people, but I rarely meet devs who don't baulk at estimating (and thereby committing publicly) how long their work will take up-front. I've barely met these guys, much less earned their trust, which means I've got some making up to do. Jack has not left his desk. Fine, if that's how it's going to be.

'Hi. Thanks everyone for taking time out; I know you are all busy. This shouldn't take long,' I start tentatively. A few of the devs have brought their laptops and continue to tap away. I sigh. 'If I could please have your attention, this will go quicker.'

Two of the laptops close. The owner of the third looks toward Jack who is ignoring the whole event and then continues with what he's doing.

Damn. My options now include asking him to leave if he doesn't want to be involved in the activity, which is heavy-handed given I just got here; I don't know the office politics well enough. If I do that and he calls my bluff, it could prompt the rest to entrench in what is previously unchallenged ground. Jack appears to be the current owner, and while he hasn't granted access rights, he hasn't denied them either. Yet.

'Right, thank you.' I smile widely at the devs now giving me their attention. 'I'd like to get a clearer idea of how far off we are from launch.'

'We run our own teams,' Vivek, the iOS lead immediately states.

'I understand that. I'm not trying to project manage here.' I totally am. 'But Eric tells me we need to launch in less than a month and I'd like to help make that happen.'

Everybody looks at each other at this news. The more senior leads check Jack's reaction. There isn't one. His dark head doesn't even look up.

'As you can see, I've indicated on the Post-it notes where I think a feature is complete, or at least looks so to me; please correct me if I'm wrong.' I point to the notes with the tick on them. 'The others are either partially done, or not started yet. If we could run through these and put points on the remaining work, then we'll have a better understanding of where we are.'

'We already know where we are,' says the dev who refused to put his laptop away. 'Where are you?'

He smirks, looking up and down my chic office outfit. I may not be wearing jeans and a T-shirt with the name of some random software services company on it, but that doesn't mean I haven't been doing this since before he could code.

'You're on Android, right?' It's always the Android guys who chafe most at this activity; their preferred platform attracts free thinkers who enjoy the choose-your-own-adventure approach to coding, rather than the more rule-abiding, organised iOS guys. I walk over to him and stand in front of his damned open laptop. 'When will you be done?'

'I'll be done quicker if I'm not wasting my time on this.'

'Right.' I smile thinly down at him. 'Super, when exactly will that be? Tomorrow, next week, next month? Exactly? We need to start planning the launch, so we need a date.'

He stares back at me and eventually shrugs. 'A month, if that's what it has to be. We'll get it done.'

'If you leave a Sprint for test and debug, that leaves you less than a Sprint to finish, right?' I back up to the wall and point to the Android list. 'According to this, you still haven't joined up key journeys and some sections are missing key features. Are you sure you'll be done in time?'

He gives the list a cursory check. His lack of response is all the acknowledgement I need. Now that I've made my point, I have everyone's attention. Well, nearly everyone.

'Let's start at the beginning. Do you all know what your velocity is?'

Shrugs. Vague mumbling about delivering their sections faster or slower depending on the variables outside their control, clear requirements or API readiness. Unsurprisingly, there's no clear view on how fast they deliver as a team.

'How about non-functionals? Accessibility? Load times? They aren't captured in the tickets. Are you planning on giving them their own tickets or have you tackled them within the features?'

Blank stares. Not good. Do they want to know what I mean or are they afraid to speak up? I need to assess their approach or I'm not going to have an accurate view at the end of this exercise.

'Okay, who did the payment section? When I enter my credit card details, and press pay, what is the response time supposed to be?'

'A few seconds.'

'Instant.'

I tilt my head a little to the side, a smile on my lips as I make sure nobody feels like they're under attack, as dev and test give two different answers. 'Which is it?'

'Up to three seconds,' Jack says from his desk. 'After three they receive feedback; at ten they get a "please try again" notification.'

'I didn't do a time-out message,' Vivek volunteers. 'Put an extra point on iOS.'

All right, at least one of the team has played this game before.

'How do you normally size tickets?'

Vivek shrugs. 'We just do the work.'

That's okay when there's no deadline, but this project is about to run out of runway. We need to make sure we focus on the right things in the precious remaining time.

'How about we have a go and just run through the exercise?' Jack is once again tapping at his computer, but I've kept the attention of my hold-out. That's something.

I call out feature tickets and the team quickly get into a rhythm of calling out the number of points they believe a ticket will take to do.

Most of the team head out for lunch once we finish, while I shuffle the features into priorities/completeness. This is where I can add value, stand back from the project, and start to ruthlessly cut features that aren't needed for launch. My focus here is to get out a minimum viable product that can make the looming deadline something that's good enough; perfect is a much longer-range goal.

'What are you doing?' Jack's dark tone tells me he knows exactly what I'm doing.

'My job.'

'Which is what exactly?'

'Getting this bloated mess across the line.' It's not actually that bad, but I can't seem to help myself.

'Bloated.' He repeats the word, slowly, like he's savouring it, before he plans to spit it out.

'For starters, you don't need payment in the apps to launch; you can send users to the website.' I pull the tickets for these and put them lower down on the wall. 'Same goes for account management, possibly even registration.'

His eyes turn into slivers as he glares at me so hard I don't think I would be shocked if blue lasers were emitted and cut through me where I stand.

'So you will decide what our finished product looks like?'

'You could have taken part in the exercise with the rest of the team,' I grit out.

'This is a participatory exercise? Seems like you're the only one who gets to play.'

Does he mean to refer to what had happened between us? That we didn't really have sex together. Just one of us. But his face couldn't look more innocent.

'If you don't want to be told what to do, then you're more than welcome to take part.'

'Am I?' His tone is suspiciously silky this time but still not openly inappropriate.

'I get it.' And I do. I should have tried to discuss my plan with him earlier; that's what I would have done any other time in any other office. 'You don't like being told what to do.'

I pause. That's it. I totally put his back up. Some devs get really involved in their projects and take ownership to a different level. He's one of those. I need to offer an olive branch, work through this.

'Not like some, hey?' This time there's no question that he's referring to our night in Paris. The look he gives me – that knowing dirty, dirty sex look – I can practically hear the words as we lock eyes. *Come for me.*

How dare he? I can't believe he's crossing the line like this. My head is on a swivel as I check that nobody's close enough to watch this exchange, though he has said nothing I can use against him.

Smug.

Asshole.

This feeling, this discombobulated wrong-footed feeling, I hate it.

'Look, let's be clear. If I had known we would ever meet again... I would never have—'

'Let someone like me anywhere near you?' he finishes for me.

And he had been near me. Way too near me.

'You come in here, all process and whatever your fancy degree has told you that makes you think you're better than us.' His face is dark with anger.

I'm barely listening.

I'm still fuming. And embarrassed.

I have never wanted to strike a person so badly in my life.

I take a breath. *Don't respond. Don't react.*

Do it for Mike.

My exhale is released in a juddering breath. I've got this.

'Right. So if we can just do our jobs and forget we ever met before, that would be great.'

'Not that memorable, darlin'.'

Wow. I stare after him as he strolls back to his desk. My blood is on fire.

With rage. Definitely with rage. I want so badly to storm off and never see his ass again, but that's not an option.

Go for drinks? Play nice?

With him?

I wouldn't drink water with him in the middle of the Sahara at the height of summer in a draught. No, I'm going straight home tonight.

I'm too angry to go for lunch, but I force myself to go for a walk, storming up and down the backstreets and converted offices of Clerkenwell until I'm clearheaded enough to return and finish my to-do list for the afternoon.

I stomp back to my seat after I've taken pictures of all the Post-its, which are far too close to Jack's desk for comfort. Transferring them to an Excel sheet and listing them out for the Android and IOS teams and assessing the website as best I can is methodical, familiar work and when I finish, I find once again that there are only three people left as everyone has drifted off for the evening.

I arrange the tickets in priority order. If we're going to get this done in a month, then the team needs to focus on finishing what they've already started – ensuring the flows are seamless and ditching unnecessary features that we can live without for launch.

The team lead in Buenos Aires emails to let me know he will start validating my assessment next week. I bang out a strongly worded response to the effect that I expect it to be sitting in my inbox in the morning. CC-ing in my stepbrother is heavy-handed, but I don't have time to play email tennis. We're two days in already and if the deadline is immovable, then I don't have time for this. They're a few hours behind, but as a professional outsourcing operation, if they've been running without tracking where they are, I'll be shocked. There's always the risk they've been doing only what is needed by the mobile teams as asked. Plenty of these types of outfits have multiple clients on the go at once and if you aren't measuring what they are delivering, then you're paying for time not always spent on your product.

I notice as I make my way out that Jack is yet again the last one out – not that I'm keeping track of him or anything.

The next morning the web results are in and they're not as bad as I feared. A lot of the missing features are waiting for a release planned for the end of the week. Overall, they're all on track for a comfortable launch in the summer. And we have a little over ten days to finish development and start launch prep.

I move things around on the wall, scratching some features, prioritising others, and then do the same on the board. After lunch, while double-checking the online board, I discover the tickets have been moved back to the prep column. All my work has been undone.

I click into the history of the ticket and identify the culprit. I could Slack, but I've always been a fan of walking over and having a conversation. There's a reason teams are co-located as much as possible, and it's not to keep Instant Messaging apps in business.

'Max, who is JEK?'

Max looks up from the music site she's browsing. 'Huh? Oh, right. That's Jack, Jack Keogh.'

Of course it is. I survey Jack, who has heard his name but not looked up.

I walk over and stand over him. He continues typing.

'What happened to playing nice?' I finally burst out.

'What happened to not deciding what our MVP looks like without consulting anyone else?'

Cutting RL8 back to the minimum viable product that could be finished in the short time remaining but still be worth launching is not an easy task, especially for those who are emotionally invested; one of the benefits of joining so late is that I haven't had time to get attached to pet features. Unlike Jack. But first steps first.

'So you concede you need an MVP?'

His jaw clenches. Why am I being like this? Fine, he's an ass, but I've dealt with plenty of those over the years, and this time my mom's house is literally at stake. If he really is JEK then he's the guy, the go-to guy who's been calling the shots. The same guy I've been doing my best to avoid since I got here. Three days ago. That leaves less than a week and a half to get this thing done.

'Can we…' This is for my mom. I lower my voice – Max is paying decidedly less attention to her music site now than she was a few minutes ago. 'Can we start again?'

Jack's dark head goes back and he rubs at his stubbled jaw. His blue eyes glint in my direction.

'Why?'

'Don't you want your product to succeed?'

His head tilts to one side. 'My product *will* succeed.'

'Because you say so.'

'Yep.'

'Even if your competitors get to market first.'

'I feel like we've had this conversation before.'

If I grind my teeth any harder, I'm going to spit enamel.

'I'm sorry if we got off on the wrong foot.'

'Is that what we *got off on*?'

Screw enamel, I'm going to explode. They'll be picking up Leonie pieces in the Clerkenwell area for weeks.

'Wait.' He puts a hand up. He's laughing at me. His blue eyes are dancing, not just a little but flash-mob-in-Waterloo-level. 'That was below the belt.'

His eyes drop below my waist. And there's that sinful Colin Farrell grin.

My jaw drops and then I deliberately move my heeled shoe over his soft sneakers and grind down, leaning forward. For someone so offended by what he thinks happened in Paris, he sure likes to poke at it. But I've had enough.

'We're all good then?' I smile into his face, leaning into him.

He matches my smile, giving no indication to anyone looking our way that I'm causing him pain.

'Super.' He flashes me that Hollywood smile, pushing his chair back. 'Let's review your wall, shall we?'

I release his foot. 'Let's.'

With Jack on board, identifying the MVP is the work of moments; not only does he ratify the Post-its I've already descoped but he quickly removes others I dithered over, afraid I was stripping the product of core features that made it unique in the market.

'Are you sure?' I ask as he moves a ticket Vivek asked me to include called 'Friend bubble ask'.

'Yeah, if we create a small call-to-action it will indicate to the user that it's there; we don't need a whole section.'

'Is there a design of the section?' I can't quite visualise how the replacement works.

'No, no need.'

'How is there no need?'

'It's in my head.'

'And you have time to explain it to everyone when they get to it in their priority list?'

A slight twitch on the lips is his grudging acknowledgement that my argument has merit.

'If it was on Max's computer everyone could go quicker.'

'Okay then.'

'Okay?' I blink. Did I hear that right?

'Yeah, okay.'

'Because you're giving me this one or because you believe it would be easier for the team?' I eye him suspiciously.

'Just take the win, Leonie.'

The rest of the day passes in what seems like minutes until the lights go on and I look up to realise that once again I am alone in the office with Jack. Definitely time to be going home then.

As my hand reaches for the door I freeze. I am here for one thing, and one thing only: to make sure this app succeeds. And it's becoming unavoidably clear that one person is the key to making that happen. Maybe my jackass stepbrother is right. I need to be the grown up here. The professional.

I walk back until I'm standing over him. He finishes what he's doing before he deigns to acknowledge my presence. I smile at him.

'Should we go for that drink?' *Smile* is probably too

generous a description for what I do – no teeth, possibly not even lips visible, in the shape my mouth is making. 'Clear the air?'

I can't believe I'm doing this, but it's for my stepdad and mom. I wait while he contemplates my offer.

'Okay,' he says, rolling his shoulders – to shake off the day's work or to ease the tension caused by my proximity? I really do not like this man.

He shrugs on his jacket and turns out the lights as he mockingly holds open the door to the lit stairwell for me. We make our way silently to the bar down the street. Why did I decide to do this? I could be on my way home, wrapped in the silent comfort of anonymity in the train zipping its way through the dark tunnels far, far below the city.

'I'll go to the bar. Just find a seat.'

I place our order and turn around to see if he's found us somewhere to sit, grateful for the moment to brace myself. All I needed to do was keep it professional – one drink, thirty minutes. How hard could it be?

Impossible, given my drinks partner is currently exiting the front door of the pub. My jaw drops as I watch the dark outline on the other side of the Victorian stained-glass window pass by. I've never known anyone like him to love a big exit. What have I done to offend him now?

Eurgh. I silently scream. I catch the bartender's eye and put a ten-pound note on the bar before I take off in pursuit of Jack.

I rush in the direction I saw him take, pulling my hood up against the rain, scanning the road ahead.

'Leonie.'

I turn at the sound of my name coming from the dark alley running beside the pub, backtracking and ducking gratefully into the covered lane. Jack is leaning against the wall in shadow from the light of the pub's window behind him.

'Can you stop doing that?' I ask, scowling. 'What's wrong now?'

'Stop doing what?'

On the edge of berating him for his drama-queen style, I hesitate. He hadn't left; he had just come outside and into this alley. My eyes drift downward and catch the unlit cigarette dangling from his fingers.

'You smoke?' How unusual for a Californian.

'No.' He shakes his head. 'Well, not in ten years.'

'And you thought it a good idea to start again now?' I had no idea he was so stressed. I feel a pang of guilt as the person putting him under such pressure. 'Don't do it. Another week and we'll be done. It's not worth it.'

'No?' A curious smile drifts across his face. 'It feels like it might be worth it.'

A prickle of electric current runs through me. Is he talking about the app or about something else? Ignoring the charge in the air, I refocus on the problem at hand.

'There's only a couple of points left. I know I'm here to get things done but I hope you don't feel like I'm putting you under too much pressure.'

'Lady, like a Coke tin in space.' His tone is dry.

'What?'

'You think an app launch is driving me to sin?' He

pushes off the wall behind him, invading my space. 'No, it's you, you and those damn skirts.'

'Excuse me?' I splutter, taking a step back. Enough. We are colleagues. His not-quite-hints at what passed between us have caught me wrong-footed more than once. His simmering outrage at what he thought had happened in Paris, his doubletalk that I couldn't quite counterattack on… But this, this is blatant.

'You can't talk about the way I dress. That's sexual harassment.'

'Sexual harassment?' He sounds genuinely shocked.

'And now what? You're adding gaslighting to your crimes?'

'Gaslighting? Like pretending I don't know what you're on about? Oh. I know. Sexual, I'll grant you – all day long.' His voice drops a few octaves. 'But harassment – who do you think is harassing who here?'

'What?' My inner rage clings on despite the growing warmth in my belly at his low tones.

'Well, you're the big shot who tried to use me for my body.'

He seems to be closer. When had that happened?

'I did no such thing.' I try to gather my thoughts. 'You, you're the one…'

'I'm the one, what?' His voice is a throaty purr.

I put my hand to his chest to ensure he can come no closer… Yep, that was definitely why I was now touching him. My eyes feel dilated. I must look like a cat. What is he accusing me of? My brain is no longer functioning.

I feel pressure on the side of my leg as his hand traces up the line of my skirt. Right. That was it.

'You're the one talking about my skirts.' I regroup. 'That's not on these days, you know. Skirts are appropriate officewear.'

His hand has gotten high, cupping my hip.

'What do you think I should wear?' I throw at him, since he is apparently now the sartorial judge of what's appropriate.

Nothing, his eyes tell me, and a flash of memory strikes – his warm hand caressing my bare skin in the cold Parisian morning light. A slow chuckle vibrates through him as his length presses against me.

'No,' I breathe. 'That's not what I meant.'

'What did you mean?'

I struggle to clear the fog in my mind. What had we been talking about?

'You shouldn't smoke. It's bad for you.' My voice goes from husky to prim with each word. The flicker between us is doused as I watch the heat fade from his eyes.

'A great many things are bad for us.' He steps back, glancing at the cigarette in his hand. 'I thought maybe a quick one to remind me why I quit in the first place.'

'I suppose there is some logic in that,' I agree. The danger has passed but my mouth is dry and, unthinkingly, I wet my lips.

His eyes flick to the movement. 'Do you think so?'

His tone has dropped again and just that quickly, the atmosphere lights up again. There is nothing but the awareness of him, the rain and hum of the pub, passing traffic, all fading away again.

'And after?' I ask. 'You can just walk away again. It'll be out of your system?'

His eyes haven't moved from my lips, studying their shape as I form words.

'That's the theory.'

'Interesting theory.' I know we aren't talking about the cigarette in his hand anymore. I make sure he knows it too as I take it from his unresisting fingers.

And then our lips are touching. The kiss at first is soft, checking that we're both in this together, then deeper, exploratory, testing the hypothesis. One kiss, one moment to recall that what we felt in Paris couldn't possibly be as good as we remember. That our new reality makes this a bad idea. Something not worth pursuing.

He starts to pull back. A sigh exhales from him. He's done? No way. This man makes me crazy!

If I'm going to be deemed not worth giving in to temptation, then I … I nip his lower lip crossly.

He stills for a fraction of a moment, his entire body tensing before he wraps himself around me and I hit the wall behind me with a bump. The wall provides the support I badly need as he falls into me and on me and my knees literally weaken at the sensual onslaught. His hands are on me; mine are inside his coat, on the warmth of his skin under his sweater, while his fingers thread through my hair as his kiss robs me of thought, of oxygen.

A wolf-whistle splits the air. We break apart, staring at each other in the half-light as we take in the air we had been lacking for the last few minutes, hours... I have no concept of time.

He steps back.

'Not a good idea.' His words are a mumble as he steps back out into the rain. He smiles ruefully at me as he pulls the packet of freshly opened cigarettes out of his pocket and crumples them in his hand deliberately before tossing them into the bin located at the top of the alley. The rain is already hitting him as he steps back out into the night, sluicing down the planes of his face. 'You win.'

I win? How is that possible? I feel oddly bereft but there is something about the way he can't seem to leave that sends a surge of triumph through me. Not that memorable, he'd said. Liar.

His test was a failure. He wanted to be able to dismiss the chemistry between us like the false satisfaction of nicotine – a mirage of pleasure that leaves bitter ashes in its wake. Still getting back my breath, I know the simmering embers of that kiss and the ones we shared before are what hold him there in the pouring rain.

That test was supposed to clear the air. The air does not feel clear. But he has taken another step back, further away.

He's right. It was a bad idea. I straighten up.

We work together.

I give him a jaunty wave. I don't need this.

'See you tomorrow.'

His eyes hold mine for another second, then with a curt nod he turns on his heel and is gone.

• • •

The next morning, I tackle Max as soon as she comes in. She has to be bored; I can see she is barely utilised, killing time at her desk on social media and idle browsing to punch in her hours.

An hour later, an email from Max appears with a completed design of Jack's amended feature. Max sketches it out for me: instead of having a section where the user goes to bring someone new into an active conversation, they can instead just click a link to allow someone to join. Quickly and efficiently executed, I attach it to the new ticket and put it into Sprint immediately.

I then list all the remaining or tweaked features that seem to need designs in their tickets and ping them over to Max before I go to make my mid-morning coffee. The dark, rich rinds of the earlier brew are slumping into the bin as Max comes in, her smile uncertain.

'Well done on that design,' I compliment her as I rinse out the last of the grains. 'I didn't quite understand what Jack meant, but obviously you did. Should help the iOS team make up some time.'

'Oh, that's good.' Max reties her hair in a pink bun on top of her head. 'They really want all those designs?'

'Yes, they'll be able to go ten times faster with your designs; you clearly know the product.' I pour the water in before looking up. 'You can't just agree to fit in the space they let you. You have to make the space for yourself, show your value.'

'But I don't want to piss anyone off.'

I get it – maybe it's a personality thing, or maybe it's a female thing to want everyone to get along. 'How many of those guys do you think wake up and think, *I hope I don't annoy anyone today*, and how many do you think just decide they want to do a good job, be better than the next guy?'

Max's face is a picture of dawning understanding with a side of kicking herself under the table.

'If Vivek is coding and doing the design, then he's applauded for doing a job and a half. If the design doesn't match between devices, who will be blamed? Vivek?'

'Not Vivek.' Max sighs. 'But—'

'But they won't listen to you? That's why we have processes. If you do the designs and link them to the tickets, then if the devs don't build to spec, the testers will fail the ticket until it reflects your design.'

I could practically feel the stillness at Jack's desk outside the door. Was he listening? Was he going to overrule me now in front of Max and kick the foundation I was trying to help build under her feet? Bring it on, dude.

I haven't looked at him all day. I have no idea where we stand after last night. Somehow I feel like the air had been cleared, in some ways. I palm my jeans to cool them down. If not in other ways.

'You do your job and ultimately it will make it easier for them to do theirs as they won't be sitting there figuring out what needs to go where, or worse, redoing it when the other team does something different.'

Max nods, her pink hair flipping down in front of her face.

'But my files are too big to put in the tickets.'

'So put them in the cloud, or whatever online doc

storage filing system you like and then just paste the URL into the tickets.'

Max gives me a broad smile and moves away, itching with new purpose. Beats spending the day waiting for someone who needs to be buzzed in.

Jack has resumed typing. No objections this time, then.

In fact, no objections for the rest of the Sprint; it turns out when we forget ourselves, we make a pretty good team. He's the engine that pushes the team along as I keep the tracks laid. The entire team are fuelled by the new energy, and as the Sprint slips by it increasingly looks like we're going to scrape our MVP across the line.

Sprint is supposed to close on Thursday but slips over into Friday, yet there is a jubilant atmosphere in the late afternoon as everyone starts prepping for the final push starting Monday. Buenos Aires is pushing their update later in the day and the testers have all agreed to work the weekend to do end-to-end testing, which I'll add to with more user-style testing, giving us a clear view come Monday of exactly what we're up against to have a user-ready version in two weeks. My stomach dips at the amount of work done and yet still to do.

I survey the wall. So many more ticks than only a week ago. It's amazing what can be achieved when everybody is focused and moving in the same direction. But it's Friday and that same direction after the hours everyone has been putting in is home. Long days can get to be a habit. Time to hustle everyone out as a reward.

I catch Jack's eye and circle my index finger in an upward motion. He nods his approval.

'Hey, guys,' I call, gesturing at those who manage to hear me to elbow their neighbour. 'Great job this Sprint. You're all superstars! Really well done. Now go home.'

'Leonie's right. That we're here with a launch build in less than a Sprint is testament not only to the hard work you've put in all these months but to your skill and agility when we needed to get it done. So, please go, enjoy your families and be ready to celebrate at the end of next Sprint when we will be launch ready. Night out on me, Friday two weeks!' Jack's announcement is met with a cheer.

Everyone starts to bustle out the door to the weekend.

'You look nice today.' I stop as I make for the door myself to compliment Max who is made-up to full dramatic effect. Her eyes are accentuated by extra liner and her lips are a violent shade of red – strong for an office lip. 'Hot date tonight?'

'Yep.' She glows. 'I'm trying Opp/Att. I've decided to go Full Max. If that doesn't scare the nice accountant away in the first few minutes, I'll at least know it's not a complete waste of an evening.'

'Opp/Att,' I echo. Why does that sound familiar?

'Yeah, it's a dating app, but for, like, opposites,' Max explains. 'I was showing it to Jack before; it's got some killer features.'

Oh god. That's where I heard the name – the app Alicia used in Paris before deleting it so I couldn't back out. Jack, hearing his name, lifts his head. Why can't he be stuck under headphones like everyone else?

'You put in the things you go for in a bloke and it gives you the opposite,' Max continues, gushing about the app.

'Like, I'll bet you go for smart guys, so you put that in but instead they give you the guy with an amazing body. Abs over quals any day, am I right?'

'Right,' I agree weakly. What had Jack put in to get me?

'Good luck!' I smile. *Don't look around, don't look around.* The chip Jack has on his shoulder about my usual type could double as a foundation stone for one of the great pyramids. It's Friday night. Keep going. We've been getting along so well. Maybe he didn't overhear. Maybe by Monday he'll have forgotten. Maybe he already knew what kind of app it was.

He didn't.

Nothing could be clearer as I give everyone a run-down of the bugs the test team and I found over the weekend at stand-up on Monday. Oh, he's present ... but he's not *present* the way he was last week.

Or for the remainder of the Sprint. Easy smiles and words of encouragement continue to be showered on the team but it's like I'm on the other side of an umbrella, in an Arctic box. Not a sliver of warmth is sent in my direction for the entire Sprint.

But with each day popping up new bugs that get hammered down like whack-a-mole, it's as much as I can do to keep up with the pace of new iterations that crush the most obvious snags only to reveal the next layer below. It's impressive for a relatively small team that they're issuing new builds every few days. The hours they must be putting in... It's as much as I and the test team can do to keep up. If they hadn't already covered most of the journeys with automated testing that a couple of the testers specialise in, we would be underwater.

'There's no way we can squeeze in a couple more bugs?' I ask.

Graham looks exhausted but this morning had uncovered a couple of issues that hadn't existed in the previous build.

'Leonie, I hear you, but if we tackle those we're going to push out until Monday.'

We were so close. If we could just sneak these in before we submitted to the Google Play store...

'MVP isn't about perfection,' comes a dark voice behind me. 'It isn't the total opposite of what you wanted either, is it, Leonie?'

Ouch. 'No, but...'

'Glad we cleared that up.' He turned to Graham, who, like me, had frozen in the face of Jack's sour tone. 'Finalise the build. It will just have to do.'

'If it fails certification, then we can look at squeezing them in?'

'Cos if it's not perfect it's sure to fail, yeah?' Navy-blue eyes cut coldly to me for the first time in days.

Why do I get the very strong impression we aren't talking about the app anymore? Graham looks like I feel. It's been a long Sprint, and the last thing the team needs is for it to end with Jack and me fighting publicly with each other.

So I turn and stiffly sit back at my desk. Rise above.

Me: *I need a rescue.*

Alicia: *Has Irish guy inflicted actual frostbite?*

Stella: *Please tell me he's bitten you! Vampire emoji*

Me: *I'm serious, we have to do work drinks and it's the last day and I'm super obligated to go after all the work everyone's done. But I can't.*

Can't what? Be in the same room with him any longer? Say goodbye? It was work; the work is done. I don't know why I'm so affected. Also, alcohol, and at this point I'm pissed at the way he's been for the last two weeks. I was pissed when he was goady and sexy, but the cold shoulder has made each day interminable, especially given the length of the days we've been putting in. I swear in the final hours of each day before dashing to catch the train, I've had one eye on my work and one on the other people in the room to ensure I wasn't left alone with Mr Frosty.

Nessa: *I got you, girl. Last-minute theatre tickets? Gives you a hard stop. I'll even swing by and drag you out so it looks legit.*

7:30 curtain, 6:30 exit would give time to get to the West End, grab a sandwich en route, but still give the impression I had hung out in the bar as long as possible.

Me: *kiss emoji. My angel of mercy!*

Nessa: *fist bump emoji*

Me: *6:30, The Red Lion on Woodlawn Street. Thanks emoji.*

True to her word Nessa whirls in at 6:30 on the dot, I make my apologies and promise to connect with everyone on LinkedIn. Especially as these guys may be on the market sooner than they expect. Thanks to Eric and his secret sale. The sale which is going to save Mom and Mike.

'So, which one is he?' Nessa breathes into my ear as I wind my scarf around my neck.

'Stop,' I hiss, catching her in full survey of the bar.

'Oh.' She's spotted him in conversation with a couple of devs, pint of Guinness in hand, resting easily against the bar. 'Ooh, I see what you mean now. He's like the meltiest slice of chocolate dipped in … oh, I know what I'd like to dip him in, as Stella would say.'

'Nessa.' My mouth drops open. I'm half used to Stella saying such things but from Nessa, who's still looking him up and down like she'd like to be dripping chocolate on his bare flesh? He catches her looking and his eyes flick to me, the humour fading, his lips thin as he takes in my imminent departure.

He pushes off the bar and saunters our way. There are dark circles under his eyes. He's been the last out and first in for weeks; he must be exhausted.

'You're off then?'

'Yeah.' I have more words to say. Should have said

something sooner. That he isn't the opposite of what I want. That Paris was... 'Theatre tickets.'

'Right.' His eyes are still locked with mine. So blue. Unspoken words. Can I say them? What would I say? My tongue wets my lips, my mouth dryer than a sandal in the desert.

Some of the frost recedes in that blue gaze. He leans in, his breath full of the malty sour tang of Guinness, the shadow on his jaw rubbing bristly against my cheek; a fleeting touch on my leg where I could feel it, as I wouldn't have if he had touched my shoulder. 'Goodbye, Leonie.'

'Bye.'

'Wow,' Nessa says as he takes a seat at the table I so recently abandoned. 'Are you sure you don't want to stay?'

'I couldn't be more sure.'

We make our way out the door, up the street and onto a Tube train going west.

The play is probably good – it got great reviews and Nessa was lucky to get tickets at such short notice – starring a hot guy from last year's smash hit TV show, proving he's more than a pretty face and can be a reliable West End lead. But a family drama is the last thing I need right now.

That was it. I'm never going to see him again. I should be feeling relieved. Life can go back to normal. The app will be submitted as soon as Buenos Aires releases the updated website. My work here is done. Eric has what he needs to get himself out of the mess he's in. So do I.

My phone vibrates in my bag at my feet.

No more dreading going to work in the morning. This is why mixing business and pleasure is such a disaster.

No more Jack. The soft rumble of his voice in the background, that smell of cedar and sea air as he stands close to point out something. No more temptation. No more of that fizzy feeling in my stomach at his incidental touch.

Aruba. That's what I needed to focus on. I'll take a week off before I start looking for my next gig. Golden sands, a hotel I never have to leave, a pool and some sun. That's all I need.

The audience applauds the end of the first act and Nessa goes to pick up our pre-ordered drinks from the bar while I head for the facilities.

I pull my phone out of my bag as I wait in line.

Eric: *Knew you could do it. Strong arm emoji*

Eric: *See you Monday!*

Monday? What the hell is he talking about. I start to type back a response before pausing to check my email.

There's nothing in my work email to suggest I am expected in San Jose next week. On the off chance, I flick open my personal account. Wednesday contains an email from someone in his San Jose office with my flight details for dawn tomorrow.

Me: *Eric. Just seen your email re flights!?*

Me: *I'm afraid I have other plans next week.*

I'm not sure what else to say. I put my phone back in my

bag, where it remains for the second half, the entire duration of which I sit fuming over his high-handedness. How dare he book a ticket without checking in with me? Also, the build is done and is being submitted later this evening. My work here is done.

Eric: *Flights booked. Come over. Let's do this thing.*

Eric: *I booked you in to come over for the weekend, relax and get rid of jet lag then after the launch head down and see the parents for a few days.*

Eric: *Can you bring the laptop with the automated testing code on it with you. One of the testers this side needs it.*

I close my eyes to gather my thoughts and summon up whatever patience and goodwill I can dredge up into a graceful response. I can't really plead non-essential travel as he'll hear from Mom about Aruba, but I haven't been near a beach in what feels like eternity so to me that is essential. Just no. Be calm and decline.

Me: *Eric. You really don't need me at this point.*

Eric: *It's been amazing you stepping up for the family like this. I wouldn't ask if it wasn't important. Obviously we'll pay you for the additional time. Nothing for nothing. Wink emoji.*

Eric: *C'mon, Leo. It's important. I'll tell you more when you get here, but I need your help to close the deal.*

Right.

The way he manages to guilt trip me into feeling obliged to the family is mind-blowing. We barely lived together as kids, and he certainly didn't embrace me as a new sister. I was a vague acquaintance he had to put up with at best. And now this. Like I'm the one who is risking millions of his dad's money. Paying me for my time is a nice touch.

I close my eyes. I've come this far. I do owe his dad. I can see this through. A flash of blue eyes meeting mine for a second too long as we say goodbye is completely unrelated to my motivation to make the trip over. It's for Mike and Mom.

'Nessa, I have to go back to the office,' I say as I excuse myself from our usual post-play drink and review. I can't believe I'm doing this.

The flight is at 05:40 which means I'll need to pack and be up at... I work backwards from the flight time: check-in, taxi to Heathrow ... three am.

Definitely worth splurging on a taxi. Eric can pick up the tab. I try calling Max on my way back east but there's no answer. I instruct the driver to wait when we arrive back at The Red Lion, but there's no sign of anyone from the office inside. At 10.45pm, they're all long gone, either onwards to a club or home, but there's a light on in the office. Crossing all my fingers, I wave at the driver and dash across the road.

I buzz at the familiar door, once, twice, three times, four…

'Hello?' comes a disconnected voice through the intercom.

'It's Leonie. Can you buzz me up?'

The buzzer goes and I push the door in, taking the stairs two at a time. I need to grab this laptop and get home to pack.

'Oh, hi.' I pull up short at the sight of Jack beside Max's desk.

Was he? Was she? I scan for pink hair behind him. No, no. He doesn't look like someone caught in… No, he's at her desk to answer the buzzer. My bones drain of calcium or whatever it is that gives them the density that helps me stand upright.

'You're still here?'

'You're back?'

Our questions clash over each other.

'The web release is done. I just need to finalise a few bits and pieces before I submit.'

'Need to pick something up.'

We do it again. He blinks as he registers my explanation. I nod in acknowledgement and make my way over in the dark to retrieve the requested computer.

'You planning to sleep here tonight?' I ask, spotting the hand luggage by his desk.

'I checked out this morning. My flight is early; I planned to get a hotel near Heathrow tonight.' He smiles ruefully. 'I haven't had good Guinness in a while. Stayed a bit later than I'd planned.'

'Oh.' I chew my lip. *Don't ask, don't ask.* 'Have you much left to do?'

'A couple of hours maybe.'

Shut up, Leonie. 'What time is your flight?'

'5:40.'

Of course they booked us on the same flight.

'Hardly worth getting a hotel in that case.'

A dark eyebrow lifts. 'I can save the few bob by kipping on the floor here?'

'No, no.' *Don't do it.* 'Why don't you come back to mine?'

That dark brow goes even higher and I make sure every pore in my body exudes professional courtesy and nothing else.

'I'm on the same flight. My flat is on the way to the airport. I have a spare room.

'I didn't realise you were coming back to California.'

'Neither did I.'

Chapter Ten

'What are you doing?'

Waking to find Jack standing in the doorway, a dark shadow outlined by the hall light, is disturbing, and it's reflected in my voice. Not in an alarmed what-are-you-doing-there kind of way; that's how I am supposed to sound. What my question actually sounds like is a husky invitation at finding him lingering there. He takes a step into the room just as my alarm goes off.

Who invented alarms? They're one of the single most irritating things in the universe.

I grab my phone from the bedside table and yank it free of the charging lead to figure out how to turn off the alarm I use every day of the year.

Jack steps back into the hallway and the light reveals a man who, if I saw him more clearly on waking, might have elicited more terror than invitation.

'You look awful.' He looked haggard when I left him last night; now he looks downright demented. There are dark shadows under his eyes and his face is hollowed out at the cheekbones, his skin more sallow than olive.

'Thanks. It's done. I'd have uploaded it to the app store, but I can't submit it for certification.'

'Because you don't have the key,' I finish for him. I'm cc'd on the email that Graham sent yesterday. I lever myself out of bed, thankful despite only getting a couple of hours' sleep that I donned my best full-coverage pyjamas. 'I'll do it while you hop in the shower. I'll also put the coffee on.'

'Are you saying I smell bad as well as look bad?' He quirks a dark brow as I join him in the hallway. I breathe him in – a reflex – dammit, he still smells amazing. I push past him and pull some towels out of the cupboard for his shower, pushing them into his hands and moving quickly as far away from him as I can.

The screen awaits the key to submit the app. Pulling up the email with the details, I enter them carefully into the field and run my eyes across the rest of the fields to double-check everything is in order – countries to deploy in, payment types, parental guidance info.

'Leonie,' a voice husks at my shoulder. I startle. How did he creep in so quietly? Turning, I find myself nose to navel. A superb, defined navel, those magic v edge lines visible above the waistband of his jeans, the tell-tale darkening that leads downwards.

'Leonie,' comes in an amused tone this time.

I blink, not downward, upwards. I crane my neck up so I can see up across the vast expanse of bare skin to the gleaming eyes above. Knowing eyes. My jaw is slack and my teeth click as I slam my mouth shut.

'What?'

No tattoos. I expected tattoos.

He lifts the cloth in his hands and puts it down beside me. A tablecloth. I gave him a tablecloth.

My mind is a total blank; all I can see is him. He is too close. This is so unfair.

'Towels?' He lifts a brow. He knows where my linen cupboard is. He is totally doing this on purpose. I will have my vengeance.

I rise from the chair like a queen – regal, dignified.

He trails after me as I pull the required towels from the cupboard this time. Turning around, I hand them to him, purposefully allowing my eyes to trail up and down his exposed chest.

'Very nice, Jack.' I use my most patronising tone and reach out a hand to pat him on the cheek, as I did once before. This time he catches my fingers, knowing exactly the move I am about to make.

He steps into me. There is no challenge this man has ever left unanswered and despite the mutual agreement that there is nothing and will be nothing between us, he narrows the gap between us.

I stare into his collarbone. I don't dare look up, my insides responding to the crackle of energy in the tiny sliver of air between our bodies.

'We'll miss our flights.' My voice is strangled, a wreck of its usual self.

A huff and he's gone, a predatory prowl in the direction of the shower. I don't move until I hear the water running. Can't move.

It's only a thirty-minute cab ride this early in the morning to Heathrow. There's something surreal about making a journey in London before the city has woken up. Like you're doing something secret, clandestine, as the light pushes the darkness away.

Jack is barely conscious, his head occasionally nodding forward on his chest. He worked through the night last night and who knows how little sleep he's survived on as we crushed the mountain of work this month.

But we've done it. The app is in and with any luck should be certified and ready to go live by the time we land in San Jose.

The driver helps lift our bags out of the car with a dark look at Jack, who by this stage is swaying on his feet while he waits for me. He looks like he's totally out of it.

'Hey.' I stand in front of him. 'Dude, you need to wake up.'

'Dude,' he repeats with a goofy grin, like it's the most amusing thing he's ever heard.

'Jack.' This is ridiculous; he's almost slurring. 'Have you taken something?'

'Caffeine pill,' he mumbles, his dark hair covering his eyes as he sways toward me. 'Wasssshh tired.'

This is not happening. We have to get on a plane and get to California.

He pats his jacket pocket, a beatific smile on his face.

I retrieve a see-through plastic bag from his pocket. Inside it are two sheets of pills, both with some tabs already punched out. One set are bright yellow, the foil on the pack stating 100mg caffeine contained within. Back when I was in college, we mainlined coffee out of cups. Simpler times.

The other sheet holds super-strong antihistamine pills, which could also double up as sleeping pills. No prizes for guessing which one Jack took.

Thanks to the carry-on and self-service booths, we make it through check-in, and Jack stays alert enough to take off his shoes and jacket to pass through security without incident.

'Stay here,' I tell him as he lowers himself into the seat in the lounge. If we can just make it onto the plane, he'll have all the time he needs to sleep it off before we land.

I grab some food and take it back to my now-comatose travel companion. I stand for a moment, contemplating him. Even haggard and slack from a too-deep sleep, he is magnetic, and grittily attractive. His eyelashes are dark arcs on those high cheekbones and his stubbled jaw makes him … deeply asleep. No, no, no!

'Jack.' No response. I glance at my phone. We have an hour until our flight, which means we probably only have fifteen minutes here before I need to get him moving to our gate.

Maybe a short nap will help. I take a seat and pick at the food on one plate. After about ten minutes, I try calling his name. No response. A push on his shoulders has as little impact.

Taking hold of both shoulders, I give him a more vigorous shake. Nothing. This is not good. Also not good is our location in the business lounge instead of being in the more anonymous seating areas of the airport.

'Can we help you, madam?' Great. Behind me stand two air stewards in full uniform.

'Ah, I hope so.' I try a wry smile. They'll have seen this happen before; I'm sure they've seen worse. They'll know what to do. 'My friend took the wrong pill. He's been working hard recently and…'

I lift both hands: exhibit A.

'I see.' The more senior of the two is straight-faced while the younger man behind gives me a sympathetic smile. 'What flight were you hoping to join today?'

Past tense. Uh-oh. 'He's fine, really. I'll just splash some water on his face. We'll be fine.'

The steward watches in patent disbelief as I dab water on Jack's unresponsive face.

'Your flight details, please, madam?'

Admitting defeat, I duly hand over the details of the flight I no longer see us making.

A premonition realised as the steward glances pointedly at the screen displaying the departure times. The red boarding alert already flashes beside the San Jose flight.

'When is the next flight to San Jose?' I ask as evenly as I can manage.

'Tomorrow, madam.'

So help me, if he madams me one more time I will lose it.

'Tomorrow?' My voice is definitely a tone or two higher than normal.

'Yes, we run two a day. The second is about to leave.' He

gives my slumbering travelling companion a pointed look.

I get it.

'We need to get to California today.' If we don't leave until tomorrow and there are any defects on the app, we will still be in the air during a critical period.

'There is a later flight to LAX,' the younger steward offers.

'Los Angeles is the other side of the state.'

'Yes, madam,' the other confirms.

Ugh. Is he using that word just to annoy me?

'There is a flight to San Francisco.' He consults the board where that flashing boarding alert is giving me major anxiety. 'But that leaves in thirty minutes.'

'It seems I'm unlikely to make that one either,' I state in a tone I'm desperately trying to stop becoming outright antagonistic but something about this Victorian butler routine is hitting every button all the way down to the nerve endings in my curling fists.

'That does seem unlikely, madam.' He gives that tiny shop manager smile that says *I'm trying to help you but you're impossible and I just want you to go away*.

I exhale. 'Do I have any other options?'

'You could fly with another airline.'

You passive-aggressive monster. You could... No, focus. What to do? Should I book another flight? Just walk away from these business-class flights and get us on the next flight to California that works. I look at Jack. He is deeply asleep.

I run a hand over the top of my head.

'When is the Los Angeles flight?'

'In three hours.'

'Fine.' I trot out the single most passive aggressive response in the English language.

'Very good, madam. Do you have any luggage in the hold?'

'No,' I say shortly.

'If you wish to accompany my colleague to the desk, he will make the arrangements,' Pinchface gives me that smile that says he's won.

'Thank you so much for your help,' I say in saccharine sweet style.

'Madam.' He nods and turns on his heel.

My nose scrunches in the beginning of a snarl I just can't suppress. The second steward's lip twitches.

'Let's get you sorted on that next flight' – he glances at Jack – 'maybe even rustle up a pillow for Sleeping Beauty here.'

Three hours later, I get Jack to rouse sufficiently to walk upright to the gate.

He shuffles in the direction I point him in, eyelids half-closed. We turn right instead of left and make our way to our new seats. It's only when I take my seat beside him that he seems to notice I am much closer than expected. His bleary blue gaze swivels around, taking in the cabin.

'These are not our seats.' There is a slight slur to his words.

'They are now,' I say tartly.

'What? No.' He shakes his head slowly, brows pulling together as he gathers the words together before enunciating as if I'm the one who doesn't know what's going on. 'Our seats are in Business Class.'

'Oh, you mean the seats that are halfway across the Atlantic by now? Those seats?'

His eyebrows pull even harder together, his eyes blink and open wide. 'What?'

'We missed that flight.' I show him my teeth briefly in a gruesome approximation of a patient smile. 'We're on this one.'

And I'm done talking about this. The silent part of my message seems to land, and he nods once, twice, and night, night, he's asleep again.

I exhale huffily and reach for his seatbelt. Whatever sympathy I started out with earlier this morning has worn off. At this point I too am tired and grumpy and we are going to Los Angeles. I sit back in my seat and stare at the back of the headrest in front of me.

The first clue I have that I may have finally drifted off is the awkward angle of my neck and that slight dry mouth that comes from sleeping head back and slack-mouthed.

I sit up and slowly cast my eyes toward my travelling companion. He's awake.

'This a little cosier than expected,' he offers. 'I've heard of upgraded seats, but this is the first time I've been downgraded. How did you manage that?'

I give him the strongest side-eye I can manage while trying to pull my handbag up from the tangle beneath my legs and tidy myself up somehow.

'This isn't our plane,' I say from deep within the recovered handbag. Hand wipes – not what skincare specialists recommend, but better than nothing. I wipe my face and dab on some moisturiser before turning to him. 'Apparently they don't board comatose passengers without the appropriate paperwork.'

His eyes crease at the hit, even though his expression doesn't change.

'That so? I'll be sure to arrange that for next time.'

Next time? Unlikely.

'How did you take the wrong pills?' I roll my eyes. 'Surely you perfected the correct management of wake and sleep pills when you crammed for exams at school?'

He shakes his head and, lifting the shutter, looks outside. We're mid-Atlantic, so the scenery isn't all that interesting. Fully briefed on the clouds, he pulls the shade down a little.

'What? Don't tell me you were a coffee-only type. How old fashioned. I thought it was all green pills and blue pills these days.'

His lips thin and then he turns to face me with a shrug.

'Didn't really finish school.' He takes a long drain of the whiskey on the fold-out table in front of him. This is well behind the iron curtain; this is a big admission. But he has serious skills. How did he acquire them if not at school?

My next question needs to be carefully done; this topic comes with inbuilt mines, and a misstep risks him clamming up. But ignore the comment and I'll be damned for being so high in my ivory tower I can't even conceive of where he comes from. Which I can't. My only knowledge of

Dublin is from a touristy weekend after a conference. The Guinness factory and the library at Trinity College, big Georgian streets and cobbled backstreets with lively pubs.

'How did you get into coding?' I know some people involved in coding classes in disadvantaged areas, but it's unlikely those were around fifteen years ago when Jack was in his teens.

'I was big into gaming. Me and the lads would spend hours round at each other's gaffs playing Xbox or PlayStation,' he says. The overdue rest and the whiskey must have worked enough magic on him that he provides a mellow answer to a prickly question. I wonder what causes the tension I can see creeping into his face.

'That's how you discovered coding?' I'm on the business side of things, but I can't see the connection. How do you go from shooting monsters, or whatever it is he played, to learning computer languages?

'Sort of. My cousin Domhnall from down the country moved up to Dublin to go to college.'

'Do-nal,' I repeat, attempting to repeat the name he had just used with the richness of the vowels in the way he pronounced it.

Some tension eases from his jaw as his lip curls. 'Dow-nal.'

'That's what I said.'

'It really isn't.' He laughs outright. 'Domhnall. Doe, like a female deer. Nall.'

'Ray, a drop of golden sun.'

He heaves a hefty sigh.

'Okay, okay. Doe-nall.'

'Close enough.' Though his eyes tell me I'm still a distance away. 'Now, if you ever meet Domhnall Gleeson you'll be able to say it right.'

'Who's Domhnall Gleeson?'

His head whips round, his eyes large. 'From the new *Star Wars*. Not Kylo Ren, the other bad guy.'

I've been here before. Telling a developer you've never watched *Star Wars* is tantamount to declaring the earth is flat.

'Noooo… Don't say it.'

I bite my lip. Just when things had been going so well. I give him a lopsided, apologetic smile before burying my face in my drink.

'You've seen the originals though.'

'Why is this always such a thing?'

'Because. It just is. How can you not have seen *Star Wars*?'

'I don't know. My mom is English; she wasn't into them. I guess I didn't have a strong enough male influence in my life.' I can hear myself getting defensively formal. I need to rescue it somehow. Wracking my brain, I pull a cracker out of a long-forgotten drawer. Or maybe I've just been hanging out with devs too much. 'To guide me to the Force.'

'You're not a complete Philistine then.'

'Ha, I would not have had you pegged as a geek. You'll be telling me next that you play *Dungeons and Dragons*.'

He takes a sip of his drink and peers out the window at the same view we've had for hours.

I can't help myself. A crowing sound slips out. I have him.

'I've been known to dabble a little in MMO and RPG. They're perfectly acceptable, challenging, tactical, quality gaming.' But there is a damning flush on his cheeks.

'What does that stand for?'

'What? MMO and...' He shakes his head slightly like Venus really is a whole different address to Mars. 'Massively Multi-player Online and Role Player Games.'

A smile blooms across my face, 'Like where you're a wizard and you're talking to some princess who's actually a fifty-year-old Bulgarian while some ten-year-old kid in his bedroom whoops your asses while pretending to be a monster? *Those* kinds of tactical skills you're honing there with your big bad self?'

'Anyway, my cousin,' he attempts to redirect the conversation.

'Doe-nall,' I say solemnly.

'Yes, Domhnall, he started at college.'

'And he introduced you to some fierce pixies, who knew just where to find the secret mojo juice.'

He lowers his eyebrows and gives me a stern look. 'Do you want to hear this or not?'

I put my hands up in surrender. I like this side of him – mock fierce, teasing banter, the safe space we're in high above the world, where we just are who we are. No judgement, no work, no expectations.

I purse my lips in an exaggerated signal that I won't interrupt again and nod.

'Right.' His mock ferocity has deepened his accent, so it sounds like he's using an o where the *i* should be but I make no comment.

'My cousin got a grant to come up to college, and we'd meet up for a few jars now and then. One night I'm round at his place and one of his flatmates is studying and while I'm waiting for Domhnall, I ask him about it, to be polite or whatever.' He shrugs, shaking his head as if to emphasise how this moment was no big deal then, or now. Even though I know enough about him to guess he's telling me that *this* moment, *this* casual conversation in his cousin's student flat is the moment that changed the direction of his life. 'He was in first year so the stuff was basic C++, but it's easy to demonstrate how it goes from being code to—'

'The green writing on the black screen?'

'Like in *The Matrix*?' His jaw drops. 'I know you work on the business side, Leonie, but … that's what you see when you look at the screens of the people you work with?'

I could read bits of words in the commands and codes on my colleagues' screens so I didn't quite see it as sushi recipes in a made-up cyber alphabet but – I shrug a shoulder – I don't entirely *not* see it like that.

His jaw snaps shut, his expression caught between amusement and disbelief.

'What was I saying? Yeah, how it goes from being commands – *Matrix*-style green mystery language floating in the ether, to you – and transforms into events and colours and actions on a screen that can create games, or apps, or huge databases that process unbelievable amounts of data using algorithms that—'

'You got all that from a conversation with a first-year student?'

'Ha, ha, no but it got me started. After that he'd lend me

books occasionally. But mostly I figured it out at the library and online.'

'You taught yourself?'

Was he really self-taught? To his current level? No mean feat. His shoulders are pushed back and his chin squares off at me. Whoa there, Rocky.

'That's amazing. But how come … couldn't you have got a scholarship like your cousin?' If he was smart enough to teach himself, surely he could have cakewalked a scholarship to fund his education.

'He had a grant not a scholarship. Everyone can go to college if they have the right grades. The government gives them money for living expenses if they can't afford it.'

My education cost a tiny fortune, so I could understand that it was still prohibitive, but even Ivy League schools offered scholarships that covered the fees. In the UK, the fees weren't even that much. Relatively speaking.

'You couldn't cover the fees?'

He laughs. 'Third-level education in Ireland is near-enough free.'

'No fees?'

'A registration fee, no tuition. Or it was back then anyway.' He raises his eyebrows at my shock. No wonder Ireland has such a big tech sector.

'Free. Then why didn't you go? Your grades must have been okay?'

'It wasn't too clever to get high marks where I went to school.'

Because calling attention to yourself would get your ass kicked, I guess.

'But even with average grades, given what you managed to learn on your own, surely a case could have been made.'

'No.'

'Just no?'

Did I step on one of those pesky mines? What did I say?

He turns away from me, his body stiff and his movements jerky as he flicks through the screen in the seat in front for something to watch.

Fine. I stand, unbuckling myself, and go to the bathroom. By the time I return, his headset is firmly in place on his dark head. Message received.

After a few minutes to cool down I feel rather bad. He opened up, told me about himself, and reading between the defences that surfaced from time to time, the sharpness that said he could handle himself and wouldn't be afraid to do so was earned. It sounded like his cousin was from a poorer background too, but had more opportunities than his urban cousin. Or maybe more family support. I shouldn't have pushed.

I flick through the new releases and documentaries, resorting to the full library as nothing calls to me. Over halfway through the alphabetical listings, I still haven't found anything that will distract me from the kicking I'm giving myself.

Star Wars. I glance to the closed-off face beside me. Maybe as a peace offering I could watch one.

Except there are loads of them. I flick through them, trying to figure out which one to watch. *Episode VIII* lists Domhnall Gleeson, which I now know how to say. Doe-nall.

Odd spelling. But that one is called *The Last Jedi*, which doesn't sound like the one to begin with. I flick through to the next ones. Ah, *The Phantom Menace, Episode I*, here we go.

The words roll on the screen, the famous crawling script.

Turmoil, blockade, Trade Federation, Congress. I need cliff notes for this and it hasn't even started.

I pull on my headset and settle back into my seat.

Spaceships. That's why I've never watched these movies.

Ewan McGregor. And Liam Neeson. Okay, maybe I can do this.

A hand reaches across and pauses my screen.

'Hey.'

'You can't start with that one,' he grumbles without looking my way. But he's talking again, so that's a start.

Jack stops the movie and selects a different one. *Episode IV*. I frown. He's starting me on the fourth one, but he's already settling back into his seat.

I sit through the opening credits and—

Rebel spies. Secret plans. Death Star. Princess Leia. I can do this. How bad can it be? More spaceships. It'll be worth it if it makes him happy.

I've turned into a teenage girl. Am I really about to watch some forty-something-year-old movie to please a boy? I avoided it all through high school. Laser fighting. Caped guy. I can totally do this. Ooh, Carrie Fisher and that ear bun hairstyle.

Two hours later, there are tears in my eyes as the music swells and Luke, Han and Chewie receive their medals.

I sit back, blinking as I take my headset off to the closing credits.

'Good, huh?'

'It was okay.'

I watch the final credits roll down. That was rollicking.

'I didn't finish secondary school, so I didn't have the grades.'

Oh. That's why he was so mad. I'm an idiot.

'And yet, you are strong in the Force,' I say in my best, earnest Princess Leia. Which is to say, nothing like Carrie Fisher but a lot of hands and a hammy expression.

As a reward I find myself on the receiving end of what I'm coming to think of as his trademark twisted-lip smile. My new favourite thing is watching his face transform with humour while his lips twist in conflicted cynical amusement. A twist of the lips that holds humour and awareness of life all in one sensuous quirk.

I do not need him to catch me staring at his lips. Looking up, I find he is similarly transfixed on the non-platonic part of my face. His eyes shutter and he sits back in his seat.

'You should try the next one.'

'But they've got the Death Star. Happy Ever After. Done.'

'Eight more movies, princess. They ain't done.'

'Good Harrison Ford impression.'

His lips twist again, but he doesn't turn from the screen in front.

Chapter Eleven

'**D**id he just say "Welcome to LAX"? As in the LAX in Los Angeles?'

'Yeah,' I drawl, the word drawn out as I turn to the glowering face of my travelling companion. 'Remember, they wouldn't let us on the San Jose flight because one of us wasn't able to stand upright.'

'So, you got them to put us on a flight to LA. That's the other side of the state.'

His reaction is almost verbatim what mine was. Still.

'I know where it is.' I'm from Los Angeles. 'It's late. We should stay the night and head off tomorrow.'

I look sideways at Jack. He seems sort of distant and braced. Like now we've landed back on the ground the real world has returned. Braced for what I'm not sure, but his shoulders have lifted in a definite taking-on-all-comers type of stance. Or maybe I'm just projecting.

'No more flights tonight.' He looks up from his phone. 'But we could hire a car.'

'If we leave now, we'll be there by morning.'

'It's still Friday. If we go tomorrow, you'll be home Saturday evening.' I don't know why I'm arguing this. My life will be way simpler if I just roll with his suggestion and we drive through the night. But while Mr Whoops-that's-the-wrong-pill is refreshed, I feel in need of a shower and a snooze before facing the eight-plus hour drive north. Throw in the fact that it's rush hour and we won't even be out of LA by dark and, well, other options seem survivable on balance.

'You're right. We don't need to be at work until Monday. What's the rush?' His shoulders ease a little. 'Why don't you check out flight options for tomorrow and I'll book a hotel.'

He's already taking his phone out of his pocket. All I have to do is stay quiet. They'll never even know I've been here.

'We can stay at my parents'.

Jack's eyebrows shoot up at this, which I ignore. I neither want nor am I obliged to explain.

'We can just grab a car and be there in thirty minutes.' Or so; it is LA.

'They won't mind me joining as well?'

'No. There's room.'

Taking the 405 is like being transported to another time. London might be an older city but there's something about LA and the way it exudes its own very particular brand of the twentieth century that can transport you back in time in a way that doesn't happen to me in London. I can't see myself sharing a road with Queen Victoria, but here I can totally see Steve McQueen cruising alongside. Maybe because I grew up in this city I can picture it better.

The 405 is its usual car-laden, slow trail north from the airport, but the asphalt and highway signs transport me back to my teens and the freedom of my first car.

LA is made for cars. In London it took me a while to adjust to life without one. An occasional hire car to nip out for a weekend in the country just isn't the same as climbing into your own car, regularly sailing up the wide boulevards and freeways under that wide blue sky. The outline of palm trees against the backdrop of the pastel-pink sky on the other side of the freeway barrier makes me nostalgic. For LA. I scrunch up my nose.

'Would you mind taking Sepulveda and then Sunset?' I lean forward to the driver. I want to see the city suddenly, rather than the car park that is the 405. At this time of day, it won't take much longer on the surface roads, anyway.

Sepulveda is the quintessential LA street, cracked and not what it was; a bit grubby, with the big automobile-era signs, the strip malls of the eighties, vibrant neon calling from grubby stores, Tacoria trucks with street food ... authentic in a way a hipster would shudder at. The tumble-down vans with flashing lighting and Mexican grills thrown up on the sidewalk. Random businesses and car repair shops, the gritty outer street hiding the increasingly nicer houses that sit in the streets behind.

Turning left on sunset, LA becomes leafy, and walled.

The older classic homes of Brentwood give way to the high walls of gated properties as we head towards the ocean. Until we finally turn up the drive to my mom's house. Or rather, Mike's house. I don't need to look around to feel the arched brow of my companion.

'Not too shabby,' comes the dry comment. 'When you said they'd have room, you weren't kidding.'

'It's my stepdad's,' I dismiss. The large, mission-style house with its white walls and warm, red-tiled roof has nothing to do with me. I lived here for a couple of years before I fled the temporary nest, and now make it back for as few holidays as possible.

After we extract our carry-ons from the trunk, I ring the bell. Twice, no answer.

'What now?' Jack is leaning against the porch wall. There's no way he could have driven north tonight; he's barely holding himself upright. Too many late nights, the sleep he had at Heathrow cut short as soon as I could rouse him and a couple more hours on the plane not enough to entirely restock.

'Follow me.' I lead him around the side of the house and through the perfectly landscaped semi-desert where it gives way to the fuller foliage of the oasis that hugs the back of the house and opens out to the infinity pool on the canyon edge.

'Nice.'

The observation behind me holds all the smugness of a chip being proven correct in all his little-rich-girl judgements.

As we round the back of the house the sound of voices

wafts toward us. On the patio, admiring the last orange and pinks of the fading light, sits my mother, stepfather and a couple of their friends.

My stepfather sees me first and stops mid-sentence.

'Leonora.'

Everyone stops and turns in our direction. My mother's face drops and she is the last to recover as I recognise their friends, the Taylors, and wave a hello in recognition.

'Darling.' She bounces up and sweeps toward us, floaty wrap wafting colourfully in her wake. She enfolds me in her arms for longer than is entirely necessary.

'I didn't know you were coming,' she says, a slightly hurt expression stinging her bright-blue eyes. I inwardly sigh, picturing that anonymous airport hotel where I could already be checked in and relaxing in peace.

'Didn't you get my text?'

She frowns, or as much as she can. My mother isn't a Beverly Hills plastic surgeon's dream, but she hasn't entirely disdained all intervention in holding onto her looks. Compared to Sherry Taylor, she's practically let herself age naturally.

My mother looks over towards Mike, who makes a face. No, he didn't receive my message either. The one I dashed off to them as we got into the car at LAX. That she hasn't looked at her phone in the last sixty minutes doesn't make her the world's worst parent, as her expression is now declaring to the room.

'It's fine, Mom.'

'And who is this?' The broad smile Jack gives her is one I haven't seen him do before. He hits just the right note between stranger introduction and sexy male admiration. Eurgh.

'This is my—'

'I'm Jack,' he interrupts, and my mother envelopes him.

'We work together.' I frown at his back. Let there be no misunderstanding on any level here.

'Aren't you gorgeous.' Mia gives him her best Goldie Hawn smile.

He tilts his head in the can-this-really-be-your-mother expression I've known my entire life.

'I'm Mike.' My stepfather extends his hand, making no move to give me a hug. I don't blame him really. I was a prickly teen and we've never recovered from those initial teenage years.

'Leonie,' Mrs Taylor greets me, teeth showing, no movement in her upper face at all. She looks almost identical to the woman I knew for the ten seconds I dated her son in high school. Or at least a strangely frozen version of that woman.

Her husband gives us both a polite nod of welcome.

'Oh, I don't know if we have enough. Are you hungry, darling? We can put on some extra. I'm sure it won't take Mike too long to whip up two steaks. I must see if your room is ready. I haven't been in there recently but it won't take me a minute to get it ready for you,' she says fussing over me, smoothing my sleeve and smiling her dazzling smile up at me, fizzing with reaction at my sudden arrival.

'Please, Mom.' I step back, 'it's fine. We'll just go grab our cases from the front door. You don't need to do anything.'

'Why don't you guys go freshen up. I know the first thing I need after a long-haul is a shower. Mia, honey, do a quick check they have linen and towels. By the time you come down we'll have a plate ready for you both.' He's already off in the direction of the kitchen, leaving Jack and me to follow my mom through the terracotta-tiled halls.

'Oh, if you had let us know you were coming I could have had all your favourite things in. But it's so lovely of you to drop in.' Her bright eyes drink me in as she turns around, reaching back to give my hand a squeeze. 'How long are you staying?'

'Just the night.'

'We don't need to be in San Jose until Monday.'

Her crestfallen expression is overturned as I glare over at Jack.

'Oh wonderful, wonderful, every moment you can spare us is precious.' She pulls open the heavy door to reveal our two bags waiting outside.

'Wonderful,' I echo.

The shower is everything I need as I stand under its highly pressured spray. California has been in a drought for as long as I can remember, but the showers here put London to shame, the water a cascade that washes away every hour of travel in minutes.

Jack is already outside when I make my way back out to the now candlelit patio in the growing purple dark.

I take a seat beside him as my mother pours a glass of Zinfandel and hands it to me. I sip and smile my thanks.

'You guys staying long?' Mike asks from over by the grill.

'Ah, no, we'll head off in the morning. We need to drive up to San Jose,' I reply, grateful that I have an excuse.

'Stay a day, Leonie. Your mother and I don't see enough of you,' Mike insists. 'I'll make it worth your while. I've got a little something for you.'

My heart sinks. This is typical of Mike. He gives me a gift that I don't want nor need, and then I'm obliged to do something for him.

'I don't need anything, Mike, really.'

'You guys have to drive north, don't you?'

'I … uh, we were going to fly up.' We had talked about driving but flying would be the fastest, if we're going to launch in a few days. There are hundreds of bugs we could resolve. If the first version gets approved, we should have an update ready to go almost immediately after release.

'It's already in the garage. We'll say no more. But I think you're gonna be real happy,' Mike states, closing the subject to discussion as he puts the plates down in front of us. Mike is a good person, but he believes he knows best about everything.

I cut into the overdone steak and smile as best I can, searching for a way out.

'Jack said you don't need to be up there until Monday,' Mia offers gently. 'Couldn't you stay one more day and then head off on Sunday morning? It will be a lovely drive.'

I grit my teeth against the surge of teenage resistance

that blindsides me. There is something about the two of them managing me that makes the sixteen-year-old inside me want to scream. Feelings and behaviours long behind me in every other part of my life rise perilously close to the surface.

'You and Jack could have a day to rest, go to the beach, let some sunshine into your soul tomorrow,' Mia suggests, happy for me just to be in the same town.

'Then we'll take you out somewhere nice tomorrow night,' Mike puts in.

I glance at Jack for support, and he just gives a small shrug. Super. Now he decides to be accommodating.

'That sounds great.' I cave as gracefully as I can manage.

Mia's blinding smile makes me feel even more guilty.

'You live in Europe?' Sherry Taylor asks from across the table.

'Ah, yes. London.'

'It rains a lot,' Mrs Taylor observes.

I throw her a polite smile, this line of conversation not helping me recover from the sixteen-year-old sulk inside me at all. 'Yes.'

'Not as much as it does in Ireland.' Jack, fresh from the shower, looks clean yet still sexy, the faint smell of whatever soap he used doing little to disguise his own sea-salt woodsy smell.

'You're Irish.' Howard Taylor neatly puts two and two together. 'We love Ireland; we've been there twice. Hit The K Club; you know it?'

'No.'

'You've got to know it, great place. We went for the

Ryder Cup. You guys beat us that time, but we had a wild time there. Plenty of the 'black stuff',' Mr Taylor delivers the local nickname for Guinness with a heavy *Far & Away* type accent.

'It's a golf course?' Jack asks.

Howard frowns momentarily before his expression clears. 'You work for Leonora, is that right?'

Is it wrong that part of me feels peevishly pleased at Jack's darkening expression that his lack of familiarity with one of Ireland's premier hotels has allowed Howard to put him in a box and label him. Welcome to my world, chip boy.

'Not exactly,' Jack replies curtly, continuing to eat his meal.

'Terence lives locally.' Sherry moves the conversation on neatly, dismissing Jack as beneath further notice having been established as the help – a classification I know Jack hasn't missed. 'You and he were so good together, Leonora, I always thought it would have been just wonderful. Imagine you two could have linked our families together.'

'Imagine.' I smiled blandly, not the vibe she had exuded back in the day.

'He married Tonya Stirling. You remember Tonya – she was head cheerleader when you guys were seniors.' Oh, the sweet cliché of it all. Did I remember Tonya? Of course I did. The blonde junior had made it her business to tell me that Terence had only taken me to prom because his parents wanted to do business with my stepfather, otherwise there was no way he'd be caught dead with trash like me.

'Yes.'

My mother has also sensed where this is going and has started to flutter.

'They have two kids – Todd is about to go to Pali High,' Sherry tells me, like my experience of Pali High would make me want to change places with her grandson if I could. I shudder at the thought of heading through those gates again. No offence to the school, but they weren't the best years of my life. 'You never considered having any kids yourself, Leonora?'

I exhale lightly. 'No.'

'Leonie has a great career and wonderful friends. She's free as a bird to enjoy her life, not like you and I were at her age, Sherry.' Mia does her best to intervene, but it's a long time since I felt the need to defend myself against the successful grandparent who seems to think I've failed my mom. 'Why, she was in Paris just the other week, weren't you, Leonie?'

She had to bring up Paris.

'All sorts of adventures to be had in Paris.' Jack can't help himself, it seems.

Mia's defence has reminded me of one thing: I am free. I put my utensils neatly on my plate as I push back from the table. 'Thanks for the dinner, Mike. If you all don't mind, it's been a long day and the jet lag is hitting. If you'll excuse me.'

It's only nine o'clock, but why suffer through an hour of this. Perhaps an early night will help not just with the jet lag but with my attitude. I know it's not fair. I just need to shake it off; tomorrow will be better.

The next morning after breakfast, Mike insists we meet him out the front while he goes to get my gift from the garage. I take my place outside, unable to shake off the stiffness in my movements. Mike has always been generous – too generous. He showers my mom with everything his money can offer and I like that, but as soon as he turns his wallet in my direction it feels heavy-handed, like he's trying too hard and always leaves me feeling ungrateful. Like now, I'm here for a few days every couple of years and he's no doubt gone out and bought me some ridiculously expensive high-powered car.

'Oh my god.'

Mike pulls around in front of the house and steps out of a navy-blue Audi Quattro that has seen too many Southern California summers, and hands me the keys, his face beaming.

I take the keys from him and sit down into the cracked leather of the low tan seat, curling my hands around the wheel. Putting the keys in, I turn it on and pull on the button and the hood folds back slowly, hitching for a moment like it will stick mid-fold before continuing again.

'But, how?' My teeth dig into my lower lip to constrain the smile that is bursting out of me. God, I loved this car. When I left LA, I sold it.

'Isn't it amazing? Mike spent ages tracking it down. Said it was the only thing he gave you that you ever really liked. So, he wanted to do it again.' Mom is practically bouncing up and down on her toes. 'So you could have a run around for when you come to visit. Even just having it there in the garage makes me feel like a piece of you is still near.'

I lift a hand to cover the tremble that has taken hold of my chin and adjust the seat to cover for the tears I need to blink away.

I step out of the car and give my stepfather a big hug, my arms reaching to stretch around the bulk of him.

'Thanks, Mike. It's amazing.'

Mike nods, his grin so wide it's threatening to meet his ears. 'You kids have fun. We'll see you later for dinner, yeah?'

Jack lowers himself into the passenger seat and we're off, pulling out of the drive and turning right, heading towards the sparkling vista of the Pacific Ocean.

'I take it this was your car when you were in high school?'

I sweep a hand over the hand-smoothed steering wheel, the wind in my hair, the light pedals of the automatic at my feet.

'Yeah, it was. I can't believe he found it. God, I hated this car.'

I sense Jack's head turning my way to appraise my grinning profile. 'You have a funny way of showing it.'

'Oh no, by the end I loved it. Loved the freedom. Whenever I needed it, I could just sit in this car and take off down the PCH. In some ways, there's nothing like being a teenager in Southern California. It's hard to hold on to the angst when you can put the top down and drive up the coast to the beach.'

'So why did you hate it?'

'It was a bit much when I was sixteen.'

'Poor little rich girl.'

Of course that was his response. I refuse to let him bring me down as we make our way out onto the PCH and turn left towards Santa Monica, endless sand on our right, palm trees appearing at the top of the cliff face to the left.

I pull into the Annenberg car park.

'Walk on the beach?'

'Sure.' He may live in California but after a dark, wet month in London, stepping out onto the sand on a sunny early April day is a treat for him too.

I pay for parking and put the ticket on the dash before I shuck off my shoes and leave them in the well of the driver's seat. Jack copies my move so we're both walking barefoot across the tarmac to the sand.

'You aren't going to put the hood up?'

'Nah, nobody here is going to rob used shoes out of a twenty-year-old car. Besides which, there are eyes on the cars here.' I nod in the direction of the café parking attendants.

The warm sand gives way to the spring cool grains below as we cross to where the waves hit the damp shoreline before the freezing cold of the Pacific hits our bare feet.

'Ah, that is cold,' Jack comments. 'I guess I expect it to be warmer down here.'

'Nope, same ocean hits here that sweeps down from Alaska, just cos the sun shines more down here doesn't mean it heats up any more than it does off the coast of Seattle or San Francisco.' I turn to take him in. He is fit and I can't see him pounding out hours in the gym for the sake of a neater waistline. 'You don't surf then.'

'No, not for me. I like to head into the mountains, do a bit of climbing.'

'Mountain climbing? Like that guy who went up El Capitan.'

'Nothing like Alex Honnold.' He identifies the freeclimber who scaled Yosemite's toughest climb without ropes. 'I prefer to use ropes, but I go to Yosemite quite a bit.'

'I've never been.' It is on my list though. The Douglas Adams poster hung on my wall as a teen, the majestic landscapes epitomising the great world waiting to be explored.

'You're from California, but you've never been to...' He shakes his head. 'You're missing out.'

'How much of Ireland have you visited?' I ask, not entirely idly.

'What? Outside of Dublin?'

'Yes, you know, Ireland beyond the pale, the hills of Donegal, the Atlantic coastline, the pubs alive with music in Clare, the great peninsulas of Kerry, the rolling green hills of Cork.' I list out the highlights from the road trip I took with Niall a few years back. You can take the girl out of America but you can never take away her love of a good road trip, and the romantic misty idyll of the Emerald Isle was irresistible. Practically on my doorstep in London, it would have been rude not to go.

He throws back his head and laughs that rare full-throated chuckle.

'Kiss the blarney stone while you were there, did you?'

'As a matter of fact...' To Niall's amusement I had insisted on it, unaware that it involved leaning out over the parapet of a castle to tip my head and place a kiss on a stone with a ninety-foot drop beneath me.

'Anyway, the point I was making is that you're as bad as me; we travel the world, taking in the sights of places we visit but forget to appreciate the things right under our noses.'

'Mmm.' Somehow he's standing closer and I'm right under his nose. Flustered, I take a step back and the surf washes over my leg, hitting hard enough that my jeans are soaked to my knees.

I pretend the moment never happened and stride up along the sand, the great navy of the ocean rolling towards shore, the heavy crash of the surf lulling me. The Malibu mountains are purple in the low cloud stretching in the distance; the sun warms my skin.

'Leonie!' A passing jogger hails us, slowing to a halt as an easy smile breaks across his face.

'Terence Taylor.' He looks good, filled out some since high school, his bare chest trim and tanned.

'My mom said you were in town. How are you?'

'I'm good, thanks. And you? Your mom tells me you and Tonya have a couple of kids, one heading to Pali High. You still live in the area then?' A slightly sour expression twists his face.

'Tonya and the kids do. I'm in Venice these days.'

Oh. So everything isn't the perfection his mother made out then.

He looks behind me as I feel Jack draw close. Even

though the encounter is destined to be brief, the pause calls for introductions.

'Jack, this is Terence, Mr and Mrs Taylor's son,' I begin. 'This is—'

'Hi, nice to meet you.' But instead of putting a hand out to shake hands he wraps it around my waist.

'Yeah, you too.' Terence edges forward on his toes. 'If you're staying in town, give me a call, I'd love to catch up.'

'We're leaving tomorrow,' Jack answers for me.

Terence flashes me an open yet rueful smile.

'Well, it was great seeing you, Leonie.' He waves before he jogs on.

'What the hell was that?' I snap at him, but his hand is still a warm glow on my hip and I am reluctant to move away.

'Ashamed to be seen with me?'

My head goes back. 'No, of course not.'

'So, that's Mr Stanford, huh?'

'What?'

'That's where he went, right? Good school, good job, right background. He the kind of guy you usually go out with?'

'He didn't go to Stanford.'

'No?'

'No.' He went to Columbia if I remember correctly.

'But you went out with him, right?'

'For like five minutes,' I scoff.

Jack looks at me, his blue eyes brighter than the sky above us, even as his jaw hardens. 'How many of your criteria does he meet?'

'What?'

'You're a lists kind of girl, right? How many does he meet? You have to put ten in the OPP/ATT.' My expression gives me away as his eyes light up at my non-verbal admission. That list has a lot to answer for. 'If he meets more than five, I pick our next activity.'

I mentally scroll through the list.

At my stage in life i.e. interested in long term. It sounds like Terence is divorced or at least separated; he probably isn't looking to play the field. Educated, tall, American, good communicator, well-travelled – all checks.

Open to children. Maybe. He has two so may or may not want more.

Good-looking, good sense of humour – check, check.

Good in bed – we never went there, so I can fairly say *unknown*.

'It's more than five.' I don't need to tell him it's almost full marks.

Jack doesn't look all that pleased to be proven right. I knew he was pissed when he found out the logic to the dating app we met on, this is the closest he's come to bringing it up. But while I'm still trying to figure out how to finally meet it head on, he catches my hand and heads back in the direction of the car.

'So, what is it we're doing?'

He slants me a grin.

Ten minutes later we're cycling towards Venice Beach on rented bikes.

'I can't believe you're making me do this.'

'You're the one who said people should act more like tourists at home.'

'I know but...' As a born and bred Angeleno, abandoning my car for another mode of transport is alien, but as we head down the bike path, past the amusements at Santa Monica Pier and groups of volleyballers, taking in the skateboarders under the Venice palms and the iron pumpers at Muscle Beach, I find I'm thoroughly enjoying myself.

We grab two poke bowls and pick a spot near the breakwater at Venice to watch the surfers wait for their ride.

'I can't believe you gave this up for London,' Jack says into the companionable silence.

I contemplate the blue in front of me.

'This isn't exactly the life I walked away from,' I start and then stop, trying to figure out how to better explain. 'I never felt like I fit in here. I wanted to go somewhere where I could start fresh, where nobody knew me or my parents.'

'Poor princess, too much sun, too much easy living.'

I turn around to look him full in the face. He's one to throw labels around. 'That's what you think?' I stand up. 'Let's go.'

We throw the remains of our lunch in one of the heavy-lidded trash cans and climb back on our bikes. I take us down Venice Blvd, past the beach houses and the canals, the boutiquey vibe of Abbot Kinney, across Lincoln and keep going until we're nearly under the blocky view of Sony Studios before swinging left.

After a couple of wrong turns and a little backtracking, I finally find 3620 Kelton Ave. The small cottage is familiar and yet nothing at all like I remember it. Mature trees shade the wooden porch with a swing seat, and chimes tinkle in a neighbour's garden. The cracked paving is the only recognisable remnant of the street I grew up in. The peeling paint and iron bars over the windows are long gone.

'This is what you wanted to show me?'

I wanted to show him where I grew up, but where I grew up was gone, replaced by an area that homes comfortable middle-class families.

'It didn't use to be like this.'

'What?'

'Palms.' I gesture at the quiet suburban neighbourhood. 'My mom and I, we lived here when I was a kid, back in the Eighties and early Nineties.'

'What was it like?'

'Not like this.' I can't quite get over it. It's like someone waved a Technicolor wand over the area. Before we turned off, I caught a glimpse of the rainbow commemorating the Wizard of Oz soaring high in the local Studio, I felt like Dorothy. What once was drab and grey has been transformed. 'It was grim when we lived here, bars on the window, my mom scraping by on two jobs.'

A slight head tilt is his only reaction as he readjusts his perception of who I am.

'Is that why you left LA? To get away from the city where you were poor?'

I tilt my head as I contemplate my old home. 'No, it was to get away from the city where I became rich.'

'Okay.' Jack's tone is balanced, neutral.

I shake my head. 'I know it sounds stupid but growing up here, I knew how to face down kids tougher than me, to ignore gang cars rolling slowly by. I never figured out how to face the rich kids I ended up joining in high school after my mom remarried.'

'It doesn't sound stupid,' Jack offers quietly. 'I left to find somewhere I fit too.'

'You haven't found it?'

'Not yet.'

Partly for him, partly for me, the rest of the day is a whirlwind driving tour of some of LA's landmarks, taking the 66 from Santa Monica up to Hollywood, a short visit to find our foot twin in the concrete outside of Mann's Chinese Theatre, a swing through the faded and rejuvenated glory of the art nouveau scrapers downtown, then up into the hills to watch the sunset with everyone else at the Griffith Observatory before we make our way home for dinner.

'He's cute.' My mom links arms with me as we exit the chrome and hardwood restaurant Mike brought us to. The ambience was a little too noisy, too on show for my taste and Mike's grilling of Jack left me on edge. Though Jack held his own as Mike gave him the third degree.

'Mom.' I can't stop myself sounding like a teenager.

'What, sweetie?' She squeezes my arm. 'I'm old, not blind.'

'He's too young.'

'I'm a happily married woman.' Her eyes crease teasingly as she pretends I meant for her. 'But I don't think a year or two should matter.'

'More like ten.'

'If you were a man, and he was a woman, nobody would blink.'

'But we're not.'

'I thought you were a modern woman,' she admonishes.

'Modern women don't sleep with men they're working with.' If I had known who he was when we met there's no way I'd have crossed that line.

'They don't? I know plenty of couples who met at work.'

'He's not right for me.' A slouchy, moody, hot mess is not even close to what I'm looking for in a partner.

'He isn't? Why not?' There's that Goldie Hawn speculative look of a woman who has never failed to appreciate an attractive man and can't fathom why I would pass on this one.

'Mom.'

'You've got to stop waiting for the perfect man Leonie; he doesn't exist. Besides, imperfect has its own…' She pauses as she searches for the right words and I know I'm about to be smacked with a quote. *There's a crack in everything, that's how the light gets in.*'

'The wise words of…?' I prompt.

'The great Leonard Cohen.'

Ah, no wonder she's so pleased with herself. Leonard Cohen has always been my mom's guru of choice.

Jack chooses this moment to turn around and throw me that twisted, amused smile – because of something Mike has said or because my mother's voice carries, I'm unsure. But damn if it doesn't curl like smoke inside me.

Chapter Twelve

'They've rejected the app.' My heart sinks as I read through the report from the app store. 'Accessibility issues in the settings area at larger viewport sizes. Likely on tablets we didn't test on because their usage isn't high, and they were too expensive to buy. Ipso facto.'

'Ipso facto?'

'You know, one thing causes the other, which causes the … never mind.' I receive some side-eye even though he's still mostly focusing on the road. 'I can forward the report to Vivek.'

'It's the middle of the night in London. I can sort it.'

'Not while you're driving the car you can't.' I pull up the map on my phone and search for accommodation. 'There's an inn just before San Luis Obispo, another ten minutes' drive. We can stay there.'

'It'll only take me an hour or so to solve the viewport issue, at most.'

'I haven't finished reading the rejection report.' I correct his belief this will be a quick fix. My attention is on trying to secure accommodation; it's short notice and a weekend. There's an option with two rooms but one price; that'll do. 'There's more – that was just the first one that caught my eye.'

'And here I thought you were trying to have your wicked way with me.'

Reserving the rooms, I look up to catch a very Han Solo smirk on his face.

'You wish.' Part of me wishes too. Maybe my mom's right. I'm too caught up on things that don't matter. Sure, we work together, but not for long once the app launches. I'll be heading back to London. And the last day has been great. He's been great – warm, funny … gorgeous.

'What else is wrong?'

'Hmm?' I've missed his question, too busy contemplating all the reasons I could cross our clearly marked lines. Coming up with all the right reasons to be with the wrong guy. 'What?'

'The other issues?'

'Oh, yeah.' I scan down the rest of the list. 'Some stuff about complying with data privacy and it looks like there's a bug in the payment process. They had issues with payment going through.'

'What kind of issues?'

'They don't say. Let me see if I can get any other details.' I close the email to give our account manager Aaron a call in Cupertino.

'Don't forget to check that they were using the right region settings.'

'You need to take exit 201 for the inn.' I ignore his backseat test advice. 'It should be coming up.'

As the phone rings on the other end, a highway sign for exit 201 appears, and I point in case he hasn't spotted it. His lip quirks at my action. Is he mocking the domesticity of it? It feels oddly husband and wifey, I have a flash of sitting in the back of a car while my mother did the same to my stepdad, Mike grumbling good-naturedly that he'd seen it, but every time she would wave her hand pointing the way even when the indicator was already on.

'Hi, Aaron, it's Leonie from RL8. Thanks for sending the report back so quickly,' I say. 'You guys turned it around so fast, we really appreciate it. We didn't expect to hear from you before the weekend was up.'

'We had some extra capacity on this week – a big submission didn't come in, so we had time.' Aaron shoos away my gratitude.

'Any chance if we get this back to you quickly that you'd be able to retest?'

'You know the rules. You go to the back of the line. We'll have to retest the whole app.'

'Couldn't you just spot test the bugs you've raised?'

'It'll go to a different team next week; they'll have to start again.'

'What if we got it back to you tomorrow, will the initial team be able to re-look at it?'

'Let me check.' The phone goes silent as he puts me on hold.

The sign for the inn is visible up high alongside the 101,

total classic Southern California highway road sign, big and kitschy, and ... dear god, is it pink?

Jack guides the car through the car park, in front of a long hotel that's a cross between the inn in *Dirty Dancing* and, well, the cottage Hansel and Gretel might have fled from. Thankfully, I can't see Jack's expression through his sunglasses. I point over to the reception sign and he pulls under the hotel where there's a bridge over the road, *Jetsons* styl-.

The line comes alive. 'You've got until tomorrow at two pm to get a new version into us.'

'Aaron, you are a legend. Thank you.'

My phone buzzes again. It's Eric.

'I'll go check us in,' Jack offers. His sunglasses are up on his head now that we're in the shade of the drive-through ... drive under? Amusement glimmers through his otherwise straight face like light through a curtain.

I nod, taking the waiting call.

'Leo,' Eric begins. I deeply dislike when he does this, this shortening of my name that suggests an affection and closeness that does not and never has existed between us. In fact, if anything, it makes me feel wary of why he's calling. 'The App Store rejected us. I need you to get on this asap. Where are you? We need this done yesterday. I've sworn that we'll be ready to launch on Monday.'

'We agreed to launch on Tuesday,' I remind him. That way the team has a day to run last checks and be fully prepped for the launch. Nobody ever launches anything on the first or last day of the week. Although Monday is preferable to Friday, there's nothing worse than launching a product when everybody will be out of the office for two days.

'We needed to fucking launch a week ago.'

I pull the phone away from my ear and take a breath. *You can take it, it's for Mike.*

'Eric. I've spoken to the store already, if we get it into them by tomorrow, they will just spot check the issues. We'll be good to go on Tuesday.'

'Right, you get Jack to do the front-end stuff.' Eric doesn't even thank me. 'I've got some guys working on the platform fixes.'

'Are you sure? London will wake up in a few hours. I can get them to focus on the aesthetic issues. It seems like Jack would be the best choice for the data issues.'

'No, no, he won't be as familiar with it as the guys here. They've been doing the heavy lifting for the last few weeks so he'll only confuse things by getting involved at this stage. If you can get him to focus on the front end and payment, I won't even bother him with the other stuff. I'll email you a list with a clear division of who's doing what. We're writing up tickets now. Get him to work on the tickets assigned to him; we'll handle the rest here.'

'If you're sure.' Eric is writing Jira tickets? It really is all hands to the pumps. I'm shocked he even knows how. He said *we*, so maybe that's more of a 'I've told someone else to do it' type of *we*.

Jack sits back into the car and puts the hotel room card on the dash as he pulls away from the reception office. A single room card.

'I've got to go,' I say distractedly. If I stare hard enough at that card maybe its twin will appear. 'We'll be in touch later once we have a better estimate on the fixes, to coordinate timelines and whatnot. We need to get it in by 2pm, ok?'

Without waiting for an answer, I end the call and reach for the hotel key card packet. My eyes do not deceive me. There is only one.

Jack only got us one room? My stomach jitters.

'Ah, I booked us two rooms.' I'm not sure whether I object. I know I should but ... over the last day or two things have been ... and I'm pretty sure I don't object in the slightest.

'You did.' He slants a grin at me. 'They showed me a picture of the room in reception.'

I'm not sure I'm following but another building has appeared in front of us, this time with a strong *Showboat* look. He parks the car and puts the hood up.

A mysterious smile is playing at his lips as he stops at a door to a room called 'Horse and Hounds'. We enter a large sitting room area with an open fireplace and a large leather Chesterfield, the walls adorned with an English riding-to-hounds motif wallpaper. Exploring the room, we discover a master suite off one side with another room upstairs. The whole upper-class English vibe has been adhered to the whole way through. Deep-pile carpets, dark greens and brown leather.

'We're still in SoCal, right?' I turn to him.

'You tell me. This place was your call.'

'I booked two rooms, though.' If I keep repeating it, maybe it will be true.

'Technically, it is two rooms,' he points out. 'I tried to rectify the situation, but they only had the Jungle Rock and The Time of Your Life rooms still available and they're in different buildings. It seemed sensible to stay closer together. I can assure you your virtue will be safe in your little upstairs boudoir.'

The upstairs does have the air of a boudoir with its kitschy wallpaper and heavy lamps.

'Hey, how come you get the master?'

'Because there's only one ensuite and I'll be the one working all night,'

I can't object to that. I'm already starting to feel guilty that I won't be able to do much, or anything at all, while he works.

He's already unpacking his laptop and settling onto the sofa with the laptop on the coffee table in front of him.

'Can you forward me the list?'

'No need. The tickets are already up in Jira. They've already divvied them out. San Jose will look after the backend if you can work through the front-end issues. If you can let me know how long you estimate they'll take, I'll coordinate with Eric and then when London wakes up, I'll get them to help pull the build together.'

I've lost him somewhere halfway through outlining my plan. No doubt he's already scanning through the tickets in Jira.

Which leaves me with an entire afternoon stretching in front of me.

'I might just go explore the grounds.'

A noncommittal grunt is all I get in response as I head

out. There's a small garden opposite peppered with eccentric statues and as I stroll around it, I notice a small tower building further up the hillside. Following the path up and around I find a terrace with a pool and a jacuzzi. The tower building I spotted from below turns out to be yet another quirky building housing a spa and a bar. I guess I've found a way to occupy the afternoon.

Returning to the room I grab my purse and hit the spa. Most of the Madonna Inn is booked out with a wedding, it seems, so despite being fully occupied there is plenty of availability and I'm ushered straight through for a massage.

The lovely Natalie kneads out all the tension in my neck and shoulders after a couple of queries about problem areas, and the stresses of the last month float away. The small store has a rack containing some floaty yoga gear and some interesting-looking on-brand swimwear.

I end up buying an itsy-bitsy teeny weenie bikini that I will probably never wear again, not only for the ultra-revealing seventies look and cut but because it is, of course, yellow polka dot.

The kidney-shaped pool isn't made for doing any kind of actual lap-style exercise so I satisfy myself with some leisurely breaststroke, which keeps my hair out of the water because I definitely do not have the energy to deal with washing my hair.

The rest of the afternoon breezes by as I enjoy the California sunshine soaking into my skin. I feel like a golden poppy basking in the warmth. I eventually pull my blissed-out ass back down to the room. I'm not sure if you can take the towels out of the pool and I'm dry and it's still warm so I don't really think about my bikini until I let myself back into the room and Jack's casual glance at my entrance snaps to full attention.

Itsy. Bitsy.

My mouth dries at the pupils-fully-dilated fixed look he gives me.

'I just need to use your bathroom to wash off, if that's okay,' I say, faking nonchalance.

The lids of his eyes drop lazily as I attempt to casually stroll across the room.

'Mmmhmm.'

If I offer him a million dollars right now, there is no way he will be able to repeat what I just said. Which doesn't entirely hurt my ego as I shut the door behind me.

In the shower I wash the chlorine off my skin, contemplating my situation. That heavy-lidded look testifies that he is definitely not uninterested in me. What if? What if something happened between us? It wouldn't be so bad. I would never in a million years have picked this guy out as a potential partner. Too young, too sexy, not at all who I saw myself with. But if the zombie apocalypse came, would I trust him to see me through it? Could I see us tucked up just the two of us in my London flat? Finding new things to cook, whiling away the hours with whatever TV series we haven't seen before? A warm glow inside me says I don't find the idea of it repulsive at all. In fact, there are *lots* of activities we could find to pass the time.

I wrap the towel around me, remembering Jack dressed only in a towel in my flat … was it only two days ago? Revenge for his thirst bomb is in my grasp. I exchange the huge industrial-size bath towel for a rather more economical size one that barely covers my ass, and at that only manage it by revealing plenty of breast. It isn't as revealing as the bikini, I assure myself; it isn't indecent; I'm doing my bit for the environment even.

The stairs to my room are beside the door to the master suite, but even without looking his way I know I have his full attention as I pad softly and carefully up the stairs.

1–1, my friend.

Coming back down, once more fully dressed, I find Jack still tapping away at his computer, though he assures me that he will be done in a couple of hours and then he will lend a hand on the platform side.

After an hour of flicking through my phone, I can ignore my stomach no longer.

'You have to eat. Come on. There's a steak house,' I say, having read the hotel information folder twice. There is also a more casual café, which no doubt does takeout sandwiches, but it seems like we're going to make the deadline comfortably. What harm can it do?

The steak house turns out to be the crowning glory of the inn. A collection of candy-pink leather booths sitting in a drop-level room with a rose motif on the carpet and fairy lights woven through the faux green, rose-dotted foliage draped across the roof from which hangs big plastic love hearts. The room is walled in mirrors, giving multiple reflections of the perfection that is the complete experience.

The waitress introduces herself and guides us to our own candy-pink booth. She hands us cocktail menus, laughing at our bemused expressions.

'First time?'

We nod and when we pull our eyes away from the impact of the room read through the list of fifties-era cocktails before finally settling on two Gin Rickys.

Jack catches me up on his afternoon's activities while I confess to my rather less industrious one. The waitress returns with what turns out to be two tall, delicious glasses of lime juice, gin and soda poured over crushed ice, and takes our dinner orders.

The atmosphere between us is light and mildly flirtatious, and I want to clear the air. Even if it means bringing up one of the cringier moments of our somewhat rocky relationship. But it's been on my mind for weeks and I just need to get it over with.

'You know that morning? I mean, after that night in Paris, the 500 euro?' *Just say it.* I look up. No help from the amused blue eyes on the other side of the table. 'I never—'

'You weren't paying me for sex.' He puts me out of my misery. 'Yeah, I know.'

'You know?' My voice goes to where only dogs can hear me. The affronted display he put on there in the café … I thought he was going to flip the table over, Hulk style. 'You could have fooled me. You were furious.'

'So maybe in the moment I did think that's what you were doing.' He gives a wry smile, slouching back in the pink booth. 'It's happened before.'

'It did not.'

'Did so.' He quirks an eyebrow, his smile still easy. 'A woman in a bar in Dublin offered me two hundred euro.' He pauses. 'We settled on two thousand.'

'*Did you...*?' My jaw has gone slack.

He totally did.

'You're shocked.'

'I'm not un-shocked,' I say carefully. 'So that's why you jumped to the wrong conclusion. I thought it was something I said, or did, that implied that I, that I thought *you*... I've never been so embarrassed in my life.'

'It was a lot of money for breakfast,' he teases. 'Even in Paris.'

'It was an accident. My friends received it as a gift and I picked it up when we were wrangling over change for a taxi and I didn't realise I had it when I put it—' I brake to a halt. 'Hold on a second here. I'm justifying why I accidentally pulled the wrong note of a currency I don't use out of my bag. You're the one who sold his ... dude.'

He laughs, not shy about this part of his past.

'It isn't the worst thing I've ever done. Or the most illegal,' he dismisses it.

'What did you do with the money?'

'Spent it on the horses.'

'You did not!?'

'No I didn't.' He laughs again. His mood is lighter than I'm used to, his laughter as rich and sexy as his accent. Throaty in a way that sends shivers through me. 'I packed my bags, bought a ticket for the States and never looked back.'

The ice tinkles as he takes a sip of the silvery drink and I do likewise.

'What happened then?'

'I fell in with some lads when I arrived, got a job under the table on one of the building sites.'

'You didn't have any papers?'

His eyes question my listening skills. He arrived in the US jobless and skill-less; of course he didn't have any papers.

'Then how?' He had to have them by now. Working on buildings as an unskilled labourer was one thing, getting work developing technology another.

'I arrived in San Francisco at the right time. It was the mid-2000s. If you were literate, you could get a foot in the door at a lot of places. Junior roles in dev were ten-a-penny. I got a job as a tester and once I revealed I could code—'

'A company sponsored you?'

'No, I got papers before that.' His lips twisted. 'I got married.'

Now my eyes are popping out of my head. He was married. Is that why nothing had really happened between us in Paris? He's *married*?

'You married for a green card?' I ask casually, focusing on his history rather than what it meant in the present, despite my heart acting like an animation from the Toon era.

'Oh no, I was mad about her. I was also twenty-two and couldn't believe this classy American girl with her fancy college and her own place would look sideways at me.'

'Where is she now?' *Please don't say at home. Please. Please.*

He looks away, and a shadow passes over his face. 'It didn't work out.'

He makes it sound like it was inevitable, like this girl was too far out of his league for it to last. How could he think that? He is magnetic and charming and clever all wrapped up in one of the sexiest packages it has ever been my misfortune to come across.

'Here you go now.' The waitress puts our plates down in front of us. 'One salmon, one rib-eye.'

'Thank you.'

'Is there anything else?'

'No, no.' *Please, just go.*

'Better get this down and get back to it, eh?' Jack picks up his knife and fork like he's about to perform complex surgery. And *he's* the one who ordered fish.

His failed marriage is closed for discussion as we move on to more neutral topics, like the gobsmacking décor.

After dinner we wander companionably back to our room, or at least as much as it can be given the tingling awareness of each other that sparks between us all the time, but instead of making me want to run a mile I want to lean in.

My mother's parting words came back to me. Another of her Leonard Cohen pearls of wisdom, misquoted as only my mother can. She leaned in as she hugged me and whispered, *Sweetheart, stop waiting for it to rain … enjoy being soaked to the skin.*

Only my mother can accuse me of being a pessimist and

blind to what is right in front of me while advising me to embrace life all in one go.

Scatterball atoms of energy bounce and rebound between us as we enter the room. I feel like everything is in slow motion, as I take one step and then another to the stairs that will take me to my bedroom. The one where he isn't.

We'll be in Palo Alto tomorrow. The app will go live and I'll go back to London. I'll never see him again. Why am I over thinking this?

'Do you have much left to do?' I ask. Am I assessing if he's free to play?

'I want to check in on what the rest of the team has done, give it a once over.' His teeth catch his lower lip. 'I suppose I should get back to work then.'

Does he think I'm shooing him away? I take another step towards the stairs that will end this conversation. My breath is hitching a little. *Dammit, Leonie.* A smile spreads across my face, mischievous inspiration hitting.

'I suppose … of course, maybe you don't have to do anything, not a thing.' I dip the words huskily in all the right places. I re-watched *To Have and Have Not* on my commute last week, not that I was brushing up or anything.

I hit the first step and look over my shoulder. He has paused mid-step on the way to his room.

'Oh, maybe just whistle.' Those blue eyes crease at the corners as he recognises the line. Meanwhile, I'm losing my nerve and unlike Bacall turn away, chickening out from delivering the next lines to his face. 'You know how to whistle, dontcha? You just put your lips together…'

Before I've hit the next step an arm curls around my waist and turns me around. His lips are on mine and I'm lost in it.

He pulls away and gives a quiet wolf whistle, and then we're backing up into his room and his shirt is off. I'm inclined to give a wolf whistle myself. With the hours he puts in sitting in front of a computer, when does he get the time to do this? My hands run up and over his biceps, and triceps – all the 'eps – as our tongues tangle together and his hands make forays of their own.

We tumble across the room, kissing against the wall before tripping into the bed in the dark, hands fumbling to turn on the brocaded lamp at the bedside, which gives the room a dark-green glow. I shimmy out of my skirt as he disposes of his own inconvenient clothing as hastily as possible, before crawling back over me. Stilling, he looks down at me, and the look that passes across his face, the one that takes him away from me, distances him from this moment.

It's a look I refuse to let win. Not this time.

No time to fear the rain.

I reach up and pull him down, back into the moment, taking his lips in a fierce kiss. A kiss that demands, that brooks no hesitancy. I am a queen and his skin touches mine in worship.

He wants this; his need surpasses mine. I feel the shadow of that younger version of him, the boy who fell in love with a girl he felt was beyond him. Is that the wound that holds him back?

His kisses trail hotly down my body. Is that why he keeps pulling away?

I feel like I see him. I know him.

Placing my hand on his head, I pull him back up to me, rolling us until I'm on top, teasing kisses, bringing his torso upright, his face and broad shoulders shadowed in the light.

His hand captures the nape of my neck, preventing me from escaping any further. My fingers are cupping the seal softness of his hair. Our lips and tongues tangle, heated, crazed.

The kiss deepens, his hands going across my hair, holding me to him as his length presses against me. His mouth explores mine, tongue for tongue. My body sings, alive with wanting him, ready for him. His body surges against me, in me, our bodies moving together, finding a rhythm.

His need to drive deeper grows. He twists us and I throw my hands behind me to protect myself from the headboard as he moves in me. He adjusts, pulling me further down the bed, my hands clawing at his back, his biceps, his shoulders, wherever I can reach, wanting to feel him, claim him as he does me.

He stills, pausing above me, and I open my eyes, catching the light of his bright-blue gaze as he stares down at me. Alert, stretching the moment. His smile is wolfish and his hands frame my face as he holds my eyes locked to his and moves in one deep thrust. I arch against him, coming apart, splintering into tiny pieces, still shivering in reaction as he moves away from me and disposes of the condom I have no recollection of him donning. Returning, he wraps himself around me. I can't move, don't want to. I am utterly blissed out.

The sun is glinting through the shutters as my eyelids flutter open. My body is utterly enervated, my muscles relaxed; I feel as if I'm floating. Short nails rake across the softness of my belly and my insides clench, reminding me of last night's activities. His hands move upwards, palming my breasts; the rough texture of his legs wraps around mine. His hands roam, claiming every inch of my skin. Turning me to face him, cupping my jaw, lips meeting lips, insistent. I moan, emergent thoughts of brushing my teeth slipping away at the open-mouth kiss. He moves along my jaw, feathering kisses. His body moves with mine, in mine, soft and sweet, the ferocity of last night sated. This morning, it's like the gentle bubble of champagne fizzing through me.

'Morning,' he breathes into the sensitive skin where my neck meets my shoulder.

A laugh bubbles up from the last remaining ounce of energy available to me.

I come to, stretched across his broad chest, my ear listening to the regular thud of his heart, searching for what has disturbed my sleep. There is an insistent buzzing on the bedside table on the other side of the body I am currently using as a pillow.

I stretch lazily across him, my hand reaching and falling short. I lift myself to grab it and quiet it before it disturbs Jack too.

His eyes open and his lips widen lazily as he catches me mid-air above him.

'Now here's a sight I could happily wake up to every morning.' He wraps his arms around my back and pulls me down onto his bare torso. Skin-to-skin, velvet and silk. His head turns to find the source of the insistent vibrating. My phone is on silent, but this late in the day the do not disturb setting is no longer keeping the call from disrupting our peace.

Jack stretches and grabs the phone, glancing at the message as he hands it to me.

'It's Eric.' His brow pulls together as he pauses in the action of passing it to me, his attention caught by whatever he's reading on the screen. His lips thin.

'Great job, I'd say.'

'What?'

He pushes up, dislodging me as he sits up and swings his legs over the side of the bed and throws the phone down into the space he left behind.

Eric: *All done this side. Don't worry about it. New build done. Uploading now.*

Eric: *Good job keeping Jack out of it.*

Eric: *Whatever you've been up to keeping him distracted!*

It reads like I was preventing him from getting involved ... in what? Eric suggested that they should divide the work up to resolve the issues efficiently, or at least that's what I understood. This makes it sound like I was in cahoots with Eric to stop Jack from seeing—

The sound of an expletive bursts in from the sitting room.

I wrap the sheet around myself and venture as far as the doorway of the bedroom. Jack is glaring at whatever it is he's seeing on his laptop screen, his jaw locked tight with anger.

He stands abruptly and pushes past me, grabbing his phone.

He stares at me with narrowed eyes, his nostrils flaring slightly. My presence not welcome, I back up into the bathroom. What the hell is wrong?

Turning on the water to the shower, I can still hear angry words being exchanged.

When I exit the bathroom, the bedroom is empty, the rumpled sheets the only evidence of the different day I woke to. I grab my phone from where it lies abandoned in the middle of the bed. Out in the lounge area I can hear the furious tapping of keys, Jack's dark head not lifting as I make my way up the stairs to my room.

I pull on some leggings and a slouchy shirt before I call Eric.

'What's going on?' I ask as soon as Eric's curt greeting sounds in my ear.

'Nothing.'

'It's not nothing. Jack is pissed. Why? What have you done?'

'We got the app uploaded on time, that's what matters here.' He exhales noisily. 'Jack is a control freak. He wants to be across everything. That's just not possible.'

'You made it sound like I was hiding things from him.'

'You haven't told him about the sale,' Eric reminds me. 'You see why now. He'll sabotage us. He thinks of the app as his baby; he won't be pleased to learn he will lose control. You've seen how he acted now over nothing.'

'I haven't told him anything.' Though I am feeling increasingly uncomfortable about it, but that is between Eric and his employee. Nor do I want to jeopardise the sale that will ensure my parents' financial security. But there is something about the way Eric is keeping the sale secret that is making me increasingly uneasy.

'Why the big secret anyway?' Jack was clearly deeply involved with this project. But that was nothing new, I'd rarely met a lead engineer or indeed any engineer who wasn't overly invested in the product they worked on. It has been known to take weeks of negotiation to persuade a senior engineer round to making changes to their vision of what was right for the product. Jack was definitely cut from this cloth. And we didn't have weeks here but my natural preference is to work transparently where key people know all the facts.

'There's no big secret. I told you I don't need him to get distracted, he loves this app but it'll be fine and he can stay with it if he chooses to go work for the buyers as part of the deal. I'll make it happen. But for now if you can just keep him busy for a little while longer and everything will work out for us all.'

'Keep him busy?' I echo. 'What do you mean?'

'Keep him focused on the front-end work, prioritise the post-launch features. You said yourself that the app needs more features if it's going to really make a mark on the market.'

That sounded reasonable.

'I'll explain more when you get here. But keeping Jack sweet is important to get this sale across the line.'

'Yeah, I suppose so.' I had seen for myself in London how much easier things went when Jack was on board. To get this sale done we just didn't have time to deal with Jack's moods. 'I'll see what I can do.'

'Good girl. See you when you get here.'

'You've been doing great so far. I can't wait to see what else you come up with,' says a dark voice behind me. Jack leans against the doorway, his gaze flinty.

I shake my head. How much has he heard?

'Were you listening in to my conversation?' I challenge defensively.

'Well, I had a free moment, what with you not keeping me busy right now.'

Chapter Thirteen

I eat breakfast alone at the carousel bar, the kitsch décor less amusing this morning. Or rather, I push around an oversized bowl of yoghurt and granola. Anything to avoid returning to the room. How had something that felt so right gone so wrong, so quickly? Things were so much less complicated before. Before, when? Before I met him? Back when I had clear sight of what I wanted in my life, what I did not need. I try one brief experiment and everything crash lands in hell. No sign of a tidy handbasket. Mess and drama. And amazing sex. My stomach dips as flashes of last night appear in my mind, slight aches reminding me of unusual but oh so enjoyable activity. Was this the price to be paid for a moment of madness where I go with my gut instead of my head? Drama, mess, hiding in hotel bars.

No sign of Jack as I sip my coffee. What was it exactly that flipped his lid? So he hadn't reviewed the build and spent all night working? Was that so bad? What kind of Machiavellian plot did he think had occurred while we were busy? So, we were stepping around him about the sale, it wasn't that unusual for start-ups to sell at this stage. Jack had been living in Silicon Valley long enough to know this was always a risk. But if he got that angry because Eric submitted a new build without this sign off maybe Eric was right. Jack was being over sensitive, after all, he knows we have to launch; he can do another release hot on the heels of the first one if he really objects to the launch build. I shake it off. Whatever his glitch is, it's not my problem; I flick through my phone determinedly. News – the usual. Weather – sunny. I open up my group chat.

Me: *So, I decided to live in the moment.*

Stella: *Please tell me that means what I think it means.*

Me: *Yes.*

Stella: *Whoop.*

Me: *But…*

Me: *Now he thinks I'm some kind of corporate saboteur.*

Alicia: *Very James Bond.*

Nessa: *Why?*

Me: *Because Eric is hiding an approach from some big tech company that wants to buy them up. I can't tell anyone. But he doesn't even know all that, I don't know why he's so pissed. I didn't really hide anything from him last night, just that the app was put together without him signing it off and he's pissed.*

Nessa: *So, you sent his baby off into the world without him checking it over first? The one he's been working on for over a year, that you just started on?*

Me: *Well, when you put it like that ... but ultimately Eric's the boss so Jack needs to grow up and get over himself.*

Stella: *Blah, blah. Never mind all that. On a scale of one to Paris, how was it?*

Alicia: *Harsh*

Nessa: *But fair.*

Me: *Maybe. Bah humbug*

Stella: *Seriously? No deets. Yawn.*

Nessa: *Ha, ha. Does this make you Scrooge's big sister. No fun!*

Stepsister.
Gah. That was worse.
I close my phone. Eric has every right to sell, it doesn't

make him a dick, that's just how the world works. I mean everyone sides with Bob Cratchit, but Jack is no vulnerable employee; he's an engineer in a world willing to throw money at someone of his talent. Sleeping with Bob was just messing up my perspective.

I square my shoulders, I have done nothing wrong here, which doesn't stop my stomach from screwing up in fluttery knots as I make my way back to the room with a takeaway coffee. Jack is at the door as I come around the corner. He takes the cup from me with a terse thanks and keeps moving towards the car, where he sits behind the wheel.

A quick glance around the room confirms that he's ready to go and I scoop my belongings back into my bag and do a quick walk around of the rooms, partly to check we haven't left anything behind, partly to absorb the quirky décor one last time, and totally to avoid entering a small, confined space with the simmering man who barged past me on my way in.

Jack is silent as we pull back out onto the freeway. Only three hours, thirty-two minutes to go.

The open rolling hills of the central coast erode my resolution that Eric is totally in the right as Nessa's words come back to me. Eric might own the app but that doesn't mean Jack's feelings are invalid. I haven't exactly connived with Eric to keep him out of the loop, but I know Eric is actively wresting control from him and I was complicit in that last night – though that was never my intention. No, I had only one thing on my mind last night.

Deep breath.

'Jack.' No acknowledgement.

'Look, I'm sorry,' I try again. 'I didn't know Eric would send the new build in before you could check it.'

Still nothing. His stony profile is unmoving behind his dark sunglasses. More than a trace of dark stubble is evident on his jaw, adding to that bad-boy vibe.

'What is it exactly you think I'm guilty of?' When defence doesn't work, attack is always an option. 'Last time I was buying your body for the night. This time … what, I'm some kind of Mata Hari keeping you distracted from the work being done with my nefarious seduction techniques?'

This time I'm rewarded by a slight twitch of the lips.

'You did put the moves on,' he says, still not looking my way, but his tone is amused, admiring even. I never thought of myself as the kind of girl who could hit on a guy and lure him into her bed. But between the itsy-bitsy bikini and the Lauren Bacall impression, even I have to admit mea culpa.

'Well, what's a girl to do?' A good quote escapes me right now but I throw out the line in my best Classic Hollywood impression. 'You won't let me pay for it; I had to bring my A-game.'

'Huh.' It wasn't forgiveness, but the Bogart/Stewart style thinking-noise indicates a slight lessening of hostilities.

'What if I promise to never do it again?' If I was any huskier, I would fall off the bottom of the chart. At octaves this low an entire spectrum of animals must be unable to hear me. Eat your heart out, Lauren Bacall.

'That's probably for the best,' Jack responds, not playing. *Ouch.*

'Humph.' A slightly winded-sounding exhale escapes me at the hit. I straighten in my seat, pushing my shoulders back, reaching around to rub at the knot that has made itself known in my neck. So much for all Natalie's fine work yesterday.

Fine. Message received.

'Right. I…' *don't know what I was thinking.* I didn't. For once in my life I didn't overthink everything, didn't measure and weigh the pros and cons, how suitable he was, what would happen after. I liked him and last night was… 'Like you said before, we're not really each other's type and we work together. So…'

'Exactly.'

I can't find another response within me. I stare ahead, unblinking as the Audi eats up the road. Once my mind stops whirling with all the clever responses I failed to come up with in the moment, I open the emails on my phone and flick unseeingly through them, anything to appear to be casually moving on from *that* moment in my life.

When I look up again, it's to find a looming rock in the ocean to our left and the equally distinctive power plant chimneys that together add up to the town of Morro Bay.

'You took the 1?' I assumed we would take the more direct Highway 101 for the rest of the way to San Jose, the jaunt element of our journey killed by this morning's argument.

'Yeah.'

'But that will add an extra hour to our journey.' I roll my

eyes inwardly. What's wrong with him? This is the road trip from hell; the sooner we get to San Jose the better for all concerned. If we leave a trail of smoke and fire on the road in our wake, we still won't be going fast enough.

'I've never driven this way; it's a better view.' He pauses and I can sense the hit coming my way. 'It's not sex; no lines will be crossed because we stick to our original route.'

'I'm so relieved,' I say as drily as I can manage.

This time his exhale has a distinct huff of laughter to it.

As we continue north, the high hills around Morro Bay open up and we're back on the coast, the Pacific Ocean sparkling in the morning sun. I've always been more of an evening girl. I suppose it comes of growing up on the West Coast; sunset is one of my favourite times of day and sun setting over water, the reds and oranges reflected in the ocean, is something I will never tire of.

'What is your type?'

'What?' The question comes out of nowhere.

'The app – you enter what you're looking for, and it turns it on its head. That's how it works, right?' Jack's explanation is a casual elaboration on his question, pitched as if we're in the middle of a perfectly amiable ride up the coast. Apparently, the beautiful view, open road and sunshine have worked their magic and thawed him out a little.

'Right,' I respond equably. Does this mean he now accepts my apology? Didn't we just agree to stick to being colleagues. If so, this was not a terribly obvious choice of subject. Not the first time he's brought it up though.

'So tell me, what did you put in?' he prompts.

'No.' I dig my heels in. I'm not doing this.

'No?'

'Why should I tell you?' I throw him some serious side-eye. We've just agreed that there's nothing between us except work. Why on earth would I entertain this conversation?

'I'm curious.' His accent has gone all soft and swirling, like cream in coffee. If he spoke to me like that in bed... My dug heels soften as my toes curl.

'Too bad.'

'C'mon. I'll pull in and get you a coffee at San Simeon.' He's looking over at me again, that lilt put to maximum effect as he matches it with that crooked, bad-boy smile.

'I've already had a coffee.' I refuse to let him get under my skin again. Black and white, no more shades of grey, no more considering possibilities I normally rule out. No coffee for me from here until the world ends.

'I'll bet I can guess half of them.' His timbre has gone all teasing and warming. This is the same guy who practically threw me out of his bed only one hour and forty-seven minutes ago. The same guy who accused me of using my body to— Don't think about bodies. Not his. Not mine. No bare bodies. Ever.

'I'm not playing.' I am not starting to weaken.

'Let's start with the classics,' he continues as if I haven't spoken.

'Jack, I said I'm not playing.'

'Tall.' Too easy. He knows I was self-conscious of my height as a teen, and I already confirmed Terence Taylor hit quite a few elements on my list, and he was tall so it wasn't rocket science. He glances across at me; I refuse to acknowledge him. A flicker of a smile plays across those perfectly curving lips. 'You didn't say dark, otherwise it wouldn't have thrown me up. So, either you're into blonds or you just didn't specify. Sticking with the classics, how about GSOH?'

'Obviously. Given that you're utterly unfunny.' I can't help myself.

'So, that's two,' he awards himself points that I have not confirmed.

'Graduate. That'll be three.'

He takes some time considering the next one as I fiddle with the radio trying to find something, anything, to fill the silence before he starts up again. There's no way he's letting this go; he's having way too much fun.

'I'll bet you had a preference for nationality – not ethnicity but something close to yourself. I'm Irish, so off-brand, but not by much. I guess you stated a preference for American. No, English... You like your life in the UK.'

He is unnervingly good at this. He surveys my face, and a grin spreads across his.

'Four.'

He says nothing as Fleetwood Mac fills the car but as soon as the tune fades away, I find him surveying me, a filthy light in his eyes warning me that the next guess amuses him mightily, making it highly unlikely to amuse me.

'Despite your advancing years, I think maybe you said you would like to have children. And given our age disparity annoys you so much, my money says you were looking to meet someone your own age or older.' He can tell he's got a hit by the murderous glint in my eye that I can't prevent. It would be so easy to dispose of a body out here. Ocean on one side, woods on the other. 'Bonus point for six, I believe.'

Dick.

I'm absolutely fuming at being so predictable. I sit mutinously silent beside him. Hearst Castle appears on our right, the legendary mansion of the media magnate a jewel atop the green hills. I went years ago on a high-school trip, my dominant memory being the stunning swimming pools. A pang shoots through me; Jack would get a kick out of the Hollywood golden-era history of the place. If it was yesterday, I could have suggested stopping to take a look.

Hearst Castle disappears in my rear-view mirror and I'm surprised to find him pulling in to San Simeon as promised. He goes into a small coffee shop and returns a few minutes later bearing two cups that smell of caffeine-laced nirvana.

He offers one to me but pulls it back when I reach for it. My mouth drops. Is he being serious?

'Tsk, tsk.' He leans a denim-clad hip against the bonnet of the car. 'Coffee is the reward for playing.'

He's not giving me a coffee? Devil's spawn.

'How many did I get right?' His dark brow arches up in counterpoint to the smirk pulling at his lips.

I fold my arms. I don't want the coffee. He waves the cup under my nose. The rich aroma wafts in the air in front of me.

'I'm driving.' Stupid macho boy. It's my car, and we're

on the Pacific Coast Highway. Why should he be the one to drive?

'Fine.' He opens the door on the passenger side to let me out.

I step out and face him, eyeballing the coffee. 'Six.'

His lips press together as he suppresses the grin that lights up his eyes. He hands me my reward for playing with a flourish. Snatching the cup, I stomp around to the driver's side of the car.

The coffee and soothing effect of driving on the coastal road weave their magic on me. The sting of our morning argument fades and I wonder what *he* put in to get me as his opposite. He's opened the door and we still have two hours to go.

'You don't want children?'

The question surprises a laugh out of Jack. 'You barely speak to me for hours and this is your opening line?'

This doesn't happen to me with other people. I'm not impulsive; I don't ask intimate questions. It's like his sheer nearness affects my thought processes, my very personality.

'You remember that I didn't enter my preferences. Max did,' he answers my question.

What a cop-out.

'Please. Max didn't make it up out of nothing. Be honest.'

I check my speed as a car overtakes us despite the windy road.

'I may have answered some questions.' He shrugs a shoulder. 'I don't remember all of them.'

'But children,' I prompt, not sure why I'm so hung up on

it. I'm not sure whether I want kids myself. As an older woman, some of that decision is no longer mine, but it's something I've given some thought to. I'm not sure, if I'm honest, but for a man his age to be squarely against it seems odd. He wasn't looking for anything serious when he went to Paris – a one-night stand – so it stands to reason. No, I recalled, he wasn't even looking for that, just some company to pass the evening with. I wasn't supposed to have ended up in his bed. He was the one to say no to sex – and stick to it, I recall with a mortification that still lightnings through me like a hot flush. Maybe it *is* a hot flash; maybe that's my punishment for—

'I've never had the best taste in women,' he says with heavy emphasis, breaking my spiralling thoughts. 'Adding children to that equation doesn't seem too clever.'

That's reasonable. He told me he married young. The split must have been a nightmare; at least he didn't drag children through that. And if he and I—

My stomach dips. No, he took care of prevention.

'Age?' Nothing like poking at that sore tooth.

'No preference.' There's an amused note in his voice. 'Doesn't bother me as much as it does you.'

'I'm educated.' I muse on the possible qualities that are likely to have been the opposite to what he requested. 'Does that mean your preference was not to be matched with someone with higher education?'

His breath leaves him in a loud exhale as he considers his answer. 'I didn't know it was an opposite thing so it wasn't quite like that.'

'Well, if you matched with me, you must have said education wasn't part of your wish list in a partner.'

'I suppose so.'

'But why? You're intelligent.'

'Not the same as having a formal education,' he admonishes me. 'People judge others who leave school early.'

'That's not fair,' I argue. 'I think you're smart – more so than the average graduate who has their education served up to them. You did it on your own, made something of yourself despite not growing up with the advantages most of the people you work with had.'

'You still walked in and assumed I was the help,' he flashes back.

'What?' I'm confused. I made no assumptions about his education. We met at a bar in Paris; I knew nothing about him. 'That's not true. When we met, we didn't discuss work, remember?'

'We did briefly. When I said I met with VCs it surprised you.'

I catch myself. He's right, it had. Had I made assumptions based on his face, body, accent?

'Maybe I did, but that's on me. I suppose you don't fit the type. My impression wasn't of a businessman, but I guess I still have some view that people looking for backers for their business are white, suited, forty-somethings, probably wearing glasses.'

'You think glasses would help?'

The reminder of that early conversation about his attempt

to find venture capital snags on his current role. I sort of presumed Eric sent him to meet the VCs in Paris, but that doesn't make sense if Eric is trying to sell. Maybe Jack is seeking investment, to leave to set up on his own? Then there is no reason for Eric's concern that Jack will be upset about the pending sale. Jack would be free to do his own thing. Maybe he would be relieved if he knew. But if he wasn't...

'I'm pretty sure that only works in movies – not that I haven't tried it.' I don't fit the stereotype convention either. I've also had to fight to be taken seriously, have sat in meetings where a client or vendor has addressed a junior male at my side instead of me. 'But surely everyone just wonders why you don't have the sense to get laser surgery or wear contacts.'

The asphalt becomes smoother as we move into Big Sur. Majestic redwood trees appear around us reaching high into the blue above.

'You want to set up your own business? Go it alone?'

I feel his eyes considering me before he responds in a sharp tone.

'Ideally.' His tone reminds me of the way he was that night in Paris after getting shot down. 'It's easier to get financing with someone like Eric as the face of the company – right school, right contacts, right background.'

'But surely you have enough experience to be taken seriously?' He's not that much younger than Eric. I have no doubt Eric could make it rain if he wanted to, if he wasn't so lazy.

'Unfortunately, I've either worked for people or had a

front guy, and those guys are never shy about taking credit for other people's ideas and hard work.'

Too true.

By the time we come out of the other side of Big Sur, relations are warm enough that I suggest taking a spin into Monterey for lunch. We park near the marina and take a seat at a little Italian on the pier. Given we're only a day or so from launch, we both end up working while we have Wi-Fi. I review the issues that were resolved in the second submission while Jack pulls out his laptop to do something more in-depth, I guess.

Heading back across the car park, my old and not-too-battered car gleams, still looking pretty good for her age. As we get back in, I smooth my hand over the dash, taking the passenger seat so Jack can drive the last leg.

'You never said why you hated this car,' Jack prompts, taking in my smile.

It's complicated, or at least it used to feel so to me.

'I got a job in a local supermarket when I was fifteen, after school and at weekends, I saved up to buy a bike. Not long after that, my mom met Mike; they were married less than a year later. Mike gave me this to go to school in.'

It symbolised everything I hated about my new life. Too big, too shiny, too unearned. Mike tried so hard, and I hated all of it. Except for this car, this I came to love, and I missed it when I moved away. That he went to the trouble of finding it and getting it back in shape meant more to me than any expensive car he could have much more easily gifted me. It made me feel guilty about not coming home more often, and under current circumstances even more determined that Eric didn't ruin him.

'I've spent a lot of years building things for other people. I want to build something, from the ground up. Show that I can do it, build it, run it. Be more than just someone who got lucky because of...' he trailed off.

'Because what?'

No response as he gazed out the window at the passing landscape. Then, 'I felt like when I met Lacy she gave me this shiny new life but she gave up so much to be with me. I feel like I let her down.' He shook his head as if throwing off the memories from that era of his life. 'I wanted to make a success of myself in my own right. Not live my life feeling like ... her father was right. That my father was right.'

He fell silent and I flicked through a crappy Rolodex of clichés trying to find the right response. Mom and I might have been poor and I knew what it was to feel like I didn't belong, but nobody had ever made me feel like I wasn't good enough.

Jack didn't look up from the road. 'I've worked hard to get where I am now. But sometimes I still feel like I drive a car that I haven't earned.'

'You should definitely do your own thing next time,' I encouraged, feeling on safer ground. 'Screw the Lacys and the Erics. It's a new world. It's about what you can do, what you can make happen. They were privileged to start with, but that doesn't mean we haven't caught up. We have every bit as much right to be at the table.'

'Right on.' Jack fist pumped the air, laughing at my impassioned speech.

'I mean it,' I said emphatically. 'You'd be better off without an Eric.'

He's a great engineer and there is no doubt he has the energy and ambition to make it on his own. Because it was true, I realised. Eric might own RL8 but Jack was undoubtedly the engine behind it. What Eric was doing might be legal but it suddenly felt really wrong. My privileged stepbrother wouldn't see it that way but I did and Jack deserved better. Eric needed to be straight up with him, at this point it shouldn't matter anyway.

Jack stayed on the 1 as far as Santa Cruz before taking the 17 and winding through the blackened Santa Cruz mountains. It must have been hit in one of the fires of the last few years. We loop down the other side into the heart of Silicon Valley, road signs increasingly informing us of the approach of some of the world's most famous Big Tech addresses – Mountain View, Cupertino, Santa Clara, Los Gatos – all of which I used to pass on my way to college, the growing giants of Google and Apple sucking up most of my classmates on graduation.

Eric's offices are in downtown Los Gatos, somewhere near Netflix HQ, I think. 'Are you far from the office?'

'Not far in human miles, but far enough in Santa Clara County miles,' he says, giving me the address. 'I live on the other side of the offices in Campbell.'

I put both addresses into my phone. Eric's is closest. 'Why don't you drop me off, then take my car? I can get a ride in tomorrow morning.'

'Sure.' He nods. He follows the directions to Spencer

Avenue, until we reach our destination, a modest enough looking house, if it was in any other suburb in the world.

'Is that Eric's Tesla?' His eyes narrow at the black car with the distinctive T and Eric's ridiculous reg: Smndz 1. 'I didn't realise you were so close.'

'We're not close.' Not in the way he means – or any other way. We're not friends; we're related, and not even by blood.

'But you're staying with him.' His tone is flat. Only minutes ago we were firmly on friendly ground once more. Now I feel like I've turned a corner where any misstep potentially leaves me bloodied.

'Well, yeah,' I say slowly. 'I'd rather not, but my parents would find it odd.'

'Your parents?'

'Yeah, Mike is Eric's dad.' How did he miss the photos in our family home? Mike is proud of Eric, though thinking about it, I suppose the family pictures probably aren't in the guestroom and we didn't really spend time in any other part of the house beyond the kitchen and patio area.

'Eric Simonds is your brother.' It feels like an accusation.

'Stepbrother.'

He pulls into the drive and parks with much more force than my not-young car needs, pulling up the handbrake unnecessarily hard.

'Are you setting me up?' His eyes search my face, trying to read a secret I'm not keeping. I don't understand what he's talking about.

'For what?'

'Does Eric know about Paris? Is that why he asked you

to help? Is that what last night was about? See if I could be—'

'Whoa! What?' Where is all this coming from? And what exactly is he implying? I laugh, from nerves or surprise. 'What is it you think I want from you? I want nothing from you.'

'Nothing?' He arches that brow again, his lips slanting in *that* smile.

And that quickly my mind seems to have some sort of implosion. Be bold. Do it. Ask the universe for what you want. Let the crack open. Change the record.

'Maybe this.' I stretch over to him and press my lips to his.

But he doesn't respond. I thought we were good.

Apparently not. I move slowly away from him, as if a sudden move will cause those blazing blue eyes to ignite and strike me down. I shake my head, raising my hands palms up to explain, or ask for an explanation.

'Hey, Leo,' Eric calls.

Please don't let him have seen what just happened. I can't look Jack in the eye. I can't believe after this morning I threw myself at him again. How could I have so badly misread the signals?

Eric swaggers down the drive to us and opens my door for me.

'Hi, Eric, how are you?' I step out with a forced smile.

'Great, great. You guys made good time. And we just got word back from your friend – the app submission for iOS has passed. Hopefully, we get the thumbs up from the Google Store in the morning and we're good to go.'

'On Tuesday,' I remind him.

He hits the car jovially, ignoring my correction. 'I can't believe Dad found the old girl and fixed her up. I wish I'd seen your face. I'll bet you were shocked. I told him he should have got you something better if he wants to lure you back more often.'

'It isn't exactly my fault I haven't been home more often,' I start defensively. It's not like the whole world stopped travelling or anything.

'Hey, I didn't mean nothing.' He looks over to my moody driver. 'Jack, great job, man. And thanks for bringing my big sis. Can I get you a car?'

'No need.' Jack stiffly levers himself out of the car, goes to the trunk and, taking my bag out, deposits it in the driveway as if it were toxic.

'Look at that. What a gent – CTO by day and chauffeur by night,' Eric jokes.

'CTO.' My eyes flick to Jack. I recall his words about my assuming he was the help.

'Sis,' Jack hisses under his breath as he storms back to the driver's seat and reverses way too fast back down the drive.

What the hell was that about?

I swing back to Eric.

'He's not just a lead engineer, he's the CTO?' Every atom in me squeezes in a full body cringe.

Eric shrugs, making a show of carrying my bag up to the door.

'So, why are you hiding the sale from him? Surely he has a right to know?'

'Well, hi, Eric, how's life? It's great to see you, it's been years, I'm so glad to be here,' Eric highlighted my poor familial greeting. 'What a great house.'

The house was lovely if you liked that showy, ultra-modern look.

'Eric,' I begin again.

'Leo,' he gives me a zillion watt smile. 'It really is good to see you. I'll bet Dad and Mia were over the moon. If me employing you achieves nothing else but getting you out here it'll be worth it.'

I stumble as I follow him up a hallway. Has he really just sidestepped the question by turning things around so *he's* the great son doing *me* the prodigal daughter the favour. Is he kidding?

I glare at his back before shaking it off.

'Are you really keeping the sale from your CTO? That is crazy, if he's that senior I assume you are paying him enough to roll with the punches. He may not like it but at that level he should be professional enough to deal with it.'

Eric deposits my bag by a door and turns, his expression clearly exasperated. 'You've met Jack, do you think…'

He pauses as his phone rings, he lifts it to his ear without hesitation, raising one finger in the universal signal for *hold, I'll be with you in one minute*. Rude.

'Ah yeah, I'll be ten minutes.' He pulls the phone down momentarily, giving me an apologetic smile before nodding at the door. 'You're staying in here, Leo. See you in the a.m.'

And he was gone.

Chapter Fourteen

Working in London, offices tend to come in two styles: big companies have big offices in various stages of modernisation; small companies and the start-ups gather in northeast London in buildings that were previously homes, shops or warehouses. Here in California, offices are newer, shinier, bigger.

The desk I'm set up at is on the ground floor, six foot of glass window looking out onto the car park, which grants me the view of a silver Aston Martin pulling up in a prime spot. Jack climbs out of it in a torso-hugging T-shirt and jeans, like some kind of thirst trap James Bond Colin Farrell mash-up.

As he pushes open the door, he does not look in my direction but is hailed by everyone as he winds his way through the room, to one of two glass offices that sit at the end of the room. Eric in one, Jack in the other. I have the beginning of a tension headache. Or it could be dehydration; California's dry air can have that effect on people.

Eric reappeared this morning and had spent the whole ride in on the phone. I can't figure out if he's doing it on purpose or genuinely is this much of a dick.

Jack's office is behind me and I feel like his mood is tunnelling into my head, driving me into my handbag for some Ibuprofen, which I down with a bottle of water. Best to cover all angles.

'You busy?' Eric asks without greeting when I enter his office per his message, which I do without coming even close to looking through the glass wall at his neighbour. At least once I'm in here there is a solid wall between us.

'Yes,' I answer shortly. While pre-launch doesn't require my core skills, my soft skills attract work like filings to a magnet, especially in a start-up like this that's without a more market-leaning product manager. So on top of things I consider my job I have a growing list of things I don't usually worry about piling up.

'Do you have something else to wear?' He looks up and then down with a faint tensing of his eye muscles. His desk is tidy, like he just walked into an abandoned office and put his laptop down.

'What?' I look down. In jeans and a button-down shirt I'm already smart by tech standards. For the few days they need me to be on hand here I'm unlikely to see anyone outside of the T-shirt on deck crew, so my shirt is actually on the dressy side.

'I need you to join me at a meeting at the end of the day.'

'This evening?' I ask. 'But we're due to launch tomorrow morning. Can't it wait?'

'No.' He gives me a speaking look.

Ah, the big tech buyers.

'What do you need me there for?'

'I need someone there who can talk to the details. You're good at that.'

'Details? Sure, if they want to talk about features and stuff, but they'll have engineering questions. Surely you need to include Jack?'

Eric runs a hand through his hair and levels me a look that says I need to worry less about his CTO's feelings and more about the family fortune.

'This makes no sense, why don't you just tell him?' I lower my voice. 'He's a grown man and you're paying him to do a job. He might not like it but he'll get over it.'

'I'm also paying *you* to do a job.' Eric's tone is cool to say the least. 'The least you could do is put our family ahead of a guy you've worked with for a few weeks.'

Well if last night he had dodged my concerns, this morning he was pulling no punches. I felt winded; of course I wanted to help Mike.

'I don't need you to pay me a cent. You asked for my help and I gave it.'

'Then having come all this way you will help me get this deal done, right?'

'Fine. I'll come, but I don't know that I know more than you. I've only been working on the app a few weeks. And hectic weeks at that.'

'If you don't know the answers then just nod and look pretty. You can at least do that, can't you?'

I grind my teeth. Not metaphorically, literally.

'Of course.' I cannot actually use more words now or I will start whacking him around the head with them, like stones. Or rocks. Boulders splatting down on him Roadrunner-style creates a satisfying image in my mind. I can't say this is a phrase I've never heard before in my career, but it's been a while. And I've *never* heard it said to a man. Big boulder. Splat.

'Can you send me whatever paperwork you pulled together in London?'

'I don't think the paperwork I did in London is what you need. The focus was to pull together a coherent vision of MVP and post-launch priorities. I'm not sure where conversations are with this buyer, but I'm sure it'll be more about kicking the tyres of the whole outfit and not just the product.'

'That's great.' Eric's phone is ringing, and he's already busy checking who it is; he answers it, signalling the end of our conversation.

Refusing to look in Jack's direction, I retake my seat and go through the documents that Max and I worked on in London. I attach them to an email and ping them off to Eric.

I might be able to avoid looking at Jack in his office behind me, but his car sits outside; sleek and gleaming in the sunshine. Catching my eye. Mocking me.

Jack is the CTO.

No wonder the London team had only started to really smash it out once he got on board with what I was doing.

And once he started to put in long hours, even as short-term contractors it was hard to walk out in the evening when the CTO was still in the office and everyone was working to a crazy deadline. JEK was the Pied Piper in the tickets and I had been so caught up in what happened in Paris that I never even thought about how the team reacted to him, too worried about my own responses. But I don't exactly have the time to think about it now either, between the imminent launch and Eric's sale talks. Priorities: Launch first. Then sale. Then Jack.

I need to focus on getting the design collateral pulled together before Max goes home. It's already the end of the workday in London, but Max is a star and has already let me know she can stay around for a few hours. I should have thought of this stuff sooner but between the rush to get the app done and the distraction that is Jack Keogh it had slipped my mind.

Jack rebounds to the top again... So I'm Eric's stepsister; so what? Why the instant backlash? Is it really such a big deal I'm distantly related to his boss? He's the CTO, and he never said anything. In fact, it's entirely possible he went out of his way to say nothing to make me look like a fool. I'm the one who should be pissed.

Me: *So turns out he's the CTO.*

No need to tell my Greek chorus who *he* is. They'll know.

Nessa: *Isn't that a good thing?*

Me: *How is that a good thing? He LIED.*

Stella: *Did he lie or did he just not wave his cock about? How refreshing!*

Alicia: *Doesn't this make him more rather than less suitable? He's a senior prof. Right?*

They're no help. I put my phone down on the desk. Face down.

Max has sent through the designs, and I scan through them. They look good but she's left in the Ipsem Lorem, the nonsense filler text I insisted she use when supplying devs with designs during build.

This not being my area, I flick through the app store to get a feel for how this type of product gets pitched.

It's the intro copy I need to work on. I'm on my tenth draft when my phone pings. My private channel with Max has lit up, joining the constant lights of the group chats I can't even imagine catching up on.

One of the chats catches my eye though – a huge string of text has just hit the website channel. I scan through it. One of the Buenos Aires engineers is having a massive fit over the lack of availability of the pre-prod environment. Surely they're running their own environments? It must be an internal communication issue. But there is no need to distract the entire team with – a couple of phrases jump out at me – a very strongly worded DM.

I click in to the new designs Max has sent. She has replaced the gobbledygook with English, but it's very

English, English. I'm not sure a Texan mom will be inspired to download an app where the participants' conversation is about a banging new gaff that Max wants to have a butcher's at after the ding-dong.

> Me to Max: *Thanks, Max. But can we avoid the cockney? The US is our primary market at launch. Give me five and I'll send over new copy.*

> Max to me: *Oh … oh yeah. Gotcha, babes. I'll swing it over asap. Gotta run though, my number cruncher just texted. He's game on for date number 2. Turns out he's got tickets to this super-private gig for this new band everyone's raving about. Stoked!*

I will stoke her. Is she kidding?

> Me to Max: *Awesome news.*

I check the time. Crap, it's after 8pm in London. We're now in the delicate zone where she is perfectly entitled to go to her hot date, but if she does, we are SCREWED.

> Me to Max: *What time is the gig?*

> Max to me: *Doors open at 10! Going to grab a bite first.*

I am jittery as I type. We need to have these images perfect. They aren't technically her job but in a start-up, if your skill set is the closest to any given job, then you'd better believe it's going to land on your desk, job description be damned.

I need to finish this copy, and I really want to do one last run-through of the finished versions on each platform before we go live. And nobody seems to have stepped in to help the engineer blocked on web.

Me to Max: *Max, we need to get these sorted before you leave tonight. I know this guy may very well turn out to be the love of your life so I get it, but totally counting on you here. Need these to be perfect.*

(New private channel)

Me to Jack: *Have you seen the web channel? Some environment issue?*

Jack to me: *typing…*

I start again on the copy. It's not working.

The new iOS build has arrived on my iPhone. I flick to the bugs that were just fixed. It's a good product. I can already see my various groups on here; even just thinking of my posse of girls it would allow us to keep our convos pure but without being exclusive, letting someone like Nessa's cousin Isabelle in, but without diluting the richness and intimacy of our thinking out loud to the mind-hive exchanges.

Maybe I just need to look at a few more apps in the social media space to get the tone right. Opening up my phone I flick through some of the apps everyone has on their phone. No, the tone is right. I just need to do more to highlight what it is we're offering, what makes us different from the rest, a place to share with your community but without everyone being invited to the party, yet still able to tell there's a party going on that they can swing by the edges of. And for sure a safe space where your privacy is respected from others and from us, including not having all your data scraped to turn to nefarious purposes.

Nefarious.

Jack has responded.

Jack to me: *Sorted. We moved pre-prod to a new environment on the Stack for launch.*

All righty. What I'm reading here is sorted. Words like Stack and environment are in the realm of commonplace words where I know what they mean, but I don't really. It's like the engine of the car. The car has an engine; I vaguely know what some of the parts are called but am I ever going to be called upon to change a valve or carburettor or whatever? Unless the oil or water need topping up, I have no clue. And even then, there needs to be a blinking light or smoke before I'll be aware.

Me to Jack: *Great.*

It's not really my place to point him at stuff like this either, but nobody wants to be the jackass who saw the broken glass on the floor and let the whole team walk around barefoot.

Jack to me: *Eat something.*

Hmm, I look around and realise that the cold remnants of pizza and some sort of sandwiches arrived and have been largely demolished in the last hour or so. Oh no, it's after two.

Max's name is lit up.

Max to me: *Have uploaded the new files. [Link] These work?*

Max to me: *Hey!!*

Max to me: *Leonie, you there? I have to go … the gig is in Camden. If I don't leave soon, he'll think I've stood him up.*

Max to me: *Aaagh. I don't know what to do? Don't want to mess you about, but I've got to dash.*

Max to me: *If they need any more tweaks, leave detailed instructions. I'll do them in the morning. You guys are launching PST morning, so they'll be ready when you get in.*

Max to me: *Okay… I'm off then.*

Max to me: *Last chance!*

Max to me: *All right. Night, babes.*

Crap. The last message was almost ten minutes ago. She's definitely gone.

I open the files and wince. They're better, but they're not launch ready. I don't normally do them, but I know what good looks like. I should have thought of this stuff earlier; in the companies I usually work for there is someone dedicated to this kind of thing. If I had been here at this desk two days ago instead of playing tourist I would have thought of it sooner.

Pushing myself straight in my chair, my hands cup my cheeks as I consider the spinning wheel of priorities. *Stop. Breathe.* Letting the wheel spin and land on whichever one is freaking me out most is not the way to go. Prioritising work is a core skill. I can apply it to myself, right?

I lift a stack of Post-its. When in doubt, Post-it.

I scribble the remaining tasks onto different notes and lay them out in front of me, evaluating them by need and knock-on impact and immovability.

I end up with:

1. Lunch. (I am starving.)
2. Web review. (It's evening in Buenos Aires but they are an agency; they will want to meet the deadline. Good reviews mean good business. As long as I alert them in time they'll stick around to help.)

3. Meeting: 4–5.
4. Android review. (Have ready for the morning, anything I feel strongly about can possibly be tackled by Jack? Or picked up in a.m. in London, if very bad?)
5. Copy and imagery. (I have until midnight or so to get this over to Max to action when she comes in.)

I grab a slightly dried-out sandwich; the pizza is long gone. Pizza may be a Silicon Valley cliché but there's always some truth to these things. It's hot, tasty and can be eaten with one hand while continuing to work. Sandwiches have much the same advantages with the bonus that red sauce is much less likely to end up splattered on my white shirt...

———

Which is still pristine when Eric and I walk into the super shiny offices of Rubicon Inc.

'Thanks for taking the time to sit with us,' Suit Number One says as he shows us to a boardroom where Suits Two and Three await sipping water imported from France. Is French water really so much tastier than—

'We know it's a big day. You guys must be super busy over there.'

'Absolutely swamped,' Eric agrees, though I have no idea what he's been doing. It looks like he spent most of the day on the phone.

'Well, we won't keep you but we're really keen and just wanted to touch base before you go live,' says Suit

Two. He's younger than the other two. Young enough to be the up and comer; he'll be the one looking for the detail. Suit One got the door, so he's probably the least influential. Suit Three hasn't spoken yet. He doesn't need to; this meeting is for him – he's the one holding the purse strings.

'Our pleasure, great to see you all again,' Eric speaks directly to Suit Three, confirming my suspicions.

'You're all set for tomorrow?' Suit Three asks.

'We sure are. Leonie here came on board,' he says by way of introduction. 'Really helped us push it over the line.'

I smile and nod slightly in a gesture that combines acknowledgement and hello. If we were playing biz-speak bingo we'd already be well underway.

'You've been on our radar for a while. We thought you were much further out from launch, but we like what you've got. The market is ripe for a product like yours and we're hungry to scoop it up and move forward before that gap gets filled by someone else,' Suit Two states their opening move. 'We're looking to kick the tyres on this ASAP.'

'Absolutely, absolutely.' Eric nods, agreeing. These guys could say anything and he would agree.

And he goes ahead and does just that as a shopping list of asks tsunamis across the table at us. They want to review everything from processes and teams, assets, patents, account contracts, commitments, shareholding, architecture to product testing and launch review.

'We'll get our ducks in a row and circle back by the end of the week,' Eric volunteers. Is he out of his mind? Unless there are documents in a secret vault in a buried room I'm not aware of, we haven't got half of this stuff.

'I'm sure we can make this a win-win for everyone involved.' Suit Two gives Suit Three a pleased nod as Suit One, who spoke almost as little as I did, shows us to the lobby where we're left to make our way down to reception.

Can we? I feel like the most gullible fish in the water. *Just a little help*, he said. *It's in the bag*, he said. It is *not* in the bag and somehow I need to magic up a truckload of documentation. Oh, the sweet temptation to just leave Eric to sort out his own mess.

If only it wouldn't drag Mia and Mike down with him.

'End of the week?' I seethe as we make our way back to his car.

'I know, I know,' Eric says, lifting his hands, 'but I have faith in you.'

Faith in me. He's out of his mind.

'There is no way this can be done in four days, maybe if everyone was on board but certainly not while we are sneaking around behind people's backs.'

'Sneaking?' Eric looks horrified. Such a word does not align with his self-image. 'Leonie. You said you could help. I'm relying on you here. If this is about us, I know we aren't close but I always wished we were. I thought paying my dad back for all the opportunities he's given you would be a chance you would jump at.'

'This is not about us,' I grind out. He always wanted to be closer! It never showed until the day he needed my help. 'This is about reality. There is no way I can do this without Jack.'

'No. I told you, Jack will bring the sale down. He doesn't want to sell, and if we don't sell, I'm ruined here, the other app will launch and the hundred million dollars on the table disappears.'

I gape at the offer he's sitting on.

'All the money we've sunk into this app will be gone.' Eric blows into the wind. 'I already have other commitments so if this deal goes away not only do we lose our investment here but I'll have to renege on my next project. We have to lock this down now.'

For a moment there is a chink in Eric's slick armour as he digests what he's saying, not just levers to put me under pressure, but the reality of what happens if he messes up here.

'Can you just do this, this one thing for our family? We know you don't like us. But really do you hate us this much?'

Is that what he thought? What Mike thought? I never intended…

'Okay. We can do this,' I reassure him.

Somehow.

Chapter Fifteen

Everything feels like it happens in slow motion the next morning, perhaps because, despite lingering jet lag, I was still working until sometime after 1am last night. Eric dropped me at his home after the meeting where I discovered my car waiting for me. He casually mentioned something about having a dinner thing like the confrontation in the carpark never happened and still hadn't come in when I finally crashed.

My to-do list for the morning is beating a tattoo in my head as I put the hood down on the car. It's still chilly at this time in Northern California, but for a girl who lives in London, the weak April sun here is still a major burst of vitamin D. The big-wheeler truck I need to fill with documentation in the next four days is threatening to play chicken with my stationary car, like it's going to roll over me before I even begin. Because it's a lot. I tighten my hands on the cracked steering wheel. I've done a lot before. Nothing is impossible, as they like to say in the tech industry. *If* you have enough time, resource and money. I'm the only resource and I'll find the time.

I pull in for a coffee stop. The quiet moment as I wait for my brew allows thoughts of Jack to creep in. I know it's ridiculous but I can't help feeling bad that his baby is being sold and he doesn't even know. He's worked too hard to get it to launch, is so passionate about it. Surely he's professional enough to understand that this is just how our industry operates.

I smile in thanks as the barista hands me my coffee. The aroma takes me back to our road trip, the feeling of connectedness I felt with him before he had his hissy fit. Twice. We sleep together and he goes crazy over a text from Eric. And then again when he found out we were related. So now he's back to treating me like the enemy.

Why should I tell him? He is…

He is…

What? A hot-headed, moody pain in the ass? What is between us anyway? Nothing really. We had a couple of encounters, but I don't know him. He's made clear on more than one occasion that he thinks I'm using him. Was I? He was a way to break out of a rut, try something new, something without strings or potential. So why am I letting my coffee go cold obsessing about him? It was an experiment, a trial, nothing more. If anything, it just showed I should stick to my lane. There is a reason my criteria exist: because they make sense.

Jack. Jack makes no sense.

That Aston Martin is already parked outside the office as I put the hood up on my substantially shabbier vehicle.

Who is he to say I'm the snob? He's the one driving around in a status mobile.

His dark head is bowed, looking at something on his screen with one of the other engineers standing at his shoulder when I enter the office. Some sixth sense causes him to look up and lock eyes with me. I break contact first; it seems the only recourse before I end up in some trembly puddle on the floor. What was that? No expression. Is he still angry? Not angry? Maybe he misses me?

Maybe my fourteen-year-old self is calling and wants me to get a grip.

Max's comps are in. *Focus*. I gaze blindly at the screen.

I shake my head and push my shoulders back. Deep breaths. We launch in two hours; I need to get shit done here.

Max has sent two versions. The first is to the spec I sent her last night – detailed directions with the copy and interactions for specific screens. Perfect. The second set have the same screens but over each one she's put a catchy little phrase of what it will add to your life and friendships. It adds an extra dimension, really capturing the essence and spirit of the app and bringing it to life.

Me to Max: *I think I love you. If the accountant doesn't mind.*

Max to me: *Grin emoji.*

Max to me: *I'm sure I can persuade the accountant to share.*

Me to Max: *Laughing tears emoji.*

Me to Max: *Seriously. Great job!*

I upload the comps and enter the main team channel.

Me to all: *Comps in. Ready when you guys are!*

Vivek: *Should I make it live now?*

Graham: *We have finger on the button.*

Jack: *Antonio?*

Antonio: *Looks good. We're happy to push out when you are.*

Jack: *Make it so!*

Jack: *Star Trek captain gif*

Lots of celebratory gifs and even one or two real-life whoops. We are live.

It was a huge push, everyone's delighted, and we've launched ahead of the other guys so as far as everyone is aware we are halfway home, all we need now is for people to find us and stay stable.

A pang of guilt cuts through me. Everyone has worked so hard, has so many ideas for the future and Eric is about to sell it out from under them. But it might be fine, hopefully the new company will keep some of them on.

Jack: *Leonie, can you keep an eye on data?*

Sure, I don't have anything else to do.

Me to Jack: *I'll do a review tomorrow. It'll take a few hours for the app to propagate out through the stores and it'll be tomorrow before I can get indicative user interaction info.*

Subtext: those who built the code, know the code, and can fix the code can also monitor the crash analysis data for the first day. I have other things to do.

Jack: *Great.*

Subtext: we've all been working hard creating and launching this product and would like to relax and you've been doing nothing besides asking Max for designs I haven't looked at.

Me: *Cool. Will see what I can do.*

Subtext: maybe I will, maybe I won't, you passive-aggressive ass.

So we'll probably both end up doing it.

I open up the email I sent Eric yesterday to try and evaluate what we already have and how I can reshape it by Friday into some sort of due-diligence documentation to walk through with the suits.

I lose myself in the mountain I need to compile while everyone moves on to whatever they need to do post-launch. It's well past the end of the day before I give a cursory glance to the Slack channels to check nothing needs my attention. The private channel I have with Jack is lit up.

Jack to me: *Can I speak to you?*

Crap.

Me to Jack: *Sure.*

Me to Jack: *There in ten.*

Am I in trouble? For back-talking the CTO? I reread our earlier exchange. Yes, it was in front of everyone but it wasn't out of line. Could I have kept an eye on the crash graphs? Sure, it's possible but it's better if the team do it. Shit, what if this is about us? Why did I say ten minutes? I should have just gone in there and got it over with.

'Hi.' I push through the glass door with forty-five seconds left on the clock.

Those blue eyes lift, looking me up and down. I'm wearing jeans again, but having run out of smart-casual tops have a wide-neck T-shirt on. It's dropped a little off one shoulder, and his eyes linger on my exposed neck and shoulder. I can almost feel the drag of his stubble across the tender skin, the low rumble of his laughter as he knows exactly the effect it's having on me; I see the light through the shutters of the inn playing across the rumpled bed. I lift a hand to cover my neck – to draw his gaze, or to protect my sensitive skin? Am I imagining this?

Work. He called me in here to discuss work.

I meet his eyes. The black has taken over the surface area normally occupied by a magical cobalt blue. He's not thinking about work either. I take a step back into the glass of the door. A slight curl of his lips informs me he hasn't missed my reaction.

I let my eyes drop and when I look up I'm all business, no hint that a flash of the other day has just leapt into my mind and heated my body.

'You needed something?' Prim. Nonchalant. Professional.

His gaze drops deliberately to my lips, causing my stomach to plummet like it's an elevator with its cables cut.

I blink and try very hard not to react. His face lights up in that dirty, sexy grin he's so proficient at.

'Please sit down.'

Said the spider to the fly.

The glass door swings closed behind me as I move forward and take a seat in one of the two chairs facing his desk. This one is a little more cluttered; Post-its and pens are scattered across its surface, and a pile of devices across the smartphone and tablet spectrum testify to his hands-on approach. He must be checking the front end of the app as well as the back end platform stuff.

There are some large and spectacular landscape photos on the walls, not behind him for show but in his eyeline – and when I say *spectacular*, they are stunning. Black and white, one is of a waterfall crashing down into a valley, a rainbow arcing across the water below; another catches the light through great redwoods; the one facing him I glimpsed on my way in and recognise as the classic view of Yosemite valley – El Capitan one side, Half Dome on the other. I take another look at the ones on the wall beside me. They are gorgeous compositions – the immensity of the redwoods, the ferocity of the water, the play of light and dark that is singular.

'You seem busy, what are you doing?'

'Nothing.'

'Where did you go with Eric yesterday?'

And there it was. Lie to Jack or protect my family's interests.

'You're an Ansel Adams fan?' I ask as I recognise the artist, dodging the question. If I tell him where we were, will he sabotage the deal? Will he accept that his dreams of building something here are done?

'Mmm. There's a gallery in the national park.' His head tilts down.

'Are they…?' I inspect the redwoods photo beside me. There's a silver quality to the photograph. 'Are they originals?'

He shrugs. This time he's the one shifting uncomfortably. Is he embarrassed?

'Yeah, well, those two are.' He indicates the two on the

side wall before throwing his eyes to the one behind me. 'That's a print.'

'They're beautiful,' I compliment, and then because I can't help myself, 'But why are you so...? You drive an Aston Martin.'

'I bought them for myself,' he admits. 'They cost a lot of money.'

'You drive an Aston Martin,' I repeat.

The head duck and backward shuffle are more pronounced this time, as is his clenching jaw. Subject closed.

'I wanted to...' He clears his throat, meeting my eyes directly. 'Thank you – for the help in getting us live.'

That's not what he wants to say. I flick my brow up, waiting.

He's been furious at me for days. And I'm furious at him. We sleep together and he loses it because I'm related to the boss.

'You should have told me.' His lips are thin. He's really pissed off about this.

'You didn't tell me you were CTO,' I say to justify my sin of omission.

His eyes light up at my coming at him. The boy likes a fight.

'I didn't tell you? When exactly should I have done that? When you picked me up for a bit of fun in Paris or when you walked into my office in London and took over without so much as a by your leave?'

'By your leave?' I splutter back to him, mocking his old-fashioned turn of phrase as my mind registers what he said. 'I did not pick you up.'

'Oh, you totally did.'

I totally did not. 'It was an app date, so it was mutual.'

'Why is it such a big deal, anyway?' I divert away from the night we met, which still leaves me floundering in embarrassment on so many levels. 'It's not a secret, but I don't see any need to broadcast it. Eric only asked me to come in to help for a few weeks.'

He stands and walks over to a cabinet, extracting a bottle and two glasses. He tilts one in my direction. I give a slight shrug of one shoulder; I'm no whiskey drinker but it seems politic to accept the Irish version of an olive branch. He pours the two glasses and perches on the end of his desk as he hands me one. I look around and realise that everyone has disappeared from the open-plan office. The sound of Eric on the phone seeps through from the office wall behind Jack's desk.

I take a sip; the peaty taste lingers on my lips as the heat hits my throat. I lick it off. Ugh, why does anyone drink this stuff? I lean forward and put the offending drink down on the desk. Looking up I find Jack's eyes have snagged on the slight movement.

'You know Eric.' I push on to cover my awareness of him, how close he is, his legs stretching out beside my chair. I need to stand up. I feel like some adoring fan looking up at him. 'We don't get on that well, you know, what with him being an ass and all.'

'Yeah, it just triggered me, I guess,' his eyes crease in amusement at his self-diagnosis, proof his time in California has rubbed off on him. He sticks a hand out to me. 'Friends?'

I grasp his extended hand, enjoying the feel of his touch. His hands are rough against my softer ones. He uses the grip to pull me upright, and face to face with him. Very close face to face with him.

'More than friends?' he whispers. The ground lurches under my feet and somehow I've fallen into him, my free hand on his chest to prevent myself from collapsing fully against him. This is treacherous ground. Does the San Andreas come this far north? I think it does. Totally the earth's fault; nothing to do with his dark, seductive gravity. All I hear is the sound of our breaths.

'Why?' I stall.

'Why what? Why was I pissed about you being related to Eric?' His voice is a low rumble as his thumb drifts down the inside of my palm, which is totally triggering me. 'Or why more than friends?'

'Um … the trigger,' I lie. Blatantly so, as his huff of laughter indicates my lack of success in my deception.

'I dunno … something about rich families, You know, money sticks to money, blood to blood. You not telling me you were related. That text earlier. It gave me an itch in the back of my neck.'

'An itch?' There is nothing between the length of our bodies, except his heat, and mine. He's not wrong. I have chosen to put my family first. I shouldn't be here.

'An itch, like Da coming in the door, and without turning around knowing he's in a mood and it will not end well for me.'

'Your dad was…?' We are so close his breath warms my

skin. I know if he knew what I was doing at my desk I wouldn't be in his arms like this.

'Oh … not like that. Temper.'

'Hard to believe.' I speak the words against his mouth.

His lips press forward and land on mine. A nibble, a caress. His glass hits the desk, that hand moving to hold the back of my head to him as he deepens the kiss. And I let him. More than friends.

'Yeah,' he murmurs. 'You just… I want a chance to explain.'

'Explain what?'

'Why I…' He pulls back and gives me the full force of his gaze. 'Before we met, I had this plan and then you came along and you reminded me of who I was. That kid who took opportunities that came his way.

'Opportunities, like this.' He slants me a smile and his eyes crinkle. 'You think this happens every day?'

The Princess Bride, I identify. Except the line is 'This is true love. You think this happens every day?' My stomach flips.

But he is kissing me again, I can feel the smile on his lips as he savours the moment. The right now.

His phone pings. We continue to kiss. My trapped hand traces up his chest, around his shoulder and holds him fast to me, not wanting the moment, the deliciousness of his whiskey-laced kiss, to end.

His phone pings again – multiple pings from his open laptop. He pulls away. Did I just moan in protest? But he hasn't stepped away. Not yet.

'Come away with me this weekend.'

I laugh, where has all this come from. Is he, does he want something more, a tomorr… No, stop, don't analyse it. Just do it. I need to be in the moment too.

'Come away, o human child,' he whispers in my ear, 'to the waters and the wild.'

Is he quoting Yeats? For real? He's really working the Irish angle right now, and I think I'd follow him to any underworld of his choosing, if that's what he's suggesting.

'Hmm?' The hand that was cradling my head has crept to the small of my back, pressing our lower bodies together, and his whispering lips have found their way to the side of my neck.

I can't do this.

'I need to…' He pulls back and meets my unfocused gaze.

'What?' More pings from his phone and laptop. He gives them a frown.

'So, what do you say?'

Didn't I just tell myself I was going to steer clear of him for the time I have left?

I can't spend more time with him while helping Eric behind his back.

But by Friday the deal will be done.

'For the world's more full of weeping,' I say, as another line of that poem pops into my head. That bad feeling Jack has, that bad feeling is not wrong. He's the CTO; it's not right that the product he's been killing himself to launch may be sold next week.

'Jack, I need to tell you something first.' He has a right to know. Eric is wrong to hide the sale; it will leave Jack free to go on and do other things, his own things. Not telling him is not right. How can I agree to go away with him and keep hiding the sale? It's Eric's business but still, it feels wrong.

'Shit.' Whatever those messages are about is pulling his brow together and he's already moving away.

'Jack, I just—'

'Shite on a bike.'

His oddly graphic exclamation cuts me off.

'I need to tell you—'

'Bollocks!' The Dublin accent is more pronounced than I've ever heard it. 'We're down. Can you tell Eric? I'll see who I can rustle up to get on this.'

'It's the middle of the night in the UK,' I calculate. It's evening here. 'They'll start coming back online about midnight.'

He frowns at his screen. 'It looks like a backend issue. Once we've solved that we can solve for—'

I've lost him as he starts typing while I can hear a ringing tone on his phone. 'Jack, yeah, I've seen it.'

I let myself out and walk straight into Eric.

'Eric.'

'The outage, I've seen it.' He dismisses it with a wave of his hand. 'Launch day, there'll always be an issue or two. The team are on it. How are you doing with prep for the meeting on Friday?'

'I don't think it's right.'

Eric's head goes back, and he narrows his eyes at me before pulling me into his office and shutting the door.

'You don't think what's right?'

'What you... I don't see why you don't just tell Jack about the sale.'

'Why would I?' He sits back in his chair. 'Why should I tell Jack about the sale?'

'I just don't feel comfortable.'

'Little cuckoo.' His sneer catches me by surprise. Not because it reveals how he really views me – unwelcome, not belonging – but the suddenness of it, the bald truth from someone who is all front, and who actively needs my help. To lash out like this he must be really feeling the pressure. '*Now* you don't feel comfortable. You didn't seem too uncomfortable when my dad gave you a home, treated you like family, spent thousands on your education.'

But I had felt uncomfortable then. And I felt it now. I didn't have to sit here and let him treat me like this. *Cuckoo*? Screw him.

'I didn't ask for any of that.'

'And yet my dad gave it to you, and he asked nothing in return. And now, the one time I ask you to do something for this family, you feel "uncomfortable". You'd see my dad and your mom out on their asses?'

'You keep saying that,' I push back. 'Like this is my mess, Eric. But let's be clear – you're the one who borrowed Mike's money, *and* if I understand correctly on top of spending it all by making this a self-funded start-up taking on all the risk instead of supplementing smaller salaries with shares, you went ahead and committed more money, money you don't have, on a new project. That's right, isn't it? That's why...' The penny flips as it drops, hits the ground and lights up my mind. 'That's why your dad is screwed, he's liable for your new debt.'

Eric dismisses my counterattack with a wave of his hand.

'You gotta bet big to win big. And this deal is more than we could have hoped for, once the deal is done I'll have plenty of cash to pursue my next venture and really play in the big leagues. So let's just focus in getting the deal done. Everyone is a winner here.'

'Even Jack?' I ask sceptically.

'Jack will do fine out of the sale if he plays along, I wouldn't worry too much about his ass.' He goes still, a smirk spreading as he quirks an eyebrow. 'Unless that's why you're so interested in Jack? Little young for you, isn't he? Good-looking guy though. How *did* you keep him busy last weekend?'

'Screw you.'

Eric's grin broadens before he huffs and leans forward across his pristine desk. 'You're supposed to be all about priorities. Why don't you get yours straight and help me fix this mess?'

Asshole. He is an absolute weasel. One good outcome out of this is that Jack will be shot of my stepbrother and can go on to bigger and better things.

Between the outages which the team are focused on for the next few days, and my full attention on pulling together everything we need for the due diligence meeting, my dedicated avoidance of Jack is relatively unobvious. Relative to what I'm not sure, but Jack is deep in resolving the recurring outages so doesn't seem to notice.

His car slips in, a silver wave beside mine as I pull up on Friday morning.

'You going to leave her here for the weekend?' he asks, nodding at my car as he walks that easy loose-hipped stroll around the front of his. For the first time all week he looks well rested.

'You slept?' I may have avoided him, but my eyes still work – and they've spent way too much time directed his way. There's a distinct improvement in the quality of his energy and those dark circles have gone away. 'Does that mean...?'

'We seem to have solved it. I'm going to have a deeper dig around in the code to find the root cause of the instability, but our fixes should hold for now. I have time to poke around in the part of the Stack that Jose led on today, see if the problem is in that area. It's not perfect, but it should hold for the weekend.' He takes in my tailored Chinese-collared shirt and wide-leg pants, and the heel that keeps me from looking cut off in them. 'We're still going, aren't we?'

Are we? By then the deal will be done. I'll tell him before we go, the ink will be drying so I can give him a heads up, so at least he won't learn the news at the same time as the rest of the employees. Maybe we can start to plot out his next steps together. If I can get him to focus on the opportunity this presents and not that Eric burned him maybe it'll all work out. Or maybe I'll be spending the weekend alone.

'Aren't you going to the party?' Eric organised drinks and food for everyone in an uncharacteristic acknowledgment of everyone's hard work.

'Sure, but I wouldn't get too excited about it. Two drinks and everyone will head off.' Unlike London where a launch party starts early and finishes late. But it's been a long week for everyone. A long month.

'You're not backing out, are you?' His eyes hold mine.

'No, of course not.'

He raises a sceptical eyebrow and I open my passenger door to reveal my bag ready and waiting. The fact that I'm living out of that same carry-on bag made it relatively easy to pack for a weekend.

Whipping it from my car to his is the work of moments. I just hope I'm not handed it back equally quickly this evening.

The office manager hails us on her way past. I feel my skin prickle in heat. Had she seen the bag? Jack steps in a little closer.

'I'll see you after, yeah?' His hand drifts across my stomach intimately as he walks away so we don't enter together. I bite my lip. After. Right.

After the meeting.

Chapter Sixteen

Suit Three gives Two a direct look, the one that will make the difference between my mother continuing in the life to which she has become accustomed or not. It's not fair. Mom worked hard all her life – worked doubly hard to make up for being a single mom – and I'm glad Mike keeps her in the good life. Glad Mike isn't going to be destroyed by his son over-extending himself. But I feel like I've betrayed Jack. It's crazy – I barely know him, and he'll be fine. He can start again or earn serious money by walking through any door in town. It's a shame Eric hadn't made this the more usual part payment in equity as was the norm in start-ups, not only would his risk have been spread but Jack and everyone else would be reaping the rewards now. Jack would still be disappointed not to be continuing but this, this payday was the goal most start-ups were looking for. The era of garage start-ups becoming huge businesses was over, now most of them were just hoping for a big payday when they got gobbled up.

Suit Two flicks through the deck in front of him, where I've laid everything out.

'Your numbers post-launch seem to plateau off for portions of each day,' he prompts and Eric gives me a blank-eyed smile that tells me I'm up. We argued about the post-launch review. Most of it is good news: users have overall shown good engagement and the level of intros to new friends is better than good, showing that our word-of-mouth is off the chart; with a few weeks in market we should be able to show high Net Promoter Scores, putting us up there with brands people not only like but also trust. Though I'm not entirely sure which of those is harder to achieve these days.

'Yes, we had some wobbles in the first days after launch. Minor outages,' I say. Always better to be transparent than be caught covering something up. Besides which, there is no way, given the amount of money on the table, that they haven't been watching us closely and are aware of the crashes. 'But as you can see, that doesn't appear to have had a major impact on downloads or engagement.'

'Mmm. How convinced are you it won't fall over again as your user numbers increase?'

'You'll see we've built the Stack to allow scale. We can easily support upwards of our target of one million users by end-of-year,' Eric says.

'That's good to know,' Suit One pipes up with a little laugh that echoes around the table. One million is an ambitious target for a small start-up with no marketing money in an already crowded market. Let's face it, no one is looking down at their phone thinking *you know what I need?*

Another app. But I don't think the target is unrealistic. There is a gap in the market that RL8 would slot into nicely, especially with the privacy angle. 'Should we decide to go that route.'

What did that mean?

'I'd be happier talking scale with your CTO,' Suit Two says. It's not the first time in what has now been nearly a four-hour meeting that he has commented on Jack's absence.

'I'm sure he'll be more than happy to speak to that, but you know how it is after launch – everyone's busting to get that next release out and with the issues this week, well, we just couldn't pry him away from his desk.'

Eric has implied more than once that Jack is fully briefed on our presence here and has substantially contributed to the deck we're presenting.

The three suits nod and lean back in their chairs in a synchronised 'we're done here' move.

'It seems everything is in order. We'll email you over a copy of the terms for you and your partner to review one last time,' Suit One says, giving the official nod that he is satisfied sufficiently to proceed.

Jack's bad feeling seems to be contagious. I just can't rid myself of the feeling that his not being in the meeting was wrong as I watch the men congratulate each other. It's just unfair, all his hard work and commitment counting for nothing as the suits decide the future of his baby without him.

'Looks like you're in the clear.' We're back in the car but I can't quite bring myself to congratulate Eric.

'Time to break out the cigars,' Eric flashes back, all smiles now that everything is going his way.

'I don't understand why we didn't bring Jack.' Or why Rubicon Inc. were satisfied to take my basic diagrams instead of in-depth documentation of the type Jack could have provided.

'I told you, he doesn't need the distraction.'

'Sure, but we resolved the outages last night. Even unprepared, he would have been able to speak to the technical issues better than us.'

Eric's frowning at the road as he puts his foot down, all the sooner to get us back to the party and away from conversations he doesn't want to have.

'Why so worried about Jack?' He casts a glance at me.

I barely react in response. 'I'm not, I'm—'

'Awfully interested in a married man,' Eric slides in.

Married. Present tense?

'I'm not. It's not like that.' I rush to defend myself. What is it like? 'I know he was married.'

'Was? *Is* married. *Very* married,' Eric says with heavy emphasis. He might not be entirely sure that there is something between Jack and I but Eric has a snake's instinct for vulnerability. And he no longer needs to keep me on side.

My mind is a fog. I'm here fighting his corner and he... he... No, it can't be true. Eric is just saying this to stop me from badgering him about looping Jack in. Jack wouldn't invite me to go away with him, there had been promise in that invitation. He wouldn't. Eric on the other hand, he's never done anything to make me mistrust him but he isn't beyond manipulating things to suit his own purpose. He's just trying to ensure I'm on his side by smearing Jack.

'Oh, I understood he was divorced or separated or something,' I say as casually as I can manage.

'No. Last time I was there his wife definitely lived there, he's definitely married.'

Married. Present tense.

Got it.

I can't breathe.

I look out the window at my side. He's still married?

'I just thought it would be helpful to have him there is all.'

He's married. Right.

Chapter Seventeen

H e's on the other side of the room when we arrive, talking to a group of people. He's married. Like, has a wife. Real time, present tense. Angela, the office manager, puts a drink of something in a red cup into my hand.

'You need food?' She waves her hand at a table set up outside Eric's office with an array of chips and dips. Far too near Jack for comfort.

His eyes are not warm as he takes in my arrival with my stepbrother. He nods at Eric indicating we should meet him in his office.

'While you were out,' he says, his eyes glaring at me – he so knows where we've been. Like I care. Liar. Rotten dirty, stinking cheater – 'we got to the bottom of the issue that's been causing us to fall over all week.'

He thinks *he's* pissed. Wait until he hears what I've got to say. I will kill him, cut him up into little pieces and throw him into the Pacific. No, that's too good for him, I will put him in his fancy car and send him to one of those car places that crushes old cars.

Eric looks unconcerned.

'I've fired Jose.' This lights a fire under Eric. Jose is the next most senior engineer after Jack. In a world where he sells the company and Jack walks out, he would need Jose to complete the due diligence with Rubicon Inc.

'You fired Jose?'

Everyone's eyes are on this office. Oh, they're all pretending to be in conversation with each other, but all attention is on the one happening on this side of the glass wall.

'Yeah, turns out he embedded code that I didn't write or want in my platform.'

'What code?' I'm not sure why I ask. Eric seems unsurprised, and it's not my top priority right now, but firing him seems harsh.

'You can't fire him.'

'I think you'll find I just did.' He steps in to Eric, not threatening bodily harm but not quite office handbags either.

'We'll see about that.' Eric is straight out of a victory and is clearly peeved at Jack's defiance, immediately throwing his weight around. 'He did what I told him to do. '

'You can't put data mining into my app.'

'Everyone else is doing it.'

'You can't do that, Eric,' I echo. The way Jack has termed it means he's not referring to the standard innocuous cookie preferences and data that most apps use to store user preferences. We're violating laws in multiple countries. 'We aren't covered to do that. It's not explicitly stated in the Ts and Cs. Our users have to give consent; California has major data privacy laws, and as for the EU's GDPR regulations…'

Jack looks at me and something in him eases at my backing him up on this. I'm supporting him on this because it's illegal, not because he isn't a toad I will make into gooey confetti.

'Then put it in the terms. All the big boys do it, and if we want to sell for the right money, we have to show that we're in the game.'

'We've made a promise to our users that we aren't going to be like them.' Jack is now less than an inch away from Eric. 'And I've told you, I'm not selling.'

He storms out.

I look at Eric, who does not look better for the exchange. He was all puffed-out chest during the exchange, but now looks somewhat consternated as he watches Jack head out the door.

'Dammit.' He looks like he has a major problem and in true Eric style immediately looks for someone else to solve it for him. 'Leo. Go after him. Tell him I'll agree- Jose is fired, it's fine, I don't care. Just get him back.'

I stare at him.

'Do it yourself.'

I'm done here.

I pretend I don't see all the curious faces turning my way as I walk over to my desk, deposit my untouched red cup, gather my keys and make my way out to my car. I feel hollow, like a battered piñata, and the next strike is the one that's going to shatter me.

The battery in the key is dead – has been for years. Mike didn't fix it and this is turning out to be goddamn inconvenient as I can't seem to put the key into the door to unlock it.

A warm body covers mine from behind. I'm not even startled. Part of me was half expecting him to appear; his car is sitting right here. I shove a shoulder behind me as I turn around, quivering with anger.

'You really didn't know?' Is he talking about his marriage? No. He doesn't know I know. He's talking about Eric getting one of their engineers to hide chunks of devious code in his platform.

'I didn't know a lot of things.' His body stiffens at my tone, my flat words. The hand on my waist tightens, then drops away. 'You're still married.'

His expression is completely unreadable in the growing dark. How did he think he could hide this? We work together. If I hadn't been so busy, so preoccupied this week, there's every chance I would have discovered him. And he wanted to go away for the weekend!

Turns out my Mr Wrong-but-maybe-right is Mr No-way-in-hell.

'Not really.' He tilts his head and gives me the Han Solo charmer smile.

No. No Han Solo, no Humphrey Bogart, no charming his way out of this one. I am stone-cold pissed.

'Not really or not actually?' My tone conveys exactly the right level of restrained calm with a side of Hannibal

Lecter. Turns out a fictional character *is* invited to this party.

'It's over.'

Oh, wow, the most cliched words in the world of cheaters.

'She doesn't understand you, you live separate lives, you see other people, you just haven't got round to it…' I trot out all the trite excuses for cheating I can think of. I stop dead. 'You told me you didn't have children. Was that a lie too?'

'No,' his lips have thinned and his eyes look stressed.

'But you're still living together,' I state. 'Bottom line, if you're sharing a front door, you aren't free to—'

'Who told you? Eric?' He has some nerve to attack me about the source of the truth. Lying ass.

'I can't believe you.'

I shove at his chest. He is too near me and I am done with this conversation, this man. He's lost it with me over the slightest thing and this whole time he—

'Wait, give me a chance to explain.' His hand grabs my wrist. *Grab* is overstating; he hasn't grabbed me. If he had I could use some of those vaguely recalled self-defence techniques from the class Nessa insisted we attend many years ago after her purse was pickpocketed in Waterloo Station. No, he's loosely wrapped his warm, tough-skinned fingers around my wrist. Softly enough that I know he won't hold on if I pull away.

'Explain what?' *Please explain. No, there is no explanation.* Those fingers, strong and gentle, remind me of his touch, remind me of—

'Oh my god, that's why... in Paris. You didn't want to have sex, isn't it?'

'No, it wasn't like that. Well, I mean it sort of...' he trails off helplessly. 'At first, I just... I never meant for anything to happen. But then... you... I couldn't help it... you made me feel—'

'What.' My eyes bug out. 'Are you blaming me for this mess?'

I take a breath in and turn back to my car. I just need to get in it and drive away, back to a place of safety where there isn't a huge, jagged hole appearing in my chest.

Voices drift across the car park as a couple of devs make their way to their cars to head home for the weekend; as predicted, the party is breaking up early. Jose's termination no doubt helped with that.

He releases my hand, and my skin feels cool at the absence of his warmth. His voice is a hoarse whisper behind me. 'Please hear me out. I'm not saying it right. Give me a chance to explain. Please.',

I want to believe him. If I leave now and don't give him a chance, I'll never feel that oddly calloused touch again.

'I didn't want to scratch the vinyl,' he tries again.

'What?' I turn around, momentarily diverted by his words.

'Why I didn't want to have sex that night. It wasn't because of her. It was because of you. That night, we barely knew each other, we didn't talk about anything much but it felt honest and I didn't want to turn something that felt so right into something wrong. I wanted that one song to not be damaged in any way.'

That morning in Paris he had said something similar, and a part of me had understood him then. Still understood now.

He takes my hesitation for the sign of weakness that it is. 'Come for a ride with me.'

It's a simple thing to turn around and get into the gleaming plush interior. Five seconds, no more, to step off the direct route to safety. I haven't committed though; this is a diversion, nothing more, a moment to consider – to *ensure* – I've heard all the facts. Product management is about not being afraid to fail, or at least understanding thoroughly what happened and learning from your mistakes. This is research, that's all. A learning experience.

The purr of the engine is the only sound as we pull out of the car park and move through the congested streets of Friday evening traffic in one of the world's most officey cities.

'You need to start using words.' I'm already regretting sitting in the car. 'Something.'

'Spend the weekend with me.'

These are not the words I'm expecting. I've just learned the man I'm sort-of-but-not sleeping with is married and his response is to fix it with … what? A trip to wine country and some quality time?

'What?' Only dogs can hear me at this octave. I reach for an extra dose of gravity and try again. 'Are you…? What is wrong with you? I learn you're married and you still think I'm going away with you for a dirty weekend.'

His hands tense on the steering wheel and he takes a moment before he answers me.

'I… Okay, I can see why that's what you think,' he ventures slowly before rushing on. 'I swear to you, it's over; it's been over for years.'

'Says every cheating dick ever.'

'Christ, it doesn't make it any less the truth.' He pushes one hand across his short, dark hair, his features softened in the light from the dashboard in the growing dark. 'Yes, we still live together but for the last year I've poured everything I have into this business. I've worked sixteen-hour days; on Saturdays I go for a twenty-four-hour break and then I come back and do it all again.'

'So, basically, your marriage is over because you've had a busy year?' My voice is even and preternaturally calm; I could be his therapist right now. 'After … what? Nearly a decade of marriage. This is the same girl you told me about, the one you married when you were twenty-two, I take it. Not a second Mrs Keogh.'

He sighs heavily.

'Yes, it's Lacy. We stopped trying to make a go of it years ago. We married young and not for the… Can you say you didn't make mistakes at that age?' If he's appealing to my younger, more foolish self, he's picked the wrong girl. I haven't made mistakes like that at any age. I can almost hear my mom telling me that that's part of the problem. Perfection isn't living; it's existing. Is he telling me the truth? Should I listen to him? I've seen enough marriages break up to know that some are simply never going to make it, aren't meant to make it. Third parties getting involved are a symptom rather than the cause of the breakup. If what he says is true then *it, us,* whatever this seedling of *maybe something* is between us, is something he couldn't let die as a fatality of bad timing, because it happened before he extricated himself from a marriage that stopped being real a while ago. 'I don't know. I've worked crazy hours for years. When we married, I was so keen to prove I was worthy, that I could make it, be a success. We just grew apart. I was busy. She got busy elsewhere.'

His tone is matter-of-fact, but his knuckles are tight on the steering wheel. I had accused him of cheating on his wife; it sounded like it was the other way round. Had been for a while.

'If that's true, why didn't you get divorced before now?'

'I can't afford to get divorced yet.' His head turns and I can feel him examining my face for any hint on how I'm receiving his explanation. 'When we got together her family cut her off, or she cut them off. Either way I can't leave her with less than she started with.'

'She cares about the money that much?'

He laughs. 'No, not at all. It's me, I need to do right by her, marrying me made her poor, that's not how I want it to end.'

'She's staying with you until you earn enough to divorce?' I'm vaguely horrified, what a waste of two lives.

'Oh no, she doesn't care about the money, that's my thing. She just isn't that bothered about the paperwork. She lives her life as she wishes to.' He slants a look my way. 'I'm a trophy, a symbol of her rebellion against her rich daddy. I swear I think her current boyfriend is a yacht-owning Harvard boy. Divorcing would be admitting to her father he was right all along and that we're a terrible match. At least if she left with more than she came in with materially they could declare it a draw.'

'You're kidding.' It sounded like the plot of a soap … from the Eighties. '*Knott's Landing: The Silicon Generation.*'

'What?' His brows draw together as he tries to place the reference.

'*Knott's Landing*?' I restate. 'The California spin-off of *Dallas*.'

'Right.' Okay, so as a child in Dublin this was probably not something he tuned in to watch.

'Never mind,' I dismiss. This is no time to dive into our different experiences of TV based on our ages and where we grew up.

'It just wasn't a decision either of us wanted to make before now.' Jack ignores my detour. 'And this is it. I'm so close. This app is my stepping stone to finally making something of myself.'

'The venture capitalists in Paris…' I recall my earlier guess about his visit to Paris sure now I was right. 'That's why you were meeting them, to get new investors to buy Eric out.'

'I believe in this product. Your brother might not – but I do. We could be huge. I want Lacy to walk out of this filthy rich, sure there's a payday now but damn… I know we could be the next big thing.'

He indicates and pulls onto the freeway. When I was a teenager, this was how I burned through my angst, putting my foot on the gas and letting the rhythm of the road, the soothing sound of the engine take my troubles away. Put miles between me and my problems. It soothes me now, even though the current cause of all my angst sits in the seat beside me.

'Yes, I knew I was on borrowed time, that he was talking to someone, that he's under pressure himself; we've both put everything into this venture. I knew when Eric was rushing to get launched that it was likely because he was lining up a sale, but it also suited me to launch. Once we're out in the world, I can prove the concept has a market and then I'm a more solid prospect to new backers, and I can buy him out,' he explains.

'Wait.' My mind stutters. 'What do you mean you've both put everything into this business. It's Eric's.

'Eric only owns fifty per cent.' Jack's tone is derisory, of my brother for acting like he is sole owner or of me for believing it isn't entirely clear.

My whole body seems to drop like I'm on one of those terrifying rides that tower above everything in some theme parks. The sensation so sudden that if I looked up I'd see a trace of the world as I used to know it.

He is co-founder. A 50:50, larger than life, in Technicolor, building it with his own hands partner. 'But post-launch, once you're a sure bet, surely that also becomes more expensive.' I feel out the new ground I'm on. A new reality where it seems I have conspired to betray him. Unforgivably so.

'What choice do I have?'

'You could sell. Start again.' Please say you would be happy to start again.

His jaw clenches. 'Start over ... from the bottom? It's taken me years to get to today. I've worked my way up through the ranks the hard way. Nobody would back me, and then Eric comes on board and suddenly it's raining money. So, instead of doing a start-up in the usual way – spreading the risk by giving a share to everyone who came in, keeping costs low – we held on to the stock ourselves. Went all in. Every cent Lacy and I have ever earned is in Synchronicity.'

Oh no. No, no, no. Sneaky, devious Eric. He hasn't been concealing the sale from his CTO, he's been backing his partner into a corner. He needed Jack to agree to the sale, and what choice would he have now; the clock had entirely wound down, they were completely out of funds.

'But if the competitor with the same concept went to market first, you'd have been sunk in the water.'

'I know that. Why do you think I agreed to let you gut my baby up like a fish for dinner?'

'I did not gut your baby,' I defend on reflex, my mind racing. Jack is out of money. And Eric is too.

'Oh yeah you did, you and your MVP.' He smiles. 'You were right though. The product I wanted to put into market would have taken another six months.'

They never had another six months. Eric would go bankrupt first and take Mike and Jack down with him.

'Which would have been too late.'

'Too late for what?'

Too late for Eric's buyers. The deal isn't signed though. What if Jack found another way, blocked the sale? Mike would be sunk. I felt sick.

'Ah, if your competitor launched and filled the gap in the market.' I bought myself another minute.

'If there even is a competitor,' he says softly, as if it's just occurred to him. As it has to me. We only had Eric's word that there was someone else breathing down our necks. What if there wasn't?

'He lied,' I breathe. 'Of course, he lied.'

'Yeah, to force the pace. Launch sooner rather than later,' Jack continues into the silence as I absorb the multiple levels of my stepbrother's manipulations. 'All the better to sell.'

I have to tell him. I have to tell him.

'But you could sell … would that be so bad? Fifty per cent of the deal Eric is talking about is not nothing. I mean I think the whole sale could be for as much as $100 million.'

'Goddamit.' He takes his frustration out on the steering wheel. 'He's still talking to those people. I've told him over and over that I'm not selling.'

I take a breath, look over and take in the scowl on his face, the anger burning in him which right now is still directed solely at my brother.

'It sounds like a lot, doesn't it?' He laughs. 'But after half of it goes on taxes, less the money I've sunk into the build, it won't be a lot. Not enough to seed something on my own, that's for sure. Especially not if I split from Lacy now, but I don't see us continuing as we are.'

'Why now?' Is he implying what I think he's implying. I feel like every moment that passes I'm falling further into an abyss from which I will never be able to climb out.

'You know why now.' My heart lurches. My poor stupid heart. My heart is not involved. We barely know each other. A month ago, Jack Keogh was an app accident waiting to happen. I don't know what that means. No, that's a lie; I know what it means. And yet the words he's waiting for, the ones that hover in the air are stolen from me. I cannot speak to that promise that he's floating out there in the world.

Not until he knows the truth.

'Jack.' I steel myself to say the words. The words that will set in train the chain of events that will ruin my stepfather. 'Eric has accepted the offer. He's going to sell.'

'What?' his tone is neutral. No reaction.

'He's selling. That's what the meeting earlier in the week was for. This afternoon they finalised the terms.'

'That's not possible. I know we have a great product but nobody finalises terms without doing their due diligence.'

They hadn't. 'I helped them.'

'What?' His tone isn't so neutral anymore. He sounds like he is barely able to form words.

'I didn't know that you were a partner.'

His hands tighten on the steering wheel. 'You helped him. Behind my back. Why?'

'I… I didn't know that you and he were partners,' I repeat, shaking my head. It never even occurred to me, not once had Eric implied there were any other investors. But in Eric's view of the world any kind of ownership automatically entitled him to full possession. I barely knew him outside of the occasional family call, but I did know that much, had seen it in the boy when we lived together as teenagers. But this level of deceit? I didn't know the man at all.

'Eric is out of money, he's seriously over-extended, and

has another investment as well. But it's my stepfather's money; he'll take his father and my mother both down.'

The silence feels palpable, like it's a pressure, building inside the confines of the car. Jack had met Mike. Did he understand the position I had been in?

'Eric is out of money?' he grits out.

'Yeah. You didn't know?'

His bark of laughter is almost painful after the low tones he's been using.

'No.'

'I'm sorry.' Have I said that already. I can't seem to remember. 'I didn't know.'

His dream of building something is gone. Their capital is blown. His hand is being forced; if there is no more money to cover their running costs then it's over.

'What are the terms?'

'I don't know.' I hadn't been part of those conversations.

'Find `out.' The seething fury in his tone wasn't concealed.

Did he want me to ring Eric and be the middleman for more of his lies? No. No way. The contract terms were being emailed earlier. What if they left me on the chain? I hurriedly open my phone and search for an email that only had a medium chance of... No, there it was. My stomach dips as I scan the terms.

'Ah, it looks like ... that is...' How to tell him he has been royally screwed in the deal that Eric negotiated without him? 'You've been bound in as part of the deal; you get a lump sum upfront but you have to continue to run the app after acquisition, earning out your part of the deal over five years.'

That was why Eric had wanted me to get Jack back. Why the suits hadn't been overly concerned in having high-spec documentation of the tech up front; they wouldn't need it after the sale, they would have the man who built it.

'Five years.' He seemed to have found a new level of rage.

'Do you want to pull over? Talk about this.'

'No.' His hands flex on the steering wheel as he forces himself to relax, focus on the road.

'Are you sure? I'm not sure you should be driving like this.'

'Just stop talking.' His voice is more controlled again. 'I need to think.'

'Okay.'

I let the silence hang; my lingering jetlag and the week I've had, not to mention the emotional punching bag this conversation has turned out to be, has left my energy low. Making the conversation a punching bag implies that I'm the one doing the swinging, but honestly, if it's possible to take a hit from one, then that's me, the fool standing in front of a bag that's swinging at her like a big old pendulum and, despite knock after knock, is too stupid to get out of the way.

I let the regular tread of the tyres on the asphalt take me and lean back and watch twilight settle over the valley. Traffic has thinned and the reds and oranges of sunset are fading into the horizon behind us.

'Where are you going?' This isn't aimless driving; we've been going due east the whole time.

'I want to take you somewhere.' There is almost no trace of the anger that had him in his grip earlier, he sounds tired though.

'Where?'

'Trust me.' Men say this to women in movies all the time; it drives me nuts. Some overly pecced, ordinary guy busts into her life followed by gun-toting crazies and at some point he will say those two words before throwing her out of a plane without a parachute.

I will never be the girl who lets a guy push her out of a plane.

'I got in this car to hear you out. I've listened.' I keep my voice carefully calm – painfully so. No point in provoking the nut-job who thinks you'll be okay with whatever mad plan he's come up with that is totally not okay. 'That is the sum total of our agreement here. And now you're taking me somewhere against my will.'

There isn't a question in my summing up of what he thinks he's doing, but he answers me, anyway.

'Yeah.'

'Kiss my ass.' No way, no how am I going anywhere with him.

'That's the plan.' His voice is a smoky caramel as he responds to the literal words.

'Argh!' A scream of frustration escapes me. 'Stop this car right now.'

'We're on the freeway,' he points out, as if it has somehow escaped my attention.

'Have you seen *Lady Bird*?' I ask, referring to the scene where the pink-haired teen opens the door and lets herself out of a moving car.

'The doors autolock,' he deadpans.

'You can't be serious.'

His hands tighten on the steering wheel. 'Leonie.'

Just my name. I can't help myself. I turn to look at him.

'I don't know what this is between us,' he continues. 'Maybe it's something, maybe it's nothing. I— Give me some time to think, twenty-four hours. Twenty-four hours before we flip a coin.'

'What coin?'

He wets his lips as they curl up before he answers.

'Well, whether you walk away,' he pauses, 'or I burn my life down.'

'What?'

'Being with me would mean burning your life down?' I ask when he doesn't say anything further, his clever brain sifting through all the scenarios.

'Yeah. RL8 is sold, I accept the big payday and I'll have done right by Lacy when we split but I'm stuck there for the next half-decade. You and I have a chance of being together but I'll be trapped, no business of my own, swallowed up in big tech.' The bitterness was evident in the glowing light of the console.

I say nothing as we cruise forward into the night. He's right, his ability to build his own business is going to catch fire as soon as he signs that deal. But eventually the flames will die, in five years he'll be able to start again. But he gets paid out at the end of the term, so his share of the payday will continue to dissipate in lieu of salary. After his divorce, after half a decade, what funds, what drive would be left in the dreamer who told me of his hopes of creating something that would be his.

I would never have stepped into this car a month ago, never have envisaged myself here. But I guess the frog never jumps into the boiling pot either. Although I think I've heard that thing about frogs and heating water by degrees is one of those urban myth type of things. It's not true. At a certain point even the stupidest of frogs is going to figure out it's time to get out of the water. Not me, though.

The smooth purr of the car lulls me despite the whirl of my brain, the pressures of the last couple of weeks seeping out of my bones into the tread of the tyres on the asphalt.

By the time we reach our destination I am fully asleep, rousing only to make my way up the steps, through a door and into a room with a bed onto which I sink gratefully.

'Leonie...' The whisper in my ear is warm, the accent wrapping itself around me in the cocoon of blankets and man I lie in. I let myself sink into it like a drizzle of honey onto a toasted crumpet on a winter's morning: the comforting luxuriousness of it; the smell of cedarwood, the tang of sea salt.

The delicious relaxation is crushed.

Jack.

His arms lift and retreat. The weight of his body sinks

and then disappears from the mattress. If I close my eyes very hard and don't think about anything, maybe it will all go away. Eric and Mike and Jack and ... men, just all the men.

'Here.' The aroma of coffee hits me as Jack comes back into the room. I lever myself up and take the coffee from him. I can't look at him. Married. Am I a fool for being here? Where *is* here?

I'm in a small log cabin type of room. All log walls and pioneery fireplace, old-timey iron bed frame and warm, colourful blankets. The blinds are drawn, but it doesn't look very bright outside.

'What time is it?' I feel like I've been danced on by elephants, bruised and battered, like yesterday's drama took a physical toll on my body.

'Nearly dawn.' He's still dressed in jeans – no shirt though. Of course, I think dully, why would he not look like he stepped out of a classic Levi's commercial? Meanwhile, I'm sure my bedhead hair will at least provide a distraction from the remains of yesterday's dried makeup and the pillow lines on my cheeks.

'Right.' I reach for the travel mug of coffee. At some point I've acquired a soft oversized T-shirt – his T-shirt.

'I want to show you something.' He pulls it further away from me.

I look at him in disbelief. He's married. He's kidnapped me and this is how he repays my letting him push me out of a plane. *Trust me.*

He'd better trust me. If he doesn't hand me that coffee immediately, I'm reverting to Plan A. It's a log cabin –

there's bound to be a wood chipper around here somewhere.

None of this is verbalised, but I'm pretty sure he can read me.

He lifts my suitcase from the corner of the room, placing it down on the bed.

'C'mon, Leonie.' He gives me *that* smile.

Weak. I am so weak. I grumblingly zip open my bag and pull some jeans and a sweatshirt out, to find he is now holding a puffer jacket out to me. Is that his wife's?

'It's mine,' he quickly asserts. 'Please, it'll be worth it.'

I go to the bathroom and wash my face and appropriate the varied and *entirely* male toiletries I find there. When I stumble out of what has turned out to be a two-room log cabin, I find man and coffee waiting in the car.

'Where are we?' I manage after I've taken a sip. Well, two sips.

'Wait,' he says. 'You'll see.'

We at least still appear to be in Northern California, with its redwoods and mountain roads, so that's something. I have no idea how long we drove last night. Maybe we doubled back. Are we in the Santa Cruz mountains? Is that his house? I had the distinct impression he still lived with his wife though.

Wife. This word is not having any less of an impact each time it rolls into my brain like a Toon-style boulder ricocheting around in there.

My brain is slowly registering that the view and mountain range on display is far grander than anything the range between San Jose and the ocean has to offer when he pulls into a car park as the other cars on the road continue on into a tunnel ahead of us.

'It's almost the same view, it's just quieter on this side,' he explains, pulling into the side of the road as I catch my first glimpse of the rising sun.

Oh.

My heart squeezes in my chest. The view stretching out in front of me is the most spectacular of my life. I barely notice as his hand takes mine to help me out of the car.

The valley itself would be stunning at any time of day, the green of the trees sweeping out across the valley floor framed by some of the most iconic peaks on earth, the escarpment of El Capitan on one side, the curve of Half Dome on another. Goose bumps break out across my skin; it's the most physical reaction I can ever remember having to a view. Behind me the sky is still nearly black but on the other side of the valley the sky has lightened to the palest of blues and the few wisps of cloud that spread across the spring sky are an entire page of pantone from purple through pink to the most glorious fiery glow of the clouds closest to the horizon reflecting the glory of the coming sun.

My chin trembles and my eyes water as I exhale into the chilly morning air.

I look at him to share the wonder of the moment, the sheer awesome gloriousness of it. His eyes aren't on the view, though.

I give him a trembly smile. I'm not thinking about anything else right now. Just this. This moment.

'C'mon.' He grins and takes my hand. No, that's not

right; he never let it go. He's firmed his grip and is pulling me towards the car.

I protest. I am not ready to leave. Not nearly ready.

'It gets better.'

And, unbelievably, it does. We drive through the tunnel and come out the other side, closer again to the spread of the majestic mountains and the rising sun. It's incredible.

Here is another car park, and he is right; this one has dozens of parked cars, a crowd gathered at the viewpoint taking photos, the inevitable selfies, and some more serious efforts with tripods, but he keeps going. The sky is eclipsed as we enter the woods.

'No, I want to see the...' But I am silenced as the road opens up again and the sheer majestic rockface of El Capitan appears above us, unbelievably close. Then we're in a meadow, El Cap soaring above us into the pink and blue sky, a waterfall cascading to our right.

'Is that...?' I gesture to the waterfall which, in any other setting, would be second to nothing, but I'm mesmerised by the size and scale of El Capitan. I've watched the documentary about the free climber who scaled it without ropes, seen how high it is, but nothing prepares you for being at the bottom, looking at it soar into the sky.

'No, that's Bridalveil Falls,' Jack answers my half-asked question. 'The one in my office is Vernal Falls; it's further in – a short hike would take us there.'

'What's your idea of a short hike?' I don't want to ruin the reality hiatus we seem suspended in; I want to be here with a guy I've just met, walking the trails through a national park at the weekend.

'Ha, it really isn't that bad. A few miles.'

Again he passes the parked cars of those who have stopped to take in the rising sun as it comes up behind the iconic mountain peak, pulling in at a small car park a little further on.

We take a trail from the corner of the carpark across a meadow to a mahogany-dark river, mist hovering over the almost-still water. As we draw closer, I see there is a beach. We are the only ones there.

'Here.' He sits down on the pebbly sands and pulls me down to sit in front of him and then he wraps his arms around me to keep me warm.

The mist is light, hovering over the water, melting as the pink glow makes way for the golden orb of the sun itself. Jack points out the three peaks on the other side of the Merced River, telling me they are known as the Three Brothers for the three captured sons of the Ahwahnechee Chief when the resistance of the Native Americans against the encroachment on their land here was crushed.

'The name for the peaks is Kom-poo-pai-zes or something like that. It translates into "mountains with heads like frogs when ready to leap".'

'Catchy.'

His chest moves in laughter.

'You come here often?' He definitely isn't commuting from Yosemite.

'Most weekends that the park is open. It's been a rough few years between snow and fires but I love it here. It's my escape,' he says, his voice flowing over me like the river through the valley, ancient and familiar. 'I hike. Climb.'

That explains the callouses on his palms then.

I sip my coffee, watching the sun rise in the still mirror of the Merced River. Nothing can ruin this perfect moment.

Almost nothing.

Dawn becomes day all too soon. And with it reality returns. I ease myself out of the warmth of his arms and stand up. He rises behind me and brushes his jeans down.

'Thank you.' Despite everything else that's going on, this perfect moment of peace is almost worth the storm.

'You said you'd never been.'

I smile up into his smile, the joy and beauty of the morning pushing upwards through the dark, rolling clouds inside me.

His warm lips descend to mine, moving softly, temptingly on mine, asking a question, making a case. Posing a problem that could be solved if I just let myself go.

When I was in college, my roommate would pull out the movie *Circle of Friends* every time she needed a duvet day. Chris O'Donnell and Minnie Driver as college students in Dublin, Ireland. Hello, friend irony. A movie of friendships and loves lost and found. A half-remembered line from it drifts into my head now. A heartbroken Minnie Driver facing the reality of her life versus the dream of the life she glimpsed.

'It's like taking me to the top of the mountain and showing me the world, and saying, "That's what you can't have, Benny, you great, fat article".'

I'm Benny on the mountaintop. I can't have this.

Can I?

God, I want this. Want to lean in and just let it take me.

I meet his blue eyes watching the expressions flit across my face. His own are shuttered. Does he think I'll say yes? No? I can't read him at all. I don't know my own mind, much less his.

I take a step out of his arms.

'What are you doing? What are we doing?' I look up at him. 'I need to know what you're thinking.'

'I've been thinking about what other options might be out there, if it has to be so black and white.'

'What do you mean?'

'What if I didn't divorce Lacy? She'd be happy enough not to, I think.'

'What?' What is he suggesting? That she wants them to get back together?

'She still loves you?' I thought he said it was over.

'No.' His eyes watch me warily. 'It's not like that for her. It's about winning. She bet on me. Bet big. She won't care about the money. She doesn't value money, she just wants the satisfaction of proving to her father that she bet right. Being rich and still married to the Irish nobody is the jackpot.'

'Seriously?' Is he really standing here proposing that he stay married, get me, and I guess sabotage the deal that will ruin Eric, not that I care, and Mike, which I do care about.

'You grew up with these people – you must know the type.'

'No, no. Are you crazy? What is wrong with you?' I huff out a noise that is laugh on the outside hysterical scream on the inside before taking a deep centring breath. 'And you two not getting divorced helps your plans how?'

'I can refuse the deal. With fifty per cent I can find another backer or get someone else...'

I cut him off.

'You want to stay married. Talk about the wrong guy.' I raise my hands in the air. 'No, you have to choose. You can't have it all.'

I step into him. 'Why not leave it? Start over, start again. Walk away from the deal.'

His jaw locks at my proposal that he walk away from the dreams he has spent a lifetime trying to achieve, what he feels he owes to the woman he married.

'Or don't. But I'm not sitting around waiting while you...'

'That's not what I'm suggesting.'

'Isn't it? Take me back.' His expression falls imperceptibly and I can see him gear up to make an argument, persuade me. 'I mean it. We're done here.'

Chapter Eighteen

'We'll talk later.'

'No we won't.'

I shake my head as I get out of the car outside of the office. How much has changed, yet at the same time, nothing has at all. It's not even noon. But between my request to leave and our arrival here, we have exchanged barely a dozen words.

I feel dazed, this is it. And then he's out of the car. Beside me.

'I've been thinking. I have a plan – I need to retain control of the company, I can talk to Lacy, see if she'll stick with me. She's not a bad person. If I can persuade her to retain her shares until I've built it to the next level...'

'So, you're going to try to cancel the deal.'

He nods, eyes concerned.

'Okay.' God. Mike. If the sale is off, that means Eric's debts rebound on my stepfather like a snapped elastic.

I need to warn Mike. But I can't ask Jack to lose his

company and five years of his life just because Eric has screwed us all. I have savings, maybe enough to help somehow.

'I'll see you later then?'

I nod and he leans in and gives me a peck on the forehead. No more than that, a gesture of comfort that all will be well.

I sit in my car trying to ground myself, to figure out what I do now.

I try calling Mike. No answer. Then my mom. Straight to voicemail.

I need to talk to them. Warn them.

I open my messages. Type.

Me: *He's married.*

What if she says no? Won't agree to his proposal. Wants to stay married?

I stare at the screen and the litter of yesterday's messages, an exchange spurred by a picture of Alicia's two-year-old son caught mid-act liberally applying some kind of white cream to his entire face. The light banter is so utterly normal, an exchange that could have popped into our feed anytime over the last few years, and no doubt would again in the next few.

Not mine, though. This is unprecedented.

There is no response. Where is my Greek chorus when I need it?

I sit in the familiar seat of my old car; the steering wheel has a few more cracks and is shinier than it used to be. The hood is new; it used to be tan and now it's a new navy one, darker than the dark blue of the car itself. Nice though. Understated. Mike or my mom? Whoever picked it out, there would be fewer such gestures from now on. I did my best. It isn't my fault if Eric's house of cards collapsed. It certainly isn't Jack's.

Stella: *The list never said he had to be single.*

What?

Me: *It was IMPLICIT.*

Stella: *You specified 'tall'.*

Me: *Everyone specifies tall.*

Nessa: *We're halfway through life. You've got to roll with a little baggage.*

Me: *This isn't a little baggage. It's cargo.*

Me: *You all are not helping. This is not about the list. We are way beyond the list.*

Alicia: *typing...*

I rest my elbows on the steering wheel and put my head in my hands. How did I get here? Where do I go from here? I feel like my car is an island, in the middle of the ocean and there is maybe one path out of here, like those tidal access ways to the mainland. Once I start driving, I'm committed. Pick the wrong direction and before I get too much further, I'll be stuck and will be unable to do anything but watch the water rise until I am submerged.

Alicia: *How married?*

Me: *On a scale of what? One being living in a separate country and ten being two kids and a dog waiting on him to get home for dinner?*

My fingers hover over the keys. I don't know how to answer. It's all really, really complicated.

Me: *Hands in the air shrug emoji. Maybe a two.*

Alicia: *That's not so married. But do what your gut tells you is right. Whatever happens we'll be here for you.*

Nessa: *Don't give up until you have all the data.*

Stella: *Fail fast. Have FUN on the way down. Wink emoji. Devil emoji.*

Me: *Right.*

I can't give them the rest of the data. I barely understand it myself. I can barely think straight at this point. The emotional roller coaster has left me drained. I try calling Mike again and again as I drive back to Eric's house.

There is no sign of Eric when I let myself in, and I'm thorough in my search. I don't just call out, I bang open every door. I have an extra-long shower and crawl between the crisp white zillion-thread-count sheets of the guestroom.

———

On waking, I lie in bed staring at the ceiling. If I lie here long enough, maybe I'll wake in London and my usual world. Not this one where I have to make *that* phone call. Where is my phone?

A door bangs shut downstairs. Eric's home.

I wrap a robe around me. Trust Eric to have a great white fluffy towelling robe hanging on the back of the en suite door like I'm staying at the Four Seasons.

'Eric.' I sweep into the main living room like a marshmallow-attired avenging fury. He needs to put this right, he should be the one to talk to his father, explain what he's done to them, to Jack.

'Sweetie.'

'Mom.' The wind flops out of my sails with a smack to the side of my head. I try to readjust to this new reality. My mother is flipping through a magazine on the cream sofa, Mike at her side. 'Mike. Hi.'

'Leonie, are you just out of bed? It's evening!' Mom admonishes me.

'It's been a long week.' *And then some.* 'I didn't know you guys were coming.'

'Eric organised it all, sent us the tickets this morning.' She beams in delight. So that's why I couldn't reach them earlier, they were in the air.

Eric walks into the room, all dressed up. I eye him up and down. He looks pleased with himself. He won't by the time I'm finished with him.

'Get dressed, honey, we're going out,' Mike chides me.

We are?

Is it too late to go back to bed? My mother is fretting with my hair in that silent communication that says she doesn't love my current hairstyle. I have just got out of bed though.

'Go, go.' Mike gives a quick clap and makes a gesture like I'm a chicken he's trying to scoot out of the coop. 'Reservations at Relish are for seven.'

Seven. What time is it now?

'Where is your phone?' my mom asks as the same thought occurs to me. 'We tried calling you back. We were half worried you were outside the door in LA you called so many times.'

I retrieve my mislaid phone from my car as our ride pulls up to take us downtown. Dressed in a floaty, colourful dress I've borrowed from Mom that I've cinched in at the waist and her heels, which are about a size too small for me, I've done the best I can to make myself presentable for a Saturday night at Relish, one of the area's more upmarket restaurants. There are over a dozen missed calls on my phone, some from my mom, but mostly from Jack. Has he spoken to Lacy? What has she said?

'What's the occasion?' I ask brightly as we sit in the car.

My mom looks at me. Too bright? What am I missing? An anniversary? A birthday?

'Why, we're celebrating Eric.'

'Eric? You haven't told her.'

Mom and Mike exchange looks of laughing surprise.

'What?' But I know.

'We sold to Rubicon Inc.'

'You did?' I show my teeth in an approximation of delight as I congratulate my stepbrother. My mind is spinning as I try to figure out what's happened while I was doing my Sleeping Beauty act. Or rather, William Tell. Instead of waking up to the kiss of a handsome prince I'm coming to in a world where everything I know has changed. Did Jack change his mind about selling? Is that why he was trying to reach me? I feel sick.

I pull Eric back as we are dropped off kerbside, and Mike and my mom enter the restaurant.

'What's going on?'

'We're celebrating.'

'But how? I thought Jack didn't want to sell.'

'Rubicon Inc. made an offer, and I told them my partner wasn't interested, so they made another offer.' Eric is already looking over my shoulder. I ceased being of use to him as soon as we walked out of the due diligence meeting so the fact he's taking the time to explain to me is because he enjoys crowing rather than that he feels he owes me an explanation.

But I don't care, this is good news. Mike will get his money back, Jack will start again with at least something from the pay-out. He said Lacy wouldn't care about the money, if he's told her everything maybe she has given him the same advice I did? Does he mean to start again with me? That's a lot of pressure; I've known him for little over a month. A smile plays on my lips.

'They were happy to move ahead with the deal without tying Jack in?'

'No.' Now I'm confused.

'But Jack is a fifty per cent stakeholder.'

'Need to read the fine print, Leo. Actually, Jack has twenty-five per cent and his wife owns the other twenty-five per cent. And she's happy to sell.'

I assumed his plan was that once Rubicon offered big enough money he was counting on Jack being unable to walk away from it. But that wasn't it. He's gone direct to Lacy.

'You're selling it out from under him? You can't do that.'

'Can't I?' He winks. 'Thanks, little sis. Couldn't have done it without you.'

And with that he swaggers into the restaurant. I need to call Jack back, warn him.

'Leonie, honey, are you coming?' Mike's voice calls from the doorway. Mike. My phone is in my hand. What do I do? I close my eyes. This is how divine inspiration strikes, isn't it? If I close my eyes and look to the heavens, I'll find the answer.

'Look who we found!' I turn to find the answer has been delivered. And it's as welcome as a notice to jury duty. In hell.

Jack. And he has an arm around a woman who can only be Lacy Keogh. Piñata pieces fluttering all over the sidewalk. I feel like I've been hit by a tank, and what remains of me is standing here pretending to be okay. I feel like I should throw a hand in the air, like, *I'm fine, I'm okay*, for the sake of any concerned observer who is worried the blow killed me.

She is exactly as I imagined: leggy, blonde, tennis-toned athletic arms, clean jawline, and a Hollywood smile, which she flashes as Mike makes introductions.

'You'll join us?' my mom asks.

It's like it's all taking place in an alternate reality and I'm going through the motions. I'm sure I've said and done all the right things.

I can hear Lacy telling Mike that they're celebrating too.

'I'll bet you are.' Mike's voice is loud as we make our way up the hallway. Mom's eyes cut to me and while her face gives away nothing about what she thinks of seeing Jack here, so clearly with another woman, she links her hand through mine and gives it a barely there squeeze. Maybe not everyone has failed to see through my act. 'Jack, you devil, you never said you were Eric's partner.'

'You never said you were Eric's dad,' Jack rejoins.

Mike hoots in laughter. 'You have me there.'

Eric has gone on ahead and is at the table already, his face greying as he sees our additional guests.

Jack's face is blank but amused, his arm draped around his wife's neat waist. We step back as the hostess arranges for extra seating to be added to the table, making the spacious table intimate rather than overcrowded.

What with Eric already being seated and due to the way we've arrived, I have no chance to configure the seating, and find myself duly seated in the worst possible scenario – in between Eric and Jack. No, not the worst; I could be between Jack and Lacy.

I sit stiffly, politely waiting for the worst evening of my life to begin, as if I'm attending the theatre and not my own personal apocalypse.

The waitress steps forward and proffers the champagne bottle to Eric, who barely glances at it before nodding stiffly. Has his deal been sunk before he's even popped the bottle in celebration? Part of me hopes so, even if it means Jack and his wife have reconciled.

'Fancy meeting you here.' Eric is making a fairly decent show of being happy to see his partner. 'What brings you?'

'Same as you,' Jack says. 'Celebrating. Can you bring another when you get a moment?' he asks the waitress.

The champagne emptied into the six tall glasses, the waitress scurries off to bring the next one. I lift it to my lips and take a fortifying mouthful. The bubbles explode in protest in my mouth at being treated so cavalierly.

'To Rubicon Inc. and their big cheque,' Eric toasts not quite as confidently as he would have ten minutes ago, his foundation clearly rocked by the sight of Lacy and Jack together. But Eric is nothing if not a believer in his own successes, so, until he has proof to the contrary, he is proceeding as planned.

Whoops, my glass is already empty. Mom catches my eye in concern as the waitress tops up my glass with the fresh bottle. I want to lean in and give her a big John Wayne, 'keep 'em coming', but I'm sure in this kind of establishment they discreetly keep glasses full. No cause for concern.

'To the hard work that went in to getting us here,' Jack follows up, now that I'm finally ready and we clink glasses.

This is happening; I'm sitting here at this table with my mother and the man I woke up next to this morning while his wife sits on the other side. Colour. I said I needed colour, didn't I? Well, this is colourful.

'That's a good deal you got there,' Mike is saying to Jack. 'You must be happy.'

Jack shrugs. 'I'd have liked to hold on to it a bit longer. Make a go of it.'

Mike raises his eyebrows in interest. 'But why, everyone has the three to four social media apps they need, why do you think the world needs another?'

'Because there are so few, people should have choices.'

'But if they wanted a different option, surely the market would provide?' Mike is engaged now. A capitalist all his life, in retirement his views have softened, become more socially aware. It may be my mother's influence, may be just the softening of a man who spent his life making money and only now notices that he has more than is fair. Or did, before Eric blew it ... and doubled it. Money goes to money. I reach over and refill my empty glass.

'No,' I say sourly. 'They don't. Because big tech buys them up.'

'Why would they do that?' Mom asks.

'So everyone remains stuck with apps that seem free but invade their privacy, so they can sell their data to other big tech companies while serving you all the ads they want, because it's not like you have other options, is it?' Turns out Jack and I, despite making our money in this industry, share a dislike of some of its more cynical practices.

'But what do these big tech companies do with them?' Mia asks, I'm guessing, less out of genuine interest in the answer but because as a practised hostess she is throwing herself all over this one in the hope the grenade won't go off.

'Squashes them. Buys them up. Never gives them a chance.' I sound bitter. I *am* bitter. This isn't even my fight, but I'm suddenly mad. Everyone settles for shit because the alternatives are hard. Or never get a chance because it's not in somebody else's interest.

'Is that what will happen to RL8?' Mike asks.

'Maybe. It's hard to say. If it's a success they'll stick it full of data-sucking programmes to make their users the real bit they make money off. But Rubicon already have a popular social media app, so more likely they'll let it live in the store for a while, but they won't promote it and when users fail to find it, they'll write it off as a fail. Not their fault; they're not monopolising their section of the industry. These new entrants simply fail to thrive.' Jack smiles thinly.

'Dead on arrival.' My hand slams the table. Those bubbles have also slammed into my bloodstream like atoms colliding in a bomb, the fusion reminding me I haven't eaten since sometime yesterday. Breakfast, maybe. The girl is already coming with a fresh bottle.

'But you are happy?' Mom asks Jack, ignoring my summation.

'I think the app we built could have succeeded, and

done so without using people, making them the product. But who knows, if I can't do it my way I'm going to move on with my life. Thankfully I had time to contact Rubicon and renegotiate the deal.' He cuts a bland glance in Eric's direction. 'Extracted myself from the terms, which obliged me to stay on and run it for them, their way. It will mean less money but so be it. So I don't know if I'm truly happy but at least I'm free.'

'But you came out to celebrate?' Mom looks confused.

'Oh, we're not celebrating the sale,' Lacy pipes up, her tones perfectly modulated, her face shining as she turns to share the moment with her husband, though her eyes look directly at me. She knows exactly who I am. 'But it's wonderful that all Jack's hard work has paid off.'

There is nothing out of place with her smile, not a flicker, but I know she knows. A single moment and that's it. She's moved on to Eric. I am not worth more than that to her.

I can't help myself. I finally turn my head to take in Jack's profile: his body language is relaxed, his expression easy, but he isn't looking at his wife, or at me. Eric is on the receiving end of some serious unblinking side-eye.

'We're celebrating our marriage.' Lacy lifts her glass to her husband. 'Ten years and still going strong.'

I've had enough. There isn't a power on earth that can make me stay at this table and I stand abruptly.

'Leonie.' Mom is opposite me and has been watching closely. She knows I'm not excusing myself to go to the bathroom.

'I'm fine, Mom.' The heeled sandals beg to differ and one twists beneath me, making me appear more inebriated than I am. I have, however, had nearly a bottle of champagne on an empty stomach, so apparently I'm gone enough to take the fresh bottle out of the nearby bucket and tip it toward the happy couple as I leave. 'Congratulations.'

It's the only good decision I've made all day – that and choosing to leave the stupid sandals behind me.

I hit the sidewalk barefoot with a bottle of champagne in one hand and my purse in the other. I look one way and then the other. *Doesn't matter, just walk, find a hotel, find another bottle once this one is disposed of.*

I have a plan.

'Leonie.'

No, don't turn around.

I walk faster.

'Leonie!' He's right behind me. I swing around wildly, losing balance a little, and his hand reaches out to save me. I get myself upright and look him warningly in the eye.

'I guess you flipped that coin for us then.'

He opens his mouth like he's going to argue the point before closing it again.

'I guess I did.'

'So, I'm walking away. That's the side it came down, right? So what are you doing out here?'

He looks momentarily confused, before those blue eyes clear and his lips twist wryly. I hate that smile.

'I tried to call you.'

'For what? To tell me you were picking her? No need.'

His lips thin and his eyes narrow as he looks down at me. He is only slightly taller than me.

'Your brother thought he was so clever. He used you to

help get the sale done behind my back. He also thought he was going to use Lacy. He thought he had her shares in the bag. He didn't need me to agree to the deal because he thought he had controlling interest. Turns out I was only half right about her new boyfriend. He doesn't have a yacht, but he did go to Harvard.'

'What?' The bubbles have diluted my brain. What does her boyfriend going to Harvard have to do with... Eric went to Harvard.

Nooo. No. it can't be. But the grim set of Jack's face confirms the slow realisation of the extra level of conniving weasledom to which Eric has descended in his devious deviousness... I don't have words for how utterly ... he dated his partner's wife to ensure she would vote for the buyout. It was incomprehensible. And still took the time to tell me Jack was married when he caught a hint that there might be something between us.

'Yeah,' Jack confirms for me slowly. 'And if there is one thing that pisses Lacy off its being manipulated by rich, privileged men. But, thankfully, she refused to sign without my consent. Unlike others.'

'I told you I didn't know.'

'Because you never asked,' he whips back.

'But it seems to have worked out for everyone. Your family get richer. And I have plenty of cash to start again with Lacy.'

'What about...' Me, I want to ask but can't quite finish the sentence. I want to cry. But I am not that girl.

'What did you want me to do? Turn my life upside

down for a woman who would never pick me? I'm the opposite of everything you want in a man, remember?'

'Oh, I remember.' What do I remember? Kisses in Paris and glorious sunrises. 'I fell for it.' People are stopping to look over at us. 'For your lies and… Stupid Leonie. *I understand him on a deeper level. He's not really married. It's over*. What an idiot.'

I swing away.

'Wait.' His tone is tangled, the anger of moments ago dissipated.

'No. Fuck you.'

Classy, Leonie. Real classy.

Chapter Nineteen

My head is thumping when my eyes unglue themselves. The room is pitch black as only a hotel in Silicon Valley can be. Used to guests keeping odd hours, night-time can be achieved at any time of day. I reach for my phone. 10:42.

Missed calls: five.

All Mom.

Me: *sick emoji*

Alicia: *Oh no, what happened?*

Me: *Champagne bottle emoji*

Me: *Champagne bottle emoji*

Me: *Champagne bottle emoji*

There are scribbles on the wall. Another local innovation – inspiration can strike at any time in Silicon Valley. One wall is outfitted with a whiteboard and non-permanent markers, which I appear to have made full use of while under the influence of the Widow.

New List

1. Single

Single. That's it.

My inebriated self also took the time to do a retrospective and a timeline, apparently.

The timeline isn't too detailed. What is shocking is how short it is. I've gone years without drama and in five weeks this guy has broken me. I'm not broken. I'm not.

I'm a little dented, that's all.

I'll be fine.

Ideation: London. The Anti-List.

Concept Development: Euro train app

Plan & Prepare: Ten mins in the pub

Design: (Reqs & Specs) Paris

Research: Paris. Missed warning signs!

Optimise: London.???

MVP Yosemite: What does good enough look like?

Launch: Skip. Go > Direct to Fail

Fail Restaurant: Winner! Learnings!!

The retro is less complete. Retrospectives are usually done by a team at regular intervals to figure out what went well and what could be better next time. They tend to have common themes: communication, time management, clarity of purpose… When these go well the project succeeds; when they don't… Well, it's not that dissimilar to real life.

What made you?

Mad: Jack.

Sad: Jack.

Glad: Jack.

Okay, that particular exercise didn't seem to go too well. I must have been in the maudlin section of the bottle. I've crossed a line through those and pushed through and done another list.

Mad: Eric (lies?)

Sad: Jack's choice.

Glad: He wasn't perfect … and it didn't matter (me either)

What does *me either* mean?

That I'm not perfect either, duh.

But whatever epiphany this may have struck last night seems to have faded with the new day.

Beside this list there are three further headings: Stop, Start, Continue. These are usually actionable items that the team agree to move forward into the next Sprint with, but it appears the *veritas* ran out with my *vino*.

Those three words make my stomach feel hollow, which reminds me that it most definitely is. I call down and order a club sandwich with fries. I'm too dizzy to locate and read a menu, but these are fairly reliable options and thankfully the operator agrees to send them.

I stare at those three words on the wall. Learnings.

What are my takeaways from this failure?

The words spin in front of me.

A shower seems like the best solution to my immediate

problems, that and a gallon of water. I step into the fall of water until I worry I will miss the arrival of my food. Deciding that my ability to judge the passage of time might be off, I check the hallway anyway and am hit by the distinctive smell of French fries. Grease and warmth. Why did I think this was a good idea?

I'll feel better. I'll feel better. The tomato sauce helps. As does the ice cube-filled glass of Coca-Cola.

Once the plate is empty, I feel substantially restored. A ping alerts me to my phone. The girls have been busy. The challenge with the time difference is that my morning is their early evening, so this is peak engagement time for them, as evidenced by the cascade of messages that arrived while I was in recovery.

Alicia: *Is that good? You were celebrating?*

Stella: *Told you, if the sex is good, everything else can be figured out.*

Kristen: *Woohoo, so we'll set a place for him at the wedding, yes!*

Alicia: *Tell us everything, what happened?*

Alicia: *Where are you?*

Stella: *Up against the wall, I hope!!*

Alicia: *Stella! There are children present.*

Kristen: *Please tell me you don't read your children the filth that Stella spews.*

Stella: *It's not filth. It's frank and open speech about a natural and very, very enjoyable part of the human experience.*

Stella: *Eggplant emoji x3*

Nessa: *Hi! What's going on? Do we have an update?*

Nessa: *Champagne? Does that mean he is less married than feared? Or is he throwing the luggage overboard to start fresh?*

Alicia: *We don't know. She's disappeared.*

Nessa: *Well, that's unsatisfactory.*

Kristen: *The suspense...*

I click in the entry field. The cursor blinks at me. I still don't have the words.

Me: *Bomb, explosion emojis.*

Alicia: *Oh no.*

Stella: *Is that a bad thing ... or a very, very good thing?*

Nessa: *What's happened? Use words.*

Kristen: *Are you okay?*

Their input comes in almost simultaneously. Even Kristen – she must not have a shift. That's nice that she has a rare weekend off. The cursor flashes insistently at me.

Me: *Not okay.*

I push at my eyes with the heels of my hands. Stupid.

Nessa: *hug emoji.*

Alicia: *Come home.*

Stella: *The only problem with dicks, all too often attached to one.*

Kristen: *Oh sweetie. Proud you put yourself out there.*

A fat tear plops on the screen.

Enough. Time to get my shit together. I look around the empty hotel room, and crossing to the window, yank the curtains open letting in the bright light. I pull on my mom's dress of last night. At least the floaty dress isn't going to totally scream *walk of shame* once I'm out on the street.

I stop at reception and sign off on the room service bill. There are some extra drinks on there that I have no recollection of but it explains the headache.

There's no sign of anyone when I let myself into Eric's house. I don't call out, don't want to meet anyone. If there is a god, I will make it out of here and to the airport without meeting anyone.

Which is the cue for my mother to walk in the door.

Mom pushes it open gently, hovering on the threshold, uncertain of her welcome. That's my fault. I smoothly progressed from prickly teenager to continentally distant daughter.

'Okay, baby?'

I meet her gentle look, and the bottom falls out of my world, and I am crying. Mom pulls me in and lets me sob it out.

'Boy trouble?'

I let out a strangled noise that's somewhere between a sob and a laugh. This is not the type of conversation we ever have. Not when I was sixteen, and not now. I pause. Communication is always the solution.

I pull away, sniffing inelegantly, which is a phrase you read but really means I am searching desperately for a tissue because ewww. I am a mess.

Mom hands me a wad of tissue she has magicked up from somewhere, some kind of mystery mom-power.

'What makes you think that?' I ask as airily as I can manage after mopping up the worst of the damage.

She gives me a look. My mom and I may not be close but the guy she admired in LA gained a wife of ten years in the week since she last saw him. And there was my dramatic exit with the bottle he was about to toast his blissful union with.

'Do we hate him?' Mom asks. She won't ask me to talk about it; she's had too many rebuffs over the years.

I suck in a wobbly breath. 'Yes. Bastard.'

Mom's lips twitch as she nods, eyes solemn.

'You didn't know?'

My jaw drops in outrage that she would even ask such a thing. Of course I didn't know. That is a hard line. I would never… He lied to—

He didn't. He didn't lie. He told me. I decided all on my own that it was in the past. He just didn't feel married. My brow scrunches up. Am I making excuses?

'Not everything is black and white, Leonie.'

'Being married seems black and white to me. You're free or you're not. I would call that a hard fact.'

'Death, that's a hard fact.' Whenever my mom refers to death I always think of my dad. She can tell me to get rid of old flowers and I go straight there in my head. I would go so far to say she avoids using the word around me. 'Everything else is shades of grey.'

I shake my head.

'Your dad wasn't perfect either, you know.' What? Where had that come from? 'Nor was it his fault he died.'

My dad died in a car accident. What kind of *Good Will Hunting* is she trying to pull here? Mom reads way too many pseudo-psychology books. She's always dropping nuggets like this in. Today is not the day, though.

'Mom.' I use the warning tone that means I will not engage in whatever navel gazing she wants to put under a microscope.

'Leonora,' she starts and then, meeting my gaze, seems

to climb down from whatever she really wants to say. 'You seemed happy. I thought you'd finally met someone who broke down that wall and discovered the wonderful, warm woman you are.'

'I do not have a wall.'

'Darling, you have the highest wall of anyone I have ever met.' Her hand reaches out to touch my face. As I bite my lip, I can feel my eyes water again. 'Your dad left you and you decided no one would ever hurt you like that again.'

I let out a huffy exhale. What a load of crap. 'Mom, Dad didn't leave me; he died.'

'I know that,' she says in that understanding therapy voice. 'Do you?'

Robin Williams, eat your heart out.

'I need to pack.' Or humiliate myself for a second time. I stand up from the bed stuffing down the pain from a direct blow I had not seen coming.

Mom looks utterly crestfallen at what she has taken to be a dismissal. Which it is.

'You're leaving?'

'I don't really have any reason to stay.' The words are out of my mouth before I consider them and Mia's face crumples on impact, which makes me feel bad; I didn't mean it like that. Maybe there is a nugget of truth in her diagnosis I seem pretty practiced in pushing her away. 'Why don't you stay while I gather my things?'

Her face lights up. I am a horrible daughter. I try to think of something to talk to her about.

'How was the rest of your night?' This is what I come up with? Face palm.

Mom blinks, but, bless her, she does her best.

'Ah, it was a little odd. Lacy did a lot of the talking; she's thinking about doing a little interior design for her friends. Eric talked about what he might do next.' She casts me a glance from under her eyelashes. 'Jack was quiet.'

I move into the en suite to gather the bits and pieces strewn about the sink. I don't care.

'Was he?'

'Yes,' Mom calls through. 'He seemed upset.'

Whether it's because we aren't in the same room or just her general mood today, her next words to me are bold.

'Please tell me what happened.'

And I do. I don't know which of us is more surprised. And I tell her EVERYTHING. From the almost-sex in Paris and my horror at finding we had to work together to our road trip to that magical dawn in Yosemite. I skip over some of the Eric-related stuff; anything I tell Mom I tell Mike. Besides, I don't need to worry her.

'He asked me to trust him and then I get back and he's selling the business and is staying married,' I finish.

Mia is silent for a moment, a moment longer than I consider necessary to agree with me that black is black here. And I'm better off without him, and he's a liar – you know, the simple stuff. Instead of which, when Mom eventually speaks it's to challenge my interpretation of events.

'What did you ask of him?' She tilts her head when I fail to supply an answer, but it's fine as she has one handy. 'To give up everything. What did you offer in return?'

She's right. I never offered him anything.

'If you could go back in time, would you rather be here or in Yosemite right now?'

'What, and be with a married man, with no idea of the mess awaiting me?' I'd rather avoid the mess.

'Okay then, if you could go back to Paris and never meet him would you do that?'

'What?' Delete that night in Paris, and every moment of the emotional roller coaster thereafter? 'Of course. If I'd known how it would turn out, I'd have run a mile.'

'But—'

I cut her off.

'Please don't tell me some better to have loved and lost than never have loved at all horseshit.' I'm swearing a lot at the moment, but strong feelings call for strong words.

'You know what Leonard Cohen said when they asked him what he meant by 'Hallelujah'?' Mom sidesteps my clear no-entry sign.

Great, more of Leonard Cohen's pearls of wisdom. Just what I need.

'Life is messy but he said you have to embrace the whole mess; that's what "Hallelujah" is, those impossible times that tear you apart and remind you that you're alive.'

'Are you comparing my brief, sordid affair with a married man with the song of a dead singer?'

'Maybe.' She angles her head at me. 'Your dad wasn't perfect. Mike isn't perfect. Nobody is perfect, Leonie. No marriage or relationship is. And sometimes the highs are worth the lows.'

Are they? I thought I understood him. Saw him. But he

chose another path, a path that meant he didn't have to throw away everything he had worked for. I can't blame him for that. Would I have acted differently?

Mom stands and gives me a hug. 'Thank you.'

'For what?'

Her head tilts to the side as she pauses in the doorway. 'I miss you, Leonie.'

And on this she moves to leave the room. 'You know you don't always have to do everything for yourself. Mike and I are always here for you.'

I huff; she's being ridiculous. It's not that big a deal. I'll be having this conversation in duplicate once I get back to London. But I should also talk to Mom more. There's an action for me.

'Mom.'

She pauses in the doorway.

'I'm sorry I haven't been home much, I'll do better.'

She leans her head against the door jamb before asking softly 'What happened to us, sweetheart, we used to be so close?'

'You got married, and I didn't fit anymore.' Okay, I'm going there. But that seems to be as much as I can get out over the shards in my throat.

And then my mom's arms are around me in a fierce embrace before she pulls back and takes my face in her hands.

'How could you feel that way? Mike did everything he could to make you feel a part of his family.'

She's right, I know she's right. But Eric had made it very clear that my entry into the family was temporary and to be considered in material items only, emotionally he was king of that castle.

'I don't know, I guess it was kid stuff, it doesn't matter now…'

'Eric made you feel that way?' she identifies astutely.

'I don't know.' I'd never really looked at it through this lens before, never realised how easily Eric had made me feel an outsider.

'Darling, if he did it's because you let him.' Underneath the Cali-hippie still beats the steelier heart of an Englishwoman. 'Now. What you do about it is up to you.'

With that pronouncement she is gone from the room in a swirl of colour. I cover my face in my hands. I am not going to cry again. I refuse. I take a deep breath and pick up a paper and pen. Action … what I'm going to do about it is take action.

I scribble the Stop, Continue, Start on a piece of paper, even though the Start item is the only one in my head, but in the act of writing a couple more tumble out.

Start: Sharing more with Mom.

Continue: Being more open to imperfection. Didn't work this time but nearly.

Stop: Hiding what you want. Keeping secrets.

Next time. Next time it will work out.

I open my phone to change my flight. My original ticket is scheduled to leave LAX in a couple of days. Days I no longer wish to spend in California. I can be back in London by tonight – or rather, tomorrow. Scarlett O'Hara had better be right.

I lock in my flight for early evening one way to LHR

via LAX. It costs a premium to make changes at such short notice, but the sooner I'm out of California, the better.

I open my messages to tell the girls I'm on my way, scanning the last messages as I confirm Alicia's directive. But it was Stella's comment that strikes me – is her label fair? Is Jack a dick? He lied, but so did I. I knew what it was to be on the outside looking in and from where Jack stood, I had supported Eric all the way; I didn't know Eric was screwing Jack over, but it never occurred to me that Jack was more than, well I was surprised to learn he was CTO. I had made judgements about who he was. I had spent my life battling other people's prejudices about my gender, my background – and I had looked at Eric and Jack and never questioned what I thought I saw.

Worse than that I did exactly what Jack believed; I protected my family's money. Mike's investment is safe, but at what cost? And Eric, Eric is getting away scot-free. White-collar crime pisses me off; every time I read about those big shots who gamble with the finances of millions, I always think about the people whose money that was, the people who worked hard all their lives whose pensions evaporated while the big shot continues to live in his big house with his fancy life because they have the legal resources to fight conviction while those whose lives are impacted all too often have no recourse. Because that's just the way it is. Kings are never cannon fodder, and millionaires become billionaires.

Eric is the dick here, and what was the outcome? A big payday. So he can go on and do it again to the next guy who digs deep and tries to get ahead and falls for Eric's credentials? Screw that.

I'm out of the door and down the stairs before I've thought too much more on it.

I've never gone to Mike for anything. If I have a problem I fix it; if I need money I work harder. I did before Mike came into our lives and I did after. Mike had Eric; he never asked for a daughter.

But when his future was on the line, I hadn't hesitated, I realised. I wanted to help, not for Eric's sake but for Mike's. Somewhere along the way he stopped being the guy who lived in a big house with my mom and became someone whose welfare I cared about. Jack was trapped, forced to sell because of Eric's conniving, and a part of me was relieved. If Jack flipped that coin and it fell the other way, Mike would have been ruined. And he didn't even know how close to the edge he had been.

'Mike?' My stepdad is on the outside deck reading a newspaper. Who even knows how he managed to find one of those in this town? He looks up and checks my side, clearly expecting me to be dashing in, luggage in hand, to give him the obligatory hug on my way to the airport.

'I'm not sure the point of telling you this,' I begin as I venture closer to him. I don't know where Eric is and I don't care. 'But you should know and I don't think it's right so, here goes.'

Mike's eyebrows lift as he lowers his newspaper.

'Eric is forcing Jack to sell. Jack doesn't want to.'

'But isn't Jack an equal partner?'

'He is, but the money ran out, Eric hid it from him, and

… Eric may have forced his hand. He never planned to sell; Eric setup the sale without telling him.'

'Jack wasn't aware that his company was being sold to Rubicon Inc.? How is that even possible?'

'I may have helped.'

'Why?' This is the first surprise Mike has shown.

How to tell him it nearly hadn't happened. And if it hadn't that Eric would have lost Mike's investment.

'I didn't want Eric to lose his money.'

'You mean my money,' Mike says shrewdly. 'Why did you think he would lose it?'

'Well, because he said that…' I never even questioned him. Eric said it would impact Mike, and I just put my shoulder to the wheel without stopping to assess the truth. But Mike was no fool. 'You wouldn't be ruined, if they didn't sell?'

Mike throws his head back and guffaws at this. Pulling himself together, he faces me again.

'Eric has never been shy about coming to me for money. He's never been made to stand on his own two feet. So he bounces from one thing to the next – success, failure, it doesn't really matter to him. As long as he gets to tell his friends all the interesting things he's doing. He doesn't stick at things though, so I told him the well was dry – not that there's no more water, but there's no more water for him. Not unless he knuckles down and sees something through. He seemed to have that here; he worked hard at it. He's not on his knees and, whatever he told you, I've never over-invested in anything in my life.' He gives a short laugh. 'Unless it's Eric himself.'

'You were never going to lose all your money if RL8 didn't sell?'

Mike kindly seems to be suppressing how ludicrous this idea is.

'Eric told me he was over-extended with a new project, that it would take you both down.'

'Leonie, I'm protected from Eric's dealings. I loaned him the money, and the liability is his alone.'

I had been totally played. A moment ago I was glad Eric wasn't here so I could speak freely to Mike. Now I really, really wish he was here. He emotionally blackmailed me to work for him, actually *dated* Lacy Keogh to manipulate the outcome he wanted, and crushed … what? Me? Jack? Any chance of a future together… Is Eric to blame for that? Or is Mom right? Did I sabotage any chance of that all on my own?

Mike is speaking again.

'Jack seems like he has a head on his shoulders, and I heard what he said last night. If he wants an investor, if he plans to make the market a little more interesting, then tell him to come talk to me. Terms may be agreed but they haven't signed on the dotted line yet.'

'Sure. Thanks, Mike.' I give him a hug.

'Leonie,' his voice stops me as I step towards the door into the house. 'You know you could have come to me sooner.'

It never occurred to me. I had dealt with the situation Eric had presented, chosen not to worry Mike and my mom with it because I thought I could handle it myself. I've never turned to anyone for help, not my family, not Jack. My friends support me, give advice when asked but do I ever really go to anyone for help? No, I've never even contemplated it, perhaps solving problems alone isn't always the only way to go.

I check the time. I still haven't responded to the girls. My flight is in three hours, but the airport is only twenty minutes away on a Sunday.

I open up the thread. My eye catches again on the previous messages.

Alicia: *Come home.*

Stella: *The only problem with dicks, all too often attached to one.*

Kristen: *Oh, sweetie. Proud you put yourself out there.*

I punch in my message.

Me: *I'm coming home. On the next flight out!*

As for Kristen's pride in me? What a crock. Mom is right. I didn't put myself out there.

And maybe it's time I did.

Chapter Twenty

I 've never minded driving up mountains, I just don't particularly like driving down them. I'm also fine with being in the passenger seat when someone else does the driving. Like when Kristen and Camille confronted each other with the truth of their feelings for each other, I positively squealed with delight at the view.

Right now, as I climb out of the car at the bottom of a drive with a contemporary glass-dominated house perched at the top, I'm reminded that I don't enjoy driving myself. The mountain at my back and the stunning views in front of me are ruined by the precipices and sheer drops just a few feet away as I crawl down the mountain keeping my eyes on the road.

I hesitate as I approach the doorway. I haven't thought this through. What if his wife opens the door? *His wife.* What the hell am I doing here at the top of this mountain? I am not a mountain person. The air is thin, and I don't like heights.

He's here though, or at least his car is. So…

The front door is opening in front of me; it's too late to run straight back down this drive and onto the nearest airplane. London is my preferred destination, but far away from here is the only real prerequisite. Anywhere.

'Hello, Leonie.' Too late.

I'm not wearing sunglasses. Sunglasses would have helped. His eyes are really blue. They might have helped protect me from the glare.

Don't look at the view. Focus on the road. Do what you came here to do. And put this in the rear-view mirror of life.

'Hi.'

We just sort of stand there for longer than necessary. There is a twist in my stomach that fears this will be the last time I'll ever see him. Don't look down.

He comes closer and then walks past me, opening the trunk of his car, continuing about his day like I'm a neighbour who's passing and stops to shoot the shit about the weather. He takes out a pile of rope and dumps it on the ground, then selects one and pulls on it until the length of it has untangled from the rest. He takes an end in one hand, loops the other around his shoulder and flexes his bicep, looping the rope around his flexing arm as he tidies it into one big circle before tying it off and throwing it back in his car.

He pauses before he leans down to arch another brow at me; his face is taut and unwelcoming, like whatever I have to say he doesn't want to hear, but I might as well spit it out.

I'm never getting off this mountain if I don't start the engine.

'I want to talk to you.' Self-evident. You're here, aren't you? Just a girl, standing in front of a boy ... I close my eyes. This is not the time for Julia Roberts; this is Sigourney Weaver time. Pack that gun over your shoulder and get on with it.

'Don't sign the deal.'

Both eyebrows rise at my opening statement I have an entire speech worked out in some parallel universe, but in this one I seem to have arrived here by screwing up my eyes and refusing to think about it until I get to the top of the ride.

'Mike will buy Eric out.'

The eyebrows lower, the lips thin, and his eyes narrow as he absorbs this.

'And buy me.' He finally says.

'That's not how it is.'

'Isn't it?' he asks. That's fair. That *is* how the world usually works but I know Mike; he's making this offer in good faith. To put the world to rights. Because his son made this mess and he can afford to, I guess.

A movement behind one of the glass walls of the house catches my eye. Lacy is standing there watching, alerted by voices perhaps. Or by a twitch at the edge of her web. No, she's not the bad guy here.

Jack follows my gaze and is utterly unmoved at finding her there.

Because he doesn't care? Is indifferent to her seeing us together?

This loveless business partnership is his future.

'Why are you doing this?'

He opens his mouth to speak then stops, squares his shoulders and shrugs. 'Because this is how it works in the real world.'

'So you stay married and sell out.' I accuse before I take a breath. 'I know how important RL8 is to you. But … you can do it. Start over.'

'At the bottom again. Finding the next Eric to screw me over.' He throws another length of climbing rope into the back of his gleaming car. 'I've had enough. This is my shot.'

'So you're just going to let them take RL8, stuff it full of data-mining software or shut it down.'

'It's only an app.'

But it wasn't only an app; he was proud of what he had built, of the team, and he had pushed himself incredibly hard to make the launch happen.

'You were only in it for the money?'

'Isn't that the point of it all? I've worked damn hard to make something of myself, to get here,' he says, slashing another wound rope into the trunk. 'Because I will not be nothing again.'

His feet are bare and the jeans he's wearing are old and worn. I look at the shiny sports car he drives to go mountain climbing, to stay in that rough, small cabin.

'You never bought that car, did you?' The man who drove all night to show me a sunrise doesn't need a car to tell other people who he is. 'I mean, you didn't buy it for yourself.'

His expression tightens before he relaxes and leans a hip on the trunk of said gleaming car.

'A wedding gift from Lacy to blow out the last of her

trust fund,' he concedes. He hadn't been overstating her lack of regard for money then. But it also revealed more than just that, this was a gift more about her own issues than it was her new husband. He had only just arrived here when they married. He would have either still been labouring on construction or at an entry-level IT job and she blew the last of their money to prove a point. They must have started out on nothing. I didn't know whether I was appalled or secretly admired the sheer high drama of it. 'So, you'll excuse me if I pass at the opportunity to swap out one daddy's girl for another.'

'That's not fair,' I protest. 'Or true.'

'Isn't it?' He leans down and untangles another rope.

'Mike's offer has nothing to do with me.'

He gives me a level look. 'At least Lacy is aware of the impact of her grand gestures.'

I don't know what to do with that. Does he mean me being here? No, he means Mike – that Mike's offer is as much about me as anything else, which would have horrified me a month ago. But now, here, for him, for me, I'm okay with it. But my being here is also a big deal. After that scene last night I'm here; if I were her…

I look up at the house. 'Last night… She knows. Knows that you and I—'

'Yeah,' he interrupts me. There's no sign of her at the window.

'She doesn't care?' She looked across the table at me and smiled, smiled in my face. If I'd been in her seat, if Jack were mine, I would scratch her eyes out just for looking at him. 'How could she just sit there?'

'Just good East Coast genes, I guess.'

I take in the car again. This is not a woman who just lets things go. I wonder what her relationship with her dad is; I work halfway across the world from my parents, but I still come home for the holidays. Some of the time.

'Why is she doing this? You don't love each other. Jesus, last week you were both seeing other people.'

He lifts a shoulder as if their reasoning is neither mysterious nor all that interesting. 'I told you. Lacy has her own code. And spiting her father is a strong part of it. This way she gets to be married to me and rich. 2–0 to Lacy.'

'That's crazy.'

This makes no sense. We have one life, and she's living it for her audience, not herself. For a man who lives on the other side of the country. Talk about daddy issues. I thought I had problems. Not that I was giving any credence to my mom's notion that I push people away because my father's premature death made me wary of heartbreak... Then why was that thought creeping into a segment of my brain in the middle of one of the toughest conversations of my life?

Well, what should be one of the toughest conversations but isn't particularly because I'm standing here talking about this woman when what I need to talk about is me. Him.

'This is your life.' I can't believe he's okay with this, okay with the deal he apparently made yesterday. I can't even imagine the words they used to discuss it. How do you agree to this? 'Married to a woman who picked you to piss off her dad.'

'But she picked me,' he says, alluding to his accusation

yesterday that I only went out with him because he isn't what I want, thereby putting my heart in no danger at all. Except, here I am, careening down a mountain.

'So you'll sell out yourself and your app.'

'But I'll be rich.'

Scarlett O'Hara standing on a hillside, "*I'll never be hungry again*".

'And what? Count your fancy cars while you cheat on your wife who you care nothing for?'

My heart twists sideways in my chest. He will really exchange his life, his dreams for a handful of silver. Though who am I to judge? I don't know what he wants out of life. Maybe this is enough for him.

'You make it sound like a bad thing.' His eyes gleam as he looks back at his house on its hill, the sun beaming down on it, with his blonde, leggy wife somewhere inside it. 'Believe me, there are worse ways to live.'

I know there are; I've lived my version. Too scared of trusting, of leaning on others, of putting my heart out in the world where it could get stomped on.

I nod.

'I know I told you that you're the opposite of everything I'm looking for in a partner' – this is it; I need to admit that that wasn't the whole truth – 'but you weren't looking for me either.'

He looks disappointed. But I'm not finished. 'And what if that's the point?'

'What's the point?'

'That despite everything…' *Say it. Say it.* 'I do pick you.'

His head tilts and he Han Solos it. 'I know.'

This is it. This is the moment he sweeps me into his arms and his lips meet mine and we live happily ever after.

He doesn't.

'But life isn't a movie and in real life this is more than I ever...' He pushes a hand over his cropped hair and shuts the trunk before walking over to me. And smiles that goddamn smile. The slightly cynical one that lifts his face.

Wanted? Expected? What is he telling me?

'Goodbye, Leonie.'

Oh.

This is it, then.

Do I say that word back to him? Is that what I say now? Goodbye?

No, that's not what I'm going to say to him as I stand here with my heart and pride on the floor. I can't help myself. It's there, and it's ridiculous and overly sentimental and funny. And you can call me what you like, but I'm going down in flames. I've exhausted my Bacall repertoire but it seems like a good time for some Bergman.

'Kiss me, Rick. Kiss me like it's the last time.'

He looks back at me expressionlessly.

Right.

'I guess we'll always have Paris.' I throw him the biggest shit-eating grin I can manage as I swing away. I'm not gutted. This is a story for the girls.

But then he's taken hold of my arm, is swinging me back for that kiss. The one that seems too good to be true when you see it high on a silver screen. *The Notebook* kind of kiss. And my heart is squishing into a bleeding, ugly mess because it's not an I've-found-you kiss; it's a goodbye kiss.

A kiss I shouldn't be having. But I asked for it. And it's deep and lights me up from the inside like a wildfire through a hollow tree, flames licking through me even as they burn me down.

He hasn't shaved since yesterday, and his stubble grazes the hand I lift to his cheek as the kiss comes to that bittersweet gentling that says it's over. I want to pull him back in, but I can't. I tried. I tried, and he's married. I press my lips to his one final time. And step back. I don't look up. Don't want to see myself reflected in those bright clear eyes one last time.

I walk back down the drive. One part proud that I said something, nine parts dead woman walking. One foot in front of the other. All the way back to my car. Don't look back. Don't cry. For god's sake, don't cry.

Turn key in ignition. Put car in drive. Move.

Arrive back at Eric's. Plenty of time to make the flight. Mike has arranged for someone to come and drive my car back to LA, ready and waiting for the next time I come home. Is LA where that is? Is London?

Is Jack…?

Stupid. Open door, get bag. Hug Mom, hug Mike. Shake head ruefully when the inevitable question is asked. Oh well, I tried. No big deal. It was barely anything anyway. I know the secret recipe now. It's not the ingredients; it's the attempt.

Go directly to boarding gate because I'm in a hurry to get home. Not even remotely because there is a sliver of me deep down inside that is rolling every movie I've ever seen in my life, montage-style of Jack getting in that stupid car and breaking all the road and parking rules of California and San Jose airport to make it in time. To stop me from getting on this plane.

Me: *Boarding airplane in a few minutes.*

Alicia: *Will have all the wine in the world waiting for you.*

Stella: *And Epoisses.*

Kristen: *We love you.*

No further questions. Who needs a man?

Everyone has boarded. I show my ticket and passport at the gate. Step onto the gangway. Take my seat. For London.

Chapter Twenty-One

'Great shoes,' 1B compliments me, looking up from her stack of post as I head out. One of my dearest friends is getting married, and as a single at an otherwise perfect table plan, the least I can do is rock the best pair of shoes ever to her big day.

The vows are exchanged in a little spot behind York Garden. This part of the river is littered with the houses of the once great and fabulous: Marble Hill House just a little further on belonged to the mistress of King George II; not much further down is the London property of the Northumberlands, where Jane Seymour, her less-lucky cousin Jane Grey, and the very young Queen Victoria spent years of their lives. Not that I'm thinking about any of that as my friend holds hands with the love of her life and vows to be there in good times and bad. It must be reassuring in some ways to start in bad times, to already know going in that the person you're promising to spend the rest of your life with will stick with you when things get hard.

The ceremony is just us and family, a civil service. If lockdown taught us anything, it's that your inner circle is your inner circle for a reason. The people who rally and keep you afloat when disaster strikes. When happiness strikes, you don't need to dilute that.

But Kristen being Kristen can't entirely shuck off tradition and other people's expectations, and Camille just gave that nonchalant shrug with which she usually greets life. Have a party, don't have a party, it's all the same to her as long as Kristen is happy.

The party is in the garden of a Twickenham pub. The Swan itself is on one side of the lane that runs along the green spaces on the Middlesex side of the river. Kristen and Camille moved out to Twickenham after lockdown eased in search of more space, and the old pub is one of their favourites. The garden is usually nothing more than a cement deck area with wooden tables, but today it is a veritable fairy wonderland. While we were watching the *I dos*, their marvellous friends descended and gave the space a makeover to properly celebrate their union. There are flowers everywhere and billowing chiffon blowing in the wind coming off the river and lanterns festooned across what promises later to be a canopy of twinkling lights.

Kristen and Camille's faces are a picture of delight as they sweep in to the newly made-over garden, exclaiming at the enchanting decorations.

'How good is this?' a familiar voice says from behind me.

I turn around to find myself face to face with unfamiliar

purple hair on top of a familiar face and the most astonishing shade of cerise lipstick.

'Max!' She throws her arms around me and I'm sure I will find I have a perfect imprint of a cerise kiss on my cheek.

'This is Caspar,' she introduces the rockabilly-attired man at her side. 'He works with the bride, that is, the *French* bride, in the accounting department.'

She pulls a face. Oh, *this* is the accountant. Where are the spectacles, the pocket protector, the conservative dress? How is this guy her opposite? I'd wager he could out Max, Max.

'How are you?' I ask, unsure if I want to know. Have they closed the office? Does she have a new job? Is she mad that her hard work was rewarded by a short exit? I don't want to know; I've cut Mike off every time he's tried to update me on what's happening with Eric.

What are the chances she'll say fine and we can move on to other topics?

'Great. I've decided to go back to college in September.' She's bursting to tell me, her face begging me to ask.

'To do what?'

'Computer programming.'

'What?' She has succeeded in surprising me.

'I think I was intimidated by the devs. They can all code and understand design well enough to insist they know better.' She smiles. 'I decided two can play that game. I'm terrified, but I think it'll be good.'

So, she's still at Synchronicity? Or not – it isn't clear. I want to ask. No, I'm not asking. It's none of my business.

'You'll be great. That's fantastic.' I'm already moving past her, an apologetic yet rueful expression plastered on my face. 'I need to… I'll catch you both later. It's so good to see you.'

Code for *I might see you later but if I successfully avoid you in this small party for the next few hours, good luck in life*.

Alicia's cherubs are entertainment for the next couple of hours as we nibble on the circulating bites and sip – well, the others sip champagne. I'm still not there. The chilled rosé is more than satisfactory in the balmy evening.

The lights are spectacular when they come on and the trio of musicians hired to provide a soft backdrop up their game to meet the expectations of the lively crowd.

'Like to dance?' I look up to find a woman in a suit extending her hand to me.

'I'd love to,' I answer. Because it's that kind of wedding. And I'm now this kind of me.

Laughing and overheated after throwing shapes on the makeshift dance floor, I find my way to the rail and lift my hair to let the river breeze cool my neck.

'Of all the gin joints in all the world,' comes a voice at my ear, lisping and broadening the accent in just the right places.

'As Time Goes By' is playing.

My stomach dips and my chest carves open. If I turn around and it's not him, I will break. If I turn around and it is, my heart might plop out onto the ground.

'What brings you to London?' Innocuous question.

'I came for the sun.' He misquotes Bogart.

'Not too much sun here.' I have no idea how the line

goes in the movie – something about water in the desert. My mouth is dryer than a sandal in the Sahara.

'I was misinformed,' he deadpans.

'Staying long?' It is him. It's him. What does it mean?

'Maybe. Even though I don't match your list.'

I turn around. He looks ... like Jack. My eyes are devouring his face, discreetly; I can't appear to care. He just happens to be here. At the wedding of one of my closest friends.

'Maybe I have a new list,' I say.

'Do you?'

'Yes.'

He seems to be standing very close. Is it normal to talk to someone you don't care about this closely?

'What's on it?' he breathes.

'Only one criteria these days,' I say crisply. 'Single.'

'That could work,' he says, like he's considering an alternative solution for a user journey. 'I filed last month.'

'You did?'

'Yes.'

'Really? And Lacy was okay with that, the last time I saw her she seemed super happy about the next ten years together.'

'That was mostly for Eric's benefit, I told you she does *not* like being used. And she thought you were in on it.'

'Oh. She doesn't anymore?' You don't?

'No.'

'So, divorced, huh.' I follow that through. 'Doesn't that mean you're broke?'

'Does that bother you?' He eyes me like I'm in the dock on trial.

'Can't say that it does.' I slip back into a Bacall type of voice. 'I may have other criteria.'

'Oh?'

'Yeah. Number two is sort of economic. Would you like to hear it?' I'm making it up on the spot. But it felt true. 'Must follow dreams.'

I don't need someone who's rich, but I want someone rich in life, like my mother, like the new me.

'I'm feeling good about this list.' He steps in a little closer, that sea and cedar smell enveloping me.

'Number three is still tall,' I say. With me in heels we are eye to eye.

'I'm still taller than you.'

'I suppose you are.'

He's close; I can't believe he's this close. I touch the side of his face; the prickle of his rough jaw is real. Is he staying? Do I want him to stay? He does fit my new criteria, and I promised I would give the next person who came along a chance. No more safe behind my wall.

'Get a room,' comes Stella's unmistakable tone. Oh, he's kissing me, or I'm kissing him. But it feels wonderful. Lights dance behind my eyelids. *Please let this be real.* A cheer goes up.

I pull away, and the world winks back into existence. The fairy lights have come on.

'No, really. Get a room.' Stella is waving her phone. 'I've called you an Uber.'

I gape at her. Is she really suggesting I leave?

'You must be Jack.' She's handing me my jacket and handbag. 'We'll meet some other time.'

Jack seems fine with Stella ushering us out into the night. I look around to see if my unceremonious departure is attracting attention. Kristen is leaning back in Camille's arms watching. She winks, her smile broad.

'Ah, here it is. You'll be home in no time.' Stella air kisses me on both cheeks. 'Have fun.'

'I take it she's the one who sends the aubergines,' comes Jack's amused tones as he shuffles in beside me.

'Eggplants,' I autocorrect him, nodding absently. I'm sitting in a car, with Jack. What if he's not here for me? For this? That kiss was just a momentary blip. What did he say before we kissed? Some usual nonsense banter – no, not just banter. He's getting divorced.

His hand comes around and turns my face to his and presses his lips to mine. 'I missed you.'

Not a blip. He's here.

And then we're at my flat.

Through the outer door and then I'm up against the hallway wall and his lips are on mine, his hands on my hips pulling me back into him as we tumble through to my bedroom.

We should talk, I think. I'm not thinking. He's here. I sink deeper into the bed and wrap my arms around him as he struggles to find the zip to my figure-hugging dress. It's on the side. I help him or he's found it. His clothes are gone as I wriggle out of this annoying dress.

Skin on skin. Whispered words. Breathing. Bliss.

I wake to a hard pillow that's moving up and down and a ticklish nose – a warm, moving pillow, with a heartbeat.

'Hi,' the pillow rumbles.

My phone pings. I don't even look in his direction as I grab it. Whatever is on here is not going to ruin this moment. I'm not going to look.

'Hi.' I turn my head to look at him. His eyes are lit up in his dark face. The California summer agrees with him – his olive skin is tanned, the black stubble giving him a relaxed look.

'What took you so long?' Bold opener.

'I made a mess. I needed to make sure my clean start was clean.'

'You said goodbye.' Of everything that we said and did, that was the single worst moment, and it had replayed over and over in my head. It had never ceased to hurt.

'I know,' he says solemnly. 'I won't do it again.'

Every part of me feels dangerously fragile right now. This is it. This is the moment the wall comes down. Once he's on this side, if he leaves, I will shatter.

Except, I won't. I won't shatter. I can be here with him, and if in the future I'm not, then that's no reason not to enjoy now.

'Good.'

But that doesn't mean he gets a free pass. I've thought about it, and while I admit to having built walls and making him feel like he wasn't enough for me, I'm still a little mad. I can't help that niggle of doubt, that suspicion, that says he cheated on her and what makes me so sure he won't cheat on me.

'You lied to me.'

His eyes darken but he says nothing, makes no attempt to deny it.

'What were you doing there? In Paris?' He told me he was testing a feature, but would Judge Judy buy that? I think not. 'You were married. Were you looking for a one-night stand?'

'No. I never intended for it to be more than a couple of drinks.' He pauses, and his mouth pulls up in a wry wince. 'Then you walked in, and you kissed me.'

'*You* kissed me.' I'm torn between being charmed and that niggling doubt. 'You aren't building a convincing defence here.'

'I know. I didn't mean to… You were everything I believed I couldn't have. Lacy moved on from our marriage years ago and it didn't surprise me; I expected it. She was a princess, too far above me. I was never going to hold onto her.' I can't believe how much these words hurt, how much he loved her, how little he thought of himself.

'This is supposed to make me feel better?' I ask. 'What am I? The consolation prize?'

'Wait, hear me out. I'd just had the worst day, a day that confirmed all my worst fears and you walked in and all that stuff fell away. I was in Paris to find some tech angels to get Plan A back on track, help me buy Synchronicity back from Eric so I could finally make it, figure things out with Lacy one way or another. But Plan A wasn't going so well, a different kind of angel walked into my life, a goddess who descended to have a drink with a mere mortal. And as the evening progressed, I found myself not minding so much. Other plans seemed possible. At least until the next morning.'

I groan, that 500 euros would haunt me forever. A rumble of laughter vibrates underneath my head.

We both made mistakes. I've lived my life waiting for the perfect man to walk into my life, someone I could trust to never leave, never die and always do the right thing. But Jack is a mortal, and so am I, and I find his words imperfect but honest. And at least we can laugh about it now ... mostly. 'You were pretty awful to me when I turned up at the office.'

He frowns as if he disagrees.

'You were totally inappropriate!'

His face relaxes. 'You need to tell your friends to be a little more discreet with their use of emojis.'

This time I feel my brows draw together. What's that supposed to mean?

'I was coming over to suggest we start afresh, forget about Paris,' he informs me. 'I saw your phone. Your friend Stella was pretty heavy-handed with the eggplant.'

'Oh.' That was why he had gone off on me.

'I felt objectified,' he says in case I hadn't followed.

I run a hand down his chest. 'Justifiably so.'

He huffs a laugh. 'That's outrageous.'

'You can report me to HR.' I recall the ping on my phone as I awoke; it's possibly the girls checking up on me. It is also the day after the wedding; I'm sure there's a brunch or something arranged. I lean back to my nightstand and pick it up.

I've missed brunch but it seems the girls aren't worried. The flurry of texts waiting may have contained an eggplant emoji. There is also a message from Mike. For Jack. My stomach dips. Until I read it. Oh, maybe this won't break the spell.

'Mike's asking if I've heard from you. He's been trying to reach you. He's filed the paperwork and officially taken over Eric's stake ... though I guess he's technically always owned it since he loaned Eric the money in the first place. He says you're the boss now.'

'Yeah.' He doesn't seem surprised.

'What happened to the sale?' When I left, the offer from Rubicon Inc. was in the mail.

'It fell through.' He eyes me carefully. 'Lacy agreed to support me if I wanted to hold on and not sell.'

'Before or after you decided to divorce?'

'Both. She's not a bad person. She told me I was an idiot for letting you go.'

'What?'

'Our marriage worked on its terms, but she said that if I found better elsewhere, I was a fool. Money doesn't matter.'

'Easy for her to say. She's always had it.'

'And has spent her life trying to get rid of it.'

'So she isn't taking her twenty-five per cent?'

'Oh no, she is. She's not stupid, I think you'll like her. She wants to be involved. We can talk about that later,' he says, waving it off at my increasingly rising eyebrow. 'Anyway, Eric and I limped along for a while, but we don't exactly see eye to eye on what RL8 is. Mike said he's bored with retirement; he's happy to be an investor with a little involvement.'

From the moment I left California, I had been clear that I didn't want to hear about either Eric or Jack. I spoke to Mom and Mike frequently, but this was a line they didn't cross, afraid to upset the fragile new ground we were on. But this was significant for them to have kept from me. It was also a pretty big turnaround for Jack.

'I don't understand. I thought you weren't going to accept his offer.'

'Turns out I may have been carrying around a chip that was obscuring my view.'

'A chip, huh?'

'Small one,' he concedes, his lip twisting in that amused, cynical quirk.

'Yeah, I never noticed.' I glance over at him. 'But chip-free Jack, that could be interesting.'

'I think so,' he says. 'What about you?'

'What about me?' Is he implying I have a chip?

'I have an opening for a Chief Product Officer.'

'You're suggesting I should move to California to work for my stepdad and my...' What is he exactly? He said he was interested in a clean start, but a clean start of what?

'Your...?' He knows precisely why I faltered.

'Erstwhile colleague.' I may be letting him in but I'm not sure I'm ready to label this yet.

'Oh, is that what I am?'

'You could be my erstwhile colleague-slash-something.' Let him do the work. 'Any suggestions?'

'MVP.'

'Minimum Viable Product?' I frown, assuming he's not making a sports reference.

'Yeah, I may not meet all the requirements but I'm hoping...' That he's good enough? Is that really what he thinks? That after everything, he's what's left after I've cut the requirements I started out with.

'I told you, my new requirements aren't that hard to meet.'

'I want to be more than just good enough.' He's rolled over now, hovering above me, his lips millimetres from mine. 'How about erstwhile colleague-slash-Jack 2.0?'

'That's quite the offer.' I don't know what I was expecting. Richard Gere climbing the fire escape of the Beverly Hilton? John Cusack with a boom box? Something a little more than a basic upgrade.

'I feel like there may be some bugs to iron out,' he says when I fail to jump at his suggestion.

'You think?'

'You know how I said life wasn't a movie?' His eyes close and he gives a faint shake of his head like he can't believe what he's about to say. 'What if I told you I bought a house?'

'A house?' I don't understand. Is this just a strange way to tell me that he no longer lives with his ex-wife? I should bloody think not.

'Yeah.' He leans in and kisses me. It's distracting; I need to focus on this conversation. I'm sure he was about to tell me something important. 'Here in London.'

'You don't live in London.'

'No.' His dark eyes gleam across at me as he rolls onto his side and props his head on his hand while I absorb the implications of this. He's bought in London; I've spent years thinking about it and he just did it. As grand gestures go it's bold and also poorly timed.

I smile over at him to soften the blow. 'I've been thinking of moving home, spending more time on the West Coast.'

His answering smile is wry but broad.

'LA has some good devs – cheaper than San Jose,' he says, rolling with it.

'I've heard that.'

'I could move the US office down there.'

'You could.'

'So, how about it? You want to be my CPO-slash-everything?' he repeats his offer. That slash something has become a substantially bigger offer. Be my everything. Is that a line from a movie? If it isn't it should be. Jerry Maguire, take a ticket.

'That's not a thing.' My heart is pulsing out of my chest, exposed, neon-lit, pounding, full Toon style.

'We could make it a thing.' Jack has gone very still. He's gone all out, and it sounds like I'm pushing back on his offer, which I am a little. When I went all out, he said goodbye, and it hurt. But he's back. Like, really back. He didn't burn down his life to do so, but getting here, saving his company, wasn't without its risks and he's had to lean on people he has no reason to trust to make it this far. He's all in.

'You love me.' I don't mean to say it, but he does, I know it. I'm positive. He loves me.

'It's possible,' he concedes. His lips are on mine again, promising CPO-slash-everything. He pulls back. 'I'd like to figure it out. Maybe take you to dinner.'

The smile I direct up to the ceiling is goofy wide. Uh-huh. Casual is totally buyable. He bought a house. Crazy boy. My stomach rumbles. It's way past lunchtime.

'How about a takeaway?'

'That could be a good start.' I lean over to him and this time I kiss him, those twisty lips, that harsh stubble, those watchful, dark eyes close as the kiss becomes more.

By the time our takeaway arrives, my neighbour from 1B is on her way out for the evening. I'm dressed in whatever I hastily grabbed to answer the doorbell – some kind of leggings and slouchy top, at least partly obscured by the huge bag of aromatic Indian we have way over-ordered.

'Staying in?' she asks as I back through the door into my flat, and to the handsome, entirely naked man waiting in my bed.

'Yes,' I tell her. 'Yes, I am.'

Acknowledgments

One of the last adventures I had before lockdown was a trip up the Coastal Highway in California, and I'd like to give credit to my passenger as we cruised along the 101 who suggested I try an office rom com in the future. I scoffed at the idea, firstly because I'd never thought of doing a rom com but mostly because I had plans for 2020 – so MANY plans.

Turns out a couple of weeks later I had a lot more time on my hands than I ever saw coming. I also was desperately in need of something to occupy my mind … besides the apocalypse. A world filled with snippets of travel and outings with friends all spun around a sparky set of characters determined not to fall in love was just the tonic.

So—thank you Thelma!

Leonie's friends are one of my favourite elements in this story – that Greek chorus on the phone, a lifeline for many of us in that strange Spring/Summer of 2020.

The inspiration and dedication for Leonie's fabulous group goes to my friends and family who were there with banter, meme sharing and hugs. I was continents away and you put home at my fingertips – you know who you are, love you!

And of course, huge appreciation and thanks to all the wonderful team at One More Chapter who give wings to these daydreams.

The author and One More Chapter would like to thank everyone who contributed to the publication of this story...

Analytics
Abigail Fryer
Maria Osa

Audio
Fionnuala Barrett
Ciara Briggs

Contracts
Georgina Hoffman
Florence Shepherd

Design
Lucy Bennett
Fiona Greenway
Holly Macdonald
Liane Payne
Dean Russell

Digital Sales
Lydia Grainge
Emily Scorer
Georgina Ugen

Editorial
Arsalan Isa
Charlotte Ledger
Nicky Lovick
Bonnie Macleod
Jennie Rothwell
Caroline Scott-Bowden
Kimberley Young

International Sales
Bethan Moore

Marketing & Publicity
Chloe Cummings
Emma Petfield

Operations
Melissa Okusanya
Hannah Stamp

Production
Emily Chan
Denis Manson
Francesca Tuzzeo

Rights
Lana Beckwith
Rachel McCarron
Agnes Rigou
Hany Sheikh
Mohamed
Zoe Shine
Aisling Smyth

The HarperCollins Distribution Team

The HarperCollins Finance & Royalties Team

The HarperCollins Legal Team

The HarperCollins Technology Team

Trade Marketing
Ben Hurd
Eleanor Slater

UK Sales
Laura Carpenter
Isabel Coburn
Jay Cochrane
Tom Dunstan
Sabina Lewis
Erin White
Harriet Williams
Leah Woods

And every other essential link in the chain from delivery drivers to booksellers to librarians and beyond!

ONE MORE CHAPTER

One More Chapter is an
award-winning global
division of HarperCollins.

Sign up to our newsletter to get our
latest eBook deals and stay up to date
with our weekly Book Club!
<u>Subscribe here.</u>

Meet the team at
<u>www.onemorechapter.com</u>

Follow us!
 <u>@OneMoreChapter_</u>
 <u>@OneMoreChapter</u>
 <u>@onemorechapterhc</u>

Do you write unputdownable fiction?
We love to hear from new voices.
Find out how to submit your novel at
<u>www.onemorechapter.com/submissions</u>